Angels Among Us

Write More Publications Angel Anthology

Featured Authors:

Monica Blanton
Susan Burdorf
Ashlea Burns
Callie Cool
Sky Diamond
Sara Drake
Stephanie Greenhalgh
Beth Hoyer
Theresa Oliver
Jennifer Paquette
Dana Piazzi
Nikki Shah
Melissa Somoza
Kim Stevens

Write More Publications
Kissimmee, Florida

Angels are among us guiding us, leading us and protecting us daily within our lives. Sometimes we see them, but most of the time we don't, as they prefer to give the glory of their actions to God. Whether seen or unseen, angels are still with us, leaving their marks upon the Earth in our lives and hearts, and spreading the love of God. This book is dedicated to all the angels out there who intervene within our lives, and also to those humans within our lives that serve as Earth angels in their own way.

Thank you, Angels Among Us.

Table of Contents

ANGEL OF LOVE
By: Monica Blanton

An angel's work is determined by the abilities they possess. There are some who show up just in time to stop a war or to help aid in one. There are some who show up in time to stop death or to be a guide for when death happens. There are also some for creativity, courage, compassion, and love. Aaraya was new to the job of being an angel of love, but with her beauty and nature, it made the jobs easy. She stood 5'3", had long brown hair, brown eyes, dark lashes, and a beautiful smile … okay … it was also easy because she only had two other jobs before.

The first was to help a lonely old woman find love and friendship in an abandoned golden lab and the other was a younger woman who thought she would never find the love of her life. With Aaraya's help, the young woman is now married to the man of her dreams and expecting a family soon.

A new job was presented to her in the form of a young man, Zak. At thirty years of age, he was having trouble trusting people and letting people get close to him. Once she got the information she needed, Aaraya headed out to a small town in Tennessee where Zak resided to see if she could help mend his heart and open it to the possibility of letting someone in.

As soon as she touched Earth, her wings went into hiding-as they always did so as not to give her away. The way this works is the angel with the job has to present themselves as an outsider, but close to the situation at the same time. In this case, she would have to play the part of a new neighbor or a new co-worker to get close. She found her way to his apartment building and noticed there was a vacancy on the floor above him. Perfect! Aaraya talked to the office manager and charmed the empty apartment out of the kind man.

She would not be staying long and she couldn't let people know who she was, so, it was the only way she could get in without any questions. When Aaraya walked into her new temporary home, she had all the necessities waiting on her for her stay. She pulled on some jeans and a white sweater she found amidst the clothes, along with a pair of socks and shoes. It was almost time for Zak to head to work. So, she headed down to the entrance of the building where she could run into him "accidentally."

She placed her hand on the bar of the door right as he placed his on top of hers. They looked up at each other and said "sorry" at the same time. What she was not prepared for was how handsome he was. Aaraya looked up into Zak's eyes, a beautiful green-blue hazel with the longest and thickest eyelashes she had ever seen. He had to be about 6'3" in height and a good, strong build with dark brown hair and dimples on either side of his heart-melting smile. She realized his smile was because she was almost drooling just looking at him. He laughed slightly and extended his hand that was just resting upon hers on the door.

"Hi. My name is Zak. Are you new here?"

"I ... um ... yes. Yes, I am. My name is Aaraya. I just moved into the empty apartment on the fourth floor."

"Ah, yes. That was pretty quick, though. The other tenants just finished moving out this morning. How did you manage that one?" he asked, raising his eyebrows quizzically.

With the most charming smile she replied, "I have my ways."

He looked at her smile, then back into her eyes. "I wouldn't doubt that," he said, forcing himself to look away. "Um, I have to go to work now. If you're going to be around later, I get home around five. You could come down to my place and we can have some coffee. I live on the third floor in apartment 3C."

She could tell he was not used to doing this. And the look on his face said that he couldn't understand why he had just invited her to his place, as well. But she thought that it was as good of an opportunity as any.

"Sure. I'd love to," Aaraya replied.

He looked up, surprised. Maybe a little surprised at himself and maybe a little because she accepted. "Great. I will see you then?" he asked.

"Yeah, see you then," she said.

With one last smile, he turned and headed out the door.

When 4:00 p.m. rolled around, she was nervous. She couldn't understand why she had butterflies as big as bats flopping around in her stomach. What was wrong with her? Angels didn't get nervous! Nor did they fall for their assignments!

Aaraya was beginning to think she was in deep trouble when there was a small knock on her door. When she opened it, Zak was standing there with two cups of coffee, one in each hand.

"Sorry to surprise you. I got home a little early and was wondering if you still wanted to have that coffee with me?" Zak asked, his smile melting away her will.

"Of course. Let me grab my keys," Aaraya replied, then turned and grabbed her house key lying on the small table by the door. She wished she had time to look in the mirror to see how she looked and if her nervousness was stamped on her forehead. She stepped out into the hallway, closing the door behind her and locked it. She turned back to him and smiled. "I'm ready."

He looked a little dazzled from her smile. So she broke his gaze by asking if he wanted her to carry one of the coffees he held.

"Oh … uh … sure. I didn't know what you liked in your

coffee, so, it's black. But I have cream and sugar in my apartment if you need it," he stammered, still a bit dazzled.

Truth be told, she never tasted coffee. Aaraya heard it was awful and bitter, but she tried it anyway. She hid the face she wanted to make and just said, "I think I might take you up on that."

They made their way down to his apartment on the third floor. When they walked in, he directed her over to his half-sized kitchen table while he grabbed some cream and sugar. Aaraya looked around his one-person apartment and decided to strike up a conversation.

"So, how long have you been here?" Aaraya wondered, stirring a spoonful of sugar into her coffee.

"Close to five years," Zak said, clutching his coffee cup in both hands.

"And you have been by yourself this whole time?" Aaraya asked.

"Yeah … well … I'm not much for company. To tell you the truth, I'm surprised at this myself." He waved his hands out between them.

"May I ask why?"

Zak looked down and sighed. "When I was growing up, I had a lot of problems with family. Disconnected mother, abusive father, no siblings to turn to … that sort of thing. Growing up like that made me realize that once I was on my own, I would never have to deal with that again. Once I left, I was on my own for a while and tried the dating thing, but it didn't go so well either. The first relationship I was in ended with her leaving me because I became disconnected. The second was because she cheated on me. The third, well, we'll just say after what I'd been through, I kind of ran her off with major trust issues. It caused lots of fights," he said, fidgeting while telling his story, but looked up at Aaraya when he was finished, awaiting her response.

Saddened by the thought of being so lonely, she replied,

"I'm so sorry you had to go through all of that, but not every relationship is going to end up like that. It takes time to heal and it's possible there is someone out there that's perfect for you. You just haven't found her yet."

"I wish I knew you were right."

"Oh, I know I am."

"How do I find the right one when I'm running them off? How do I make them stay when all they want to do is take off in the other direction when they hear about my past? Not everyone is so understanding," Zak asked, unable to believe that they were having this conversation.

"Well, see, that's the thing," Aaraya replied. "The right one will want to understand and want to help you embrace your past and won't be ashamed of it. She will love you for you."

Zak looked at her intently for a moment and said, "So, I'm looking for someone like you?"

Caught off guard, Aaraya felt herself blush. Wait; angels didn't blush! What was she supposed to say? How was she supposed to handle a situation like this? She quickly looked down at her hands that were resting around her cup of coffee.

"I'm sorry. That was a bit forward. I actually can't believe I just said that," Zak said, a little embarrassed.

Aaraya looked back up at him. "Please, don't be embarrassed. If things were different, maybe it would work out that way."

"If what things were different? Are you in a relationship?" Zak asked, truly interested.

"No, it's not that. It's just … well … it's my job. I have to travel a lot." Aaraya inwardly patted herself on the back for that one. She covered quickly without giving anything away and she didn't lie. If only she was in a position to give this a chance. She only researched these feelings and the signs were there for her, but it was not her place to have them. She was just to plant them within people who needed help.

"What kind of job do you have and how long are they keeping you here?" Zak asked, stirring his coffee.

Ah, sugar! She wasn't expecting that one! "I guess you can say I'm sort of a … consultant, and I don't know yet how long I am staying." She was getting better at this.

Zak pushed his coffee aside, crossed his arms, and leaned forward on the table. "Look, I just pretty much spilled my life story to you. You know enough to know this is not like me, but I feel like I should at least ask you out to dinner. I don't know why, but I'm compelled to try. Would you please go out with me tomorrow night? Just to eat. If you don't feel comfortable, we can end the date and I'll take you home."

Aaraya looked into those gorgeous, pleading eyes and couldn't resist. She prayed her wings would not be taken away, but she agreed to go out to dinner with him. Then again, it would be an opportunity to figure out how to manage the situation. Once they set the time for him to pick her up for their date, they said good night and she headed back to her place.

The whole way to the elevator, the lift up to the fourth floor and the walk to her door, she planned out the scenario in her head. What she was going to say, the questions she would ask, and what her next step would be. Would she personally look for someone to set him up with or put the bug in his ear on how to have a new outlook on things and how to be more open? The thought of setting him up with someone else sent butterflies fluttering within her stomach again. Aaraya went inside and straight to bed, not even bothering to change her clothes. Her mind was working on overtime, so she started to pray, asking for forgiveness and guidance, as she drifted off to sleep.

***

Aaraya awoke the next morning feeling a little better

about everything. Praying always seemed to help when you feel lost. Oddly, she felt more comforted than before — like the night ahead of her would turn out to be no big deal after all. She got up, took a shower, threw on her robe and made her a bowl of cereal. Then she headed back into the bedroom and sifted through her clothes to find something to wear for now and also something for that evening.

Aaraya found a t-shirt and a pair of sweat pants to put on and a cute skirt outfit for dinner. The skirt fell right below the knee and had a slit on one side that came up about three inches. The top that came with it was a gray sweater with a big collar. There was also a belt with the outfit that was simple and black, with a round black buckle to accent everything. She found a pair of black pantyhose and a pair of black pumps to go with.

She spent the rest of the day doing a little research here, making notes there. Memorizing little things that she may need to remember later. She worked through lunch without noticing until it was close to time to get ready. Aaraya put away her work and changed. She fixed her hair and had just finished with the last touches of her makeup when Zak knocked on her door.

She took a deep breath and told herself she could handle this. She was the one in control, she could help fix his problems, and then be on her way. Aaraya opened the door and it felt like her breath was knocked out of her. He stood in the doorway wearing a pair of jeans, a black button up shirt that was tucked in with the first button undone, and the sleeves were rolled up to his mid forearm, revealing half of a tattoo that was on his left arm. Zak had also gelled his hair into a slightly spiked style and smelled amazing.

He looked just as stunned by her appearance. "Wow … you look beautiful," Zak said, taking in all of her.

Again, she blushed and replied, "Thanks. You look very handsome yourself." Aaraya noticed the single red rose he held in his hand.

"Oh … this is for you," he said, handing her the rose.

"Thank you," she replied. She took the rose and smelled it. "It's very pretty."

"It's nothing compared to you."

She couldn't stop the smile that spread across her face. Who was she kidding? She had no control. Just in the short time knowing him, she was falling hard. "Give me just a sec. I'll put this in some water," she replied, turning on her heel.

In the kitchen, there was a crystal vase sitting in the widow seal. She placed the rose in it and added some water. Aaraya returned to the door where Zak was waiting and told him she was ready, then closed and locked the door behind them. He held out his arm like a gentleman, so, she placed hers around his.

Now she understood the feeling of giddiness when one meets another they like as they made their way down to the lobby and out to the parking lot where his truck was parked. He held the door for her while she settled in and closed the door behind her, then went around to the driver's side of his forest green Dodge. The restaurant he took her to was apparently known for their steaks and was very romantic.

It was only a twenty minute drive from their apartment building, so the trip wasn't long enough to start a conversation. He pulled into the parking lot and found the closest space to the entrance. Zak turned off the engine and walked around to open her car door. He held out his hand to help her out.

"Thank you," she said with a smile. "You know, it's very hard to understand why you aren't taken, if this is the way you are all the time."

"Yeah … well … like I said, no one has stuck around long enough to see this side and the ones who did just took advantage of me. I haven't shown this side of me in a long time, but you seem to bring it out of me," Zak replied. Then he opened the door to the restaurant and said, "After you." He waved his hand out in front of him for her to go in first. She stepped into a cozy dining area where the lights were dim and the tables were topped with candle light.

The hostess took them to their table right away. Once they were seated and had ordered their drinks, they looked through the menu, but decided on the ever popular steaks and baked potatoes. Aaraya started the questions. "So, what is it that you do for a living?"

"I work in a detail shop. I do body work on cars," Zak replied.

"Is that what you always wanted to do?" Aaraya asked.

"Yes. I've always liked working on cars and making designs for them is even better ... especially when the nice cars roll in."

"So, you haven't met anyone through your job that you found anything in common with?" Aaraya asked, clearly enthralled.

"Well, there is Joe, but I don't think he counts," Zak joked.

"Ha, ha! Very funny! I didn't know if there might be any women that work there or some that may come through as customers," Aaraya replied in her own defense.

"No. It's just us guys at the shop and most of the women that come through are younger or married," Zak replied, then asked, "May I ask you a question?"

She felt a little nervous, but nodded.

Zak leaned back in his chair and crossed his arms, then he asked, "How is it possible that you are not taken?"

She sighed and replied, "I guess you could say I wasn't made for that. With my job keeping me busy, it's just not possible."

"How is it not possible? If I can let someone in, you can too," Zak said, unable to understand.

"It's not that simple."

"Yes, it is. Like you told me, if you open yourself up to it, the right one will come along."

"But you don't understand ... I can't," Aaraya said, wishing she could tell him more, but knowing that she couldn't.

Zak seemed to realize that the conversation was going nowhere, so he let it drop for a little bit. The waitress came with their drinks of sweet tea. Aaraya was feeling hopeless. She liked this guy. She just couldn't help it. Obviously, he felt the same. But what could she do about it? It was not her place to get involved with a man, especially with her assignment.

He dropped his head and said, "I know I just met you, but I feel something for you. I've never met anyone like you before in my life. What can I do to have a chance?"

Aaraya didn't respond right away. When Zak looked up, he was afraid to hear her response. Not knowing what to say, she stared into his eyes as a tear trickled down her cheek. "I have to go," she said, then ran for the door. She waited until she was outside to let the rest of her tears spill over. She ran quickly back at the apartment complex faster than human speed, not caring who might be watching. In the apartment building, she ran through the lobby to the elevator, got off at the fourth floor and ran to her door. Aaraya was so upset, she fumbled with the lock until it finally gave and let her in. She slammed the door behind her and leaned up against it, sobbing so much it hurt. Being an angel, she never felt this kind of pain before.

That's when she noticed the parchment paper sitting on the table by the door. She looked around her apartment, wondering where it came from and slowly picked it up. In beautiful letters, it read:

Dear Aaraya,

You are right where you are supposed to be, my child. You did your job the way I wanted you to. Live and be happy, my child. Show each other how love is supposed to be.

Sincerely,

G.

It was like a big weight had been lifted off her shoulders. She burst into a new round of tears, but this time they were happy ones. Aaraya looked upward and whispered "thank you" and headed out the door. She ran back to the elevator, went down to the lobby, and rushed toward the entrance. But before she reached the door, Zak walked through, looking crushed. He looked up and she ran right into his arms. She wasn't sure how it worked, but she kissed him with everything she had. He gave in and wrapped his arms around her and returned her kiss.

Aaraya pushed away long enough to say, "Zak, I'm so sorry. I didn't mean to run from you, but I didn't know what to do. But none of it matters now, because I can stay! If you still want to give us a chance, I do, too. We were made for each other!"

He smiled and a tear appeared in his eye this time and said, "Of course I want this. I believe we were made for each other, too."

Over the next few weeks, they were inseparable. No one shared a love like the one Aaraya and Zak shared. One evening, they were cuddled up on the couch in Zak's apartment, watching the snow fall outside the window. Zak hugged her tight and said, "You know, next week is Christmas and I couldn't have asked for a better gift than God giving me one of His angels."

Aaraya just smiled, knowing he never knew and never will. She thought inwardly, *you have no idea.*

BEAUTY
By: Susan Burdorf

Alvena strode purposefully across the campus, lost in thought. Head down, arms swinging in rhythm to her stride, she did not see where she was going and found herself on the ground after running into someone. She looked up and a large, male angel was standing over her, holding out a delicate hand to help her up.

"Oh, I'm so sorry, ma'am," the angel said, blushing. He pulled her effortlessly to her feet and dusted off her gown, removing the dirt. Then he gazed at her with a concerned expression on his face. He was patting her wings down so hard that feathers were dislocating and floating in the air like wispy snowflakes.

"Stop that!" Alvena said, slapping his hands away before she was wingless.

"Yes, ma'am," he said apologetically. Behind him, his three companions sniggered at his discomfort but she ignored them. Euripedes, Clarence and Gabriel were always getting in trouble and she was pretty sure they were in some way responsible for this collision.

Without thinking about it, she reached into her pocket (she was one of only a couple of angels who were allowed pockets) and pulled out a Tootsie-Pop as she studied the four angels standing in front of her with their heads down. Well, the one who had bumped into her looked contrite. The other three were still smirking and poking each other when they thought she was not looking. They would never learn, for she was *always* looking, even when it did not look like it.

She pointed the wrapped sucker at the three of them and motioned toward the entrance to the Angel Preparatory Academy. They quickly rushed inside without further thought for their friend, confirming her suspicion they had been behind the accident after all.

She would deal with them later. She was pretty sure there was something needing to be done at the Heavenly Circus. After all, even the animals here still had to relieve their bowels, didn't they?

Now, as for the nervous angel in front of me, she thought as she unwrapped the sucker and took a satisfying lick of the candy.

"What's your name, boy?" she snapped at the angel.

He shuffled his feet and said with a sigh, "I have no name. I am called Angel, like everyone else until I graduate."

"Or until God so names you one of his Legion. Yes, yes, I know all that," Alvena said, annoyed at the repetition of the familiar edict. She had never agreed with this idea that once a soul came to heaven and was chosen as an angel they lost their earthly names. For the last century she had tried to convince the One Most High that this was the One Most Stupid Idea He had ever had, but He had remained adamant on this point.

"Makes them remember too much about what they were and not what they are meant to be once they reach heaven. I will rename and baptize them, once they complete their training at the Academy," He said.

Alvena did not lose many wars with God, but this one she had wisely decided to bide her time on.

"What was your Earth name, boy?" Alvena insisted.

The male angel refused to look her in the eye. Instead he looked up, down, around … anywhere but in her direction. She wondered why he looked so uncomfortable.

It's not like I'm ugly, Alvena thought as she sucked a little harder on the treat, nearly dislodging the candy ball from the tightly wrapped paper stick. *Maybe he's shy,* she thought as she finally bit into the sucker and found the sweetness of the chocolate center. She suppressed the sigh of pleasure that finding the center of the candy always brought to her. It was bittersweet; a lot of anticipation to get to this moment and then disappointment when it was over.

Until the next sucker, of course.

"Name?" Alvena asked, stamping her foot impatiently.

Finally the angel looked up and said in a clear strong voice that sent chills down her spine. "I was called Gaius Aurelius," he said, as if he expected her to chastise him for speaking it. As he spoke his former name, his shoulders straightened inside his gown, his wings flapped slightly in pride and his blue eyes burned bright with the knowledge of who he had been.

Alvena took a step back in shock, perhaps God was right. For she suddenly saw reflected in his eyes the man he had been on earth. Powerful, strong — both physically and in purpose — yet she saw a gentleness in his carriage that belied his violent other life. She saw the leather and shield of a Gladiator mirrored in his face. But then, his body collapsed as he realized he was wearing a gown which he clutched tightly in his hand and then released, the imprint of his grip impressed onto the gown in a dark, sooty handprint.

Alvena stared at the spot with surprise. The gowns were made of a gossamer material that shimmered and flowed. Dirt and stains were not supposed to remain for more than a minute if even that long, so how was it that his robe was still showing the dark patch of his emotion?

"Interesting," she muttered, reaching into her pocket for another Tootsie-Pop.

"May I go to class now?" asked the angel in a soft voice, afraid of what he had just spoken aloud. All his bravado was buried under his skin, like his muscular body was concealed under his angel uniform.

"Yes," Alvena said absently, her mind trying to wrap itself around the elusive thought that had entered her mind when he had spoken his name.

She watched him walk into the building, his gown flowing around him like a cloud before the rain. Shadows appeared in the folds of the gown, growing darker and lighter as he stalked away. His wings were upright and flapped agitatedly around his back; his halo, usually a sparkling gold, had turned a burnished bronze, and his whole demeanor spoke of anger — an emotion not usually found in heaven.

"Interesting," Alvena repeated as the door closed gently behind him.

She bit into the sucker, not even tasting the chocolate center this time as she pondered his reaction to her simple question.

"Who was *I*?" she whispered to herself as she walked slowly toward the castle on the hill and her appointment with God. She could not remember her life before coming here. "And why do I care now?"

***

"We have a problem," God said in his quiet voice that still managed to reach into the corners of the massive room where he was seated with Alvena.

"Lord?" Alvena asked, perplexed. Heaven did not tend to have problems. Oh, maybe an angel misplaced a harp once in a while, or a new recruit for the Academy might have an issue with fitting in to the gown or maybe, on a very rare occasion, a soul might arrive in Heaven that should have gone someplace else, but that had not happened in centuries. They did, after all, use all the modern conveniences to ensure the safe and timely arrival of their new recruits and mistakes like the one with Lucifer did not happen often.

"Yes, we have a problem. Not just a small one, but one that might escalate into something pretty large if we are not careful. We need to handle this with great skill and diplomacy," God said, pacing the room.

God *NEVER* paced. Alvena sat up straighter, waiting for his explanation.

So worried was she at the unusual behavior of her Lord that she did not even reach into her pocket for a Tootsie-Pop.

"There is a soul among us that the Dark Lord is claiming as one of his own," God began, then continued, "He says that we have to give him back. If we do not give him back, he will take him and that will mean war. I am not giving this soul up. He belongs here; he belongs to me."

Alvena looked up, shocked to hear her Lord so adamant about keeping the soul the Dark Lord wanted. Really, what difference would one soul make? "Who *was* this soul?"

Alvena did not realize she had spoken aloud until her Lord said gently, his hand warm and comforting on her cheek, "He is the One who will save us all. If I let him go, he will be lost; his purpose unclaimed."

"Who is it? Who does the Dark Lord want?" Alvena asked, thinking of all the newest angels she had come across lately and could not think of anyone that the Dark Lord could want. Unbidden, thoughts of the angel she had run into by the Academy came to mind. His beauty was hidden behind his anger.

"Yes," God smiled, grateful Alvena understood so quickly.

"Him?" Alvena asked, stunned. What could the Dark Lord want with that tortured soul?

"I need you to send him away on an assignment," the Lord told Alvena. She listened carefully, concerned, as he outlined his plan.

***

She sucked on the Tootsie-Pop as she strolled back to the Academy. She knew she should not doubt the Lord, but she was not too certain about this plan of His. Above her, as if hearing her doubts, the sky darkened slightly.

Alvena waved her hand as if to apologize and cleared her thoughts. He was right. The purpose of Heaven was not to force someone to be something they were not, but to allow them to become what they were meant to be.

If she did not believe that then she had no business here. But still, if what God thought was the truth, she had some concerns with sending an untrained angel into a battle of this nature.

There were no rules when playing with the Devil. The only thing certain about the upcoming meeting between the Dark Lord and this angel was the uncertainty of it all. Even God did not know what would happen.

When she left God, He had handed her a paper detailing the mission she was to send the new angel on, along with a small box.

"No matter what choice he makes, the box is *NOT* to be opened until the final decision is rendered," God told her to tell him only that. She was not to influence him. He was to be sent down to Earth to walk among the unclaimed souls.

Along the way, he would find three people who would guide him toward his destiny. Whatever choice he made when he met them would determine his fate. There were no right or wrong answers, only choices.

Alvena shivered to think of what could happen if this angel chose incorrectly.

***

Once she reached the Academy, she hesitated. She fingered the box she held in one pocket and the letter in the other, and thought about turning around and marching up the hill and back to her Lord. She half turned as if to carry out her plan and found her feet stuck to the stone at the entrance of the Academy.

Above the door were the words, I AM THE BREAD OF LIFE.

"I get it, I get it. I don't agree, but I get it. You can stop all this nonsense now?" Alvena muttered as she reached for the door.

Just as her hand touched the doorknob, it opened to reveal the very person she was there to see.

He was just as shocked to see her, stopping half inside and half outside the doorway. Behind him, other students coming out the door pushed him into her in their excitement to be free of the restraints of academia, forcing him to knock her down into the grass lining the walkway.

He pulled back just before he fell on top of her and rolled away. He bounded to his feet immediately with a skill that belied his battle training. Alvena watched, knowing that his familiarity with that maneuver took him by surprise, but he was not displeased to find that he still able to do that.

Alvena saw the dusty layers of his past life peeling away from him. His angelic repose suffered under the stress of remembering. It overwhelmed him. His expression changed from concern for her to wanting to walk away and leave her in the dirt where he had knocked her.

Chivalry won the day and he reached out a hand to help her up. She stood, this time brushing off her gown on her own, as he watched her with a petulant expression. He crossed his arms and his wings, never still, were opening and closing in agitation. Their movements reflected his mood, she was certain, although he kept his face still, trying to control whatever thoughts were racing through his head.

"We need to talk," Alvena finally said, unable to bear the darkness that surrounded him.

"We already did," he said, turning away from her quickly. He was nearly three strides away before she realized he was leaving her alone. The other angels who had witnessed the collision disappeared and there was no one around to help her.

"Humph!" Alvena thought, smiling smugly This angel did not realize whom he was dealing with. She was done being Ms. Nice Angel.

With that, she raised her hand and swung her arm in the direction of the disappearing back of the angel. With a quick snap she shot a wave of air into the path in front of him that caused a hole to open in the path. He fell into it with a grunt of pain and surprise.

Walking quickly, she caught him by the edge of his halo before he could make his way out of the hole. Not letting go of his halo, she leaned down into his face and said, "Would you like a Tootsie-Pop?"

He looked at her and smiled, all anger gone from his eyes at the ridiculousness of her question. She let go of his halo, but left him sitting in the hole.

"I don't know," he finally answered, his blue eyes twinkling, "I don't know what that is."

Alvena sat down next to the hole and reached into her pockets, she pulled a cherry one out of one pocket and a chocolate one out of the other. "You choose first," she held them both out for him. He looked at them and chose the cherry one. He unwrapped it and then laid the wrapper into her outstretched hand. "No littering in heaven," she reminded him as she put the wrappers in her pocket.

He took a lick — as he had seen her do earlier that day — and his eyes widened in delight. Within three licks, he bit into it and found the chocolate center. He opened his eyes wider and within a few seconds, he had finished the treat. He held out the stick which Alvena took and placed in her pocket along with the wrappers.

"Now," she said, settling her body into the sand next to the hole where he still sat, "want to tell me why you tried to run away from me?" She had taken several licks of her sucker before he spoke.

"No," he finally said, pursing his lips tightly together, as if trying to keep the words he would say inside, unspoken.

She waited, eyebrow raised, for him to surrender the words she knew he wanted to say.

"I was afraid you were here to tell me that I was not supposed to be here," he finally said in a whisper. Alvena had to strain to hear.

"Ahhhh …" Alvena frowned. Why was he afraid he did not belong here? Did he know something about his soul that even God did not?

"I am here to tell you God has a mission for you," she reached into her pocket and handed him the note.

He took it and unfolded it carefully. Sheepishly he handed it back to her and confessed he could not read. Alvena took the note and smoothed it out before reading God's request. It said:

> You have been chosen to return to earth on a special mission. On your journey, you will meet three people who will keep you on the right path or turn you from your destiny. The choice is yours.

"What does that mean?" he asked, confused.

"I'm not sure," Alvena admitted. "I was told to take you to the place where you will start your journey and to await your return. If you don't make the right choices, I'll be waiting for you for a very long time."

Then she reached in and helped him from the hole. They walked toward the starting point. It appeared to be a large tree in the middle of a field he had never noticed before along a path that he often walked.

The tree — a tall Oak with branches opened wide in a wooden embrace — revealed a dark doorway in its ancient trunk.

The angel stepped forward as Alvena pointed him to the opening. Then she reached into her pocket and pulled out the box. Putting a hand on his arm, she held the box out to him "This is not to be opened until the end of your journey," she said softly. She placed the box in his hands and closed his fingers around it.

There was a flash of light and a warm breeze that smelled faintly of sulfur and he was gone.

Alvena sighed, settling in under the branches of the tree and took another slow lick of her sucker, hoping she had enough of them to last until he came back.

***

The angel stepped onto the path, shaking his head to clear his thoughts. Ahead of him was a cemetery. The early morning mist was curling around the gravestones in a moist embrace and he shivered in the early morning chill. He looked down and saw with surprise that he was wearing clothes, regular clothes.

He whipped around to look behind him and saw the wings that he had been wearing just moments ago were gone. Instead, he was wearing a backpack and light cotton shirt and a pair of pants. A pair of sandals completed his outfit.

Ahead of him, the graveyard seemed to be calling to him. As he wandered among the stones he noticed an old man sweeping dried leaves from a grave. He was stooped with age and the weight of his sadness was almost a physical presence around him.

The angel moved toward the man, almost against his own will. The old man ignored him and continued sweeping the grave of debris. But the more he swept, the more debris remained on the grave. He could not seem to clear it.

"Hello, sir," the angel finally spoke.

The old man paused at his task and turned to look at the angel.

No words were spoken for a minute or two until the angel finally said, "I wonder if you could help me?"

The old man leaned on his rake and waited, not speaking, but he didn't appear to be angry, either.

Encouraged, the angel spoke again, "I'm on a quest and I think you are to help me."

The old man spat into the dirt at the angel's feet and then turned back to his task.

The angel felt the man's anger growing, becoming a dark presence that began to shape and form in the mist surrounding them. The angel felt a sadness overtake him, as well. He sat down on one of the gravestones nearby and bit his lip to keep from crying. He was not worthy of this quest. He was not worthy at all. His helplessness overwhelmed him.

The angel knew the old man was part of his quest. He also knew he had to help him, but he was not sure how. The anger and sadness became a weight pressing into his very heart and he wondered how he could go on with this mission, bearing the burden of this man's sadness.

The gravestone said, *Here lies Mary Goode, Beloved Wife, May God Take Her Soul and Keep Her in His Heart.*

Without thinking about the words, "Do no grieve, for the joy of the Lord is your strength," came from his lips and he straightened his shoulders. Then he reached out to take the rake from the old man and began to sweep the gravesite clear. Although the wind rose and swept it all back, he continued his mission. The angel continued to pray to the Lord and, within a short while, he had made some headway.

As the sun rose — he had worked through the night — the cloying mist disappeared from the graveyard and so did the debris on the grave. He had finished the task. The gravesite was clear, and the old man stood tall within a blinding light that banished the last of the anger and sadness from the angel.

He bowed down, dropping the rake, as he realized who the presence bathed in the golden light in front of him was.

"Go, my son," the vision spoke softly into his mind, "your quest is not complete. But you have done well."

And then he was gone.

The Angel raised his head to find that he was in a marketplace of a busy town.

Around him people were bustling to and fro as they went about their daily business. The bread makers were hawking their products, the weavers had displays of vibrant colors set on tables and one tried to sell him a brilliantly hued rug, but he gently shook his head.

The angel was not surprised to find himself dressed in robes of the desert dwellers with his sandals and a turban on his head. He strode purposefully through the throng of people, certain he would find the next part of his quest somewhere in this mob. On his back, instead of wings, he wore a woven basket attached to a leather harness that crossed his chest and buckled in front of him. His basket contained tree branches cut for convenience to be used in fires.

As he walked, he tried to still his stomach as he smelled the meat pies and other culinary delights of Earth. While the smells appealed to him, he surprisingly was not hungry, so he ignored their tantalizing possibilities.

After many hours of searching he still had not found the person he knew he was to meet. Tired and thirsty, he stopped by the well in the center of the town just as night began to fall.

As he drank from the well, he pondered what he was doing here. Men stroll by wearing the armor of their Lord and his thoughts returned to who he had been. One like those, he remembered, as memories rushed back in bits and pieces. Holding swords and thrusting, taking the lives of others in anger and purpose. Hardly the stuff of angels and he wondered again, doubted again, his reason for being in Heaven instead of elsewhere. He tried to push the negativity aside, but it began to crowd in as the night darkened around him.

Shifting uncomfortably on the bench by the well, he noticed a small boy trying to light a tall lamp for the night. The sounds of a whip cut through the night as an older man, perhaps the boy's grandfather, struck the boy with a thin, leather strip to encourage the boy to get the lamp lit.

The old man was lame, hence his insistence that the tiny lad light their lamp. But the boy, barely ten, was unable to do so. He had stacked boxes and some other debris in an effort to reach the tall lamp, but he still could not do it. A small amount of the precious oil spilled and the old man struck the boy again.

The angel, unable to stand the scene any more, stood up. He shouldered his basket and strode quickly to the pair. Around them a small crowd had gathered. The entertainment was the beating they were all sure the boy would take for his carelessness.

The angel hurried and grabbed the frail wrist of the old man before he could strike the boy again. "Let me help, old father," the angel said kindly. He turned to the boy and reached into his basket for a long stick. Dipping it into the precious oil that had spilled onto the ground, he soaked the end of the stick and then gave it to the boy light the lamp. Together, he and the boy lit the lamp, holding the stick and the flame to the wick until it beamed brightly into the night like a golden star captured as it fell to earth.

Disappointed that their game was over, the crowd dispersed leaving the old man, the angel and the small boy to face each other.

"Why did you do that?" asked the old man gruffly. The small boy had moved to stand next to his grandfather as if to protect him.

"I am the light of the Lord," the angel said quietly, bowing his head. Visions of the transgressions of his past life seemed insignificant at this moment.

The old man laughed, throwing off his dirty raiment as he stood tall, glowing in the night's darkness. He held out a hand and smiled, "You are that and more, my son."

He touched the angel on the shoulder and then was gone.

The angel then bowed his head, looked up, and was not surprised to find he was once again in a new location. This time he stood before a church that glowed and shimmered in the pale gray light of early morning.

He tried to step forward, reaching for the door of the church, but found he was glued to the spot. Looking down, he saw his feet were encased in stone and that his skin was rapidly becoming the same gray granite as his feet. As he shifted his body, he felt the familiar weight of wings upon his back. He looked to see bare flesh from the waist up and a small white loincloth around his middle.

He was an angel, a *real* angel, now. Had he finished the quest? Had his trials ended?

But if that were so then why was he turning to stone?

He turned hastily and saw two birds resting on the top of the church's door. The crow blinked its eyes and its beak appeared to be curled into an evil smile. The other, a tiny sparrow, fluffed its wings and sang encouragingly to him. The crow, irritated, flapped its wings and cawed in response to the song.

The angel felt the lightness of his being when the sparrow sang, and the heaviness of his past transgressions when the crow sang and found himself caught in the middle. All his doubts returned, nearly crushing him with their weight.

How could he enter the house of the Lord with all the sin he carried in his heart? How could he ask forgiveness for the unforgiveable?

As he stood before the door, doubting and fearing for his very soul, the stone crawled up his body encasing him to the waist now. Feeling nothing but shame, it was almost too much to bear. He hung his head and tried to breathe slowly, hoping to find something, some way to forgive himself.

Suddenly, like a breath of fresh air, he heard the words, "If we confess our sins, He is faithful and just to forgive us our sins, and to cleanse us from all unrighteousness." Looking up, he stared into the kindly eyes of the sparrow and ignored the agitated cawing of the crow.

"Unfair, unfair!" cawed the crow, flapping its wings and nearly unseating the sparrow from its perch next to it.

The sparrow remained quiet watching the angel, tilting its head, as if concentrating.

The angel straightened his shoulders, looked to the sparrow and said, "I ask your forgiveness and your blessing, Lord." He bowed his head as the stone crawled slower and slower up his body.

Would the Lord forgive him? Would He be able to see past the sins of war and forgive him?

Suddenly, the stone cracked and flew off him in great chunks, nearly clipping the wings of the crow as he launched himself off the plinth of the doorway toward the angel.

Rushing through the door that was no open, the angel gained the sanctity of the room inside. Outside, the crow continued to rail against the unfairness of the test, but the sparrow followed the angel inside.

Transforming into the God he knew, the angel stood tall before the Lord to face his fate, for he was not saved yet. The Lord pointed to the angel's hand and he was surprised to find the box in it. The angel opened the box to find a beautiful, silver cross hanging on a chain of silver links and black beads. Clutching the rosary, he looked at his Lord with tears in his eyes. He was forgiven!

Turning toward the light that poured from the windows, he closed his eyes and held the rosary tightly to himself. It was warm and comforting. He said a silent prayer of thanks.

When he opened his eyes once more, he was at the tree.

Alvena stood, staring at him with tears in her eyes that she quickly wiped away.

Blowing her nose on the sleeve of her gown (something no self-respecting Angel would ever do) she reached into her pocket and pulled out a cherry sucker for him and a chocolate one for herself.

He took it with a rapturous look in his eyes, "I am to be called Bannister," he told her with such joy on his face that surely all the heavens were smiling on them. "He gave me a name."

"Yep," said Alvena with a smile and a slap on his back that dislodged a few of the snowy white feathers, "and a job too. You are now my assistant."

Bannister bit into the center of the Tootsie-Pop without a single lick. Somehow he knew he would need all that sweetness he could get.

MY BABY'S ANGEL
By: Ashlea Burns

"What are you doing?" Sammy asked from across the hall.

"Nothing," I replied as I headed toward him and placed my notebook in my bag.

"Looks like you're doing something," Sammy said as he pointed to my bag. I glanced toward my bag, then back at Sammy.

"It's nothing," I said. "Just a notebook." Sammy gave me a strange look, then put his arm around my shoulder.

"Alright then," he said. "Lets go." We headed up the hallway to the waiting room. I was a little nervous. I was 9 months pregnant with my first baby and was going for my last doctor's visit before having my special bundle of joy.

Even though Sammy wasn't the daddy, he was such a great friend in my time of need. We've known each other for almost 20 years and he promised to be there for me no matter what. I was excited about having this baby. I even wanted the baby's sex to be a surprise, so I didn't let them see what it was. Sammy helped me fix up my spare room in my apartment for the nursery. He painted it a pale yellow and put up some stars as the border. It looks so adorable!

As we sat in the waiting room I watched as several other pregnant women went in the office, then back out again. Some were really small and most likely newly pregnant, and some were really showing and getting ready to have their babies, as I was. I was looking through a magazine when a little old lady sat down beside me.

"Is this seat taken?" she asked in a soft, sweet voice.

"No Ma'am," I replied with a smile. The lady sat quietly, never saying another word. She seemed so sweet. I wanted to ask her what brought her there today, but I didn't want to pry into her business.

After about a half hour, the nurse called my name. "Ms. Bell?" she said looking up from the clipboard. "The doctor will see you now." I stood up and headed toward her and glanced back over my shoulder to make sure Sammy was coming, too.

"I'm coming, I'm coming," he said, putting down the magazine and catching up to me. I just smiled as we headed through the door.

We followed the nurse down the hallway. There were several rooms on both sides. When we got to the end of the hall the nurse set the folder down on the table beside the scale.

"All right, Ms. Bell," she said. "Please step on the scale." I handed Sammy my purse and I stepped on to the scale. The nurse adjusted the little bar so that it balanced and wrote down the number, then picked up the folder. "Right this way," she said, leading me to a small room in the corner.

Sammy and I walked into the room as the nurse placed the folder in the slot on the door. "The doctor will be in soon," she said then she left the room, closing the door behind her.

I sat up on the table looking across at Sammy who was on the chair. "Are you nervous?" Sammy asked.

"A little," I replied trying not to show a lot of fear.

"It'll be alright," Sammy said, trying to comfort me. "I'm here for you." I smiled at him when the door opened and the doctor and nurse walked in.

"Hello there, Isabelle," he said as he placed the open folder onto the table. "How are you today?"

"I'm alright," I replied. "A little nervous about the delivery."

"That's common," he said as he laid me back and pushed on my belly. "You'll be just fine." He measured my belly, then listened to the heartbeat. He motioned to the nurse, who promptly went out the door. I was a little puzzled as to why she had left. A few minutes later, she came back in with the ultrasound machine. "Isabelle," he said, "We're going to do an ultrasound to see how the baby is doing."

"Um, alright," I said, a little puzzled. He placed the cold gel on my belly, then the began moving the hard, cold hand tool over m belly, beginning the ulrasound. Sammy got up and stood beside me as we both looked at the screen.

There it was. There was my beautiful baby on the screen. I was so overwhelmed that I began to cry. The doctor moved the wand around to different places then he hung up the wand, wiped off my belly and helped me to sit up.

"Alright," he said in a concerned tone. "The baby seems to be ready, but I'm not sure if it will be able to be born naturally." I was confused.

"What's that mean?" Sammy asked as I sat there wordless.

"It just means that the baby is bigger than I had previously thought. And if it can't come through the canal, then we'll have to do a C-section. This suddenly made me freak. My tears of joy turned to tears of fear.

"It's alright," Sammy said trying to dry my eyes with a tissue. "Nothing will happen to you. I promise."

"You'll be fine," The doctor said. "It's a common surgery nowadays." He patted me on the shoulder. I knew he was trying to calm me down, but my nerves were still a wreck and I was shaking. "How about we do it in the morning?"

"What?" I said almost falling off the table. "Why so soon?"

"Well," he replied. "If you go into labor on your own it may harm the baby before he's born. So we will admit you into the hospital tonight and then we will try to put you in labor in the morning. This way if something goes wrong, we can help you as soon as we can."

I wasn't sure what to say. Could this really be happening? They wanted me to have this baby tomorrow? I was in such shock I wasn't sure what to say. After a few minutes I had to say something. Sammy, the doctor and the nurse were all staring at me.

"I guess," I replied. "Do I get to go home and get my stuff?"

"Of course," he said. "Just be back here by 8pm so we can get you into a room and ready."

"Alright," I replied, then paused slightly. I was so scared.

Sensing my fear, Sammy gently rubbed my shoulders. "You will be fine," the he said. "I'll be with you." I looked up and smiled at him then the doctor grabbed the folder and opened the door.

"See you later tonight," the doctor said, then smiled as he walked out the door.

Sammy and I followed the nurse out of the room and up the hall. A million things ran through my mind in that short walk, things such as why me? Would I be all right? Would the baby? When we went back out to the waiting room I saw the little old lady sitting in the same spot, alone. She was looking toward the door I had just come out of with a smile on her face. It seemed a little odd to me, but I didn't think much of it.

Sammy helped me out to the car. I was still crying, some were tears of joy, but mostly they were tears of fear. I was so scared. I knew it would be scary anyway, but for it to be this way made it even worse. I was worried something that would happen to me or the baby. I couldn't handle losing a baby after carrying it all this time. I also couldn't stand the thought of bringing a baby into this world and not being there for it. The ride home was quiet. I just stared out the window as

Sammy drove. I didn't want to talk right now. I had too much on my mind and every time I opened my mouth, I wanted to cry.

It didn't take too long to get home. Sammy helped me out of the car and up to my apartment. Luckily I lived on the first floor and didn't have to go up and down the stairs. Once outside of my door, I got my key out, unlocked the door and headed inside. Then I sat down on the couch and began to cry.

"Oh, Isabelle," Sammy said, sitting beside me, hugging me close. "It'll be alright."

"I hope so," I replied in a blubbery, teary voice.

When I finally got hold of myself and the tears stopped flowing, I headed to my room to get my things. I had already packed a bag for the hospital and most of the baby's things were already ready. My baby shower was just a few days ago, so I was still sorting through all my gifts. I got out the brown diaper bag with gold swirls that my mom got me. The baby could be for either a boy or a girl, so most of the clothes were unisex. A lot of people just gave me gift cards or said they would buy something for the baby after it was born, when they knew the baby's sex. I packed some sleepers, diapers, wipes and socks. I also packed blankets, a hat, and a special outfit to wear on it the day it came home. It was a cream colored shirt and pants set that had little ducks on it. There was even a duck hat and booties to match. It was so cute.

Once our things were packed, Sammy carried it to the car. I stood in my living room looking around, knowing this would be the last time I would be here alone. This time tomorrow I would have my baby, hopefully, and we would be coming home to this place.

"Are you ready to go?" Sammy asked as he stood in the doorway.

"Yes," I replied heading toward the door. "Let's go."

We walked down the hallway to the car. When we got to the front door of the hospital, I glanced over and noticed the little old lady that I had seen today at the doctor's office. She was sitting in the rocking chair in the lobby of the building and, if I didn't know better, she was staring at me. She still wore the same smile on her face as she did in the waiting room. I froze for a moment, looking at her. Who was she? Why was she here? I was unsure about her, and I had an uneasy feeling that she was following me.

"Isabelle?" Sammy said tapping me on the arm. "You alright?"

I looked at him then back at the old lady and she was gone. I blinked a few times but all I seen was the rocking chair and it was empty. "Um," I replied, confused. "Yeah." Then I shook my head and headed out the door.

I walked up to the counter and check in. They ushered me to a room and began prepping me while Sammy waiting out in the waiting room. I was still puzzled by the old lady. Was she just in my mind? Did she really exist? After I was hooked up to the wires, they let Sammy come in. He sat there with me for a long time talking, watching TV and even playing cards. Suddenly, the door opened and my mom came in to see me.

"You alright, dear?" she asked, then kissed my cheek and rubbed my head.

"I'm fine, Mom," I replied.

"Your brother is in the waiting room as well with your dad. They will be here for you, as well," she said.

"Thanks, Mom," I said. She gave me another kiss on the cheek, and then headed out the door.

It was getting late and I was really tired, as was evident with my yawning.

"Well," Sammy said as he rose from the chair. "I'd better let you get some sleep."

"Where are you going?" I asked, slightly panicked.

"I will be in the waiting room with your mom, dad and brother just outside of the double doors," he replied with a smile. "I won't go anywhere. I promise." Then he gave me a quick hug then walked out the door.

I turned off the lights and lay back against the pillows to relax. So much was going through my mind. I was scared and exited, but mainly, I just wanted this to be over with. Soon, I drifted off to sleep.

I woke up with a start in the middle of the night, unable to catch my breath and sweating all over. I hurt everywhere. I couldn't move and I didn't know what was going on. I started feeling around trying to find the call button so I could get the nurse in here. Finally, I found it and rang for the nurse.

"Yes?" she asked, flipping the lights on as she came into the room.

"I hurt," I said with a raspy breath. She took one look at me and ran out. The next thing I knew, she is getting me up out of bed and putting me into a wheelchair.

"You will be alright, dear," she said frantically. "Just hang on."

But all I could see were lights. So many lights as she wheeled me down the cold, white hall. I don't remember anything but the bright lights. Except that as I was going down the hall, I swear I saw the little old lady again. She was standing against the wall, smiling at me. It couldn't have been her again, could it?

The nurse took me into a big room that had a bed, chairs, TV and little cube thing. It was probably for the baby. I was transferred to the bed and hooked up to more wires.

"Just relax," she said as she put something into my IV. "This will help you with the pain a little. I wasn't sure what it was, but it made me hot and tingly all over.

"Where's Sammy?" I asked looking around. He promised to be here, and so did my mom.

"Who is Sammy?" she asked.

"Sammy," I replied. "My friend I came in with."

"Oh yes," she said. "I'll go get him." Then she headed out the door.

I lay in the room alone, glancing around trying to see where I was. I figured she took me to the delivery room, but this wasn't anything like I had pictured. It looked more like a hotel room, only with a hospital bed in the center instead of a regular one. Then as I looked around, I saw her — the little, old lady. She was standing in the corner at the bottom of my bed, smiling.

"Who are you?" I asked, wondering how she got in here. She didn't say a word, but just smiled. I was confused. I didn't know if she was really there or just within my mind. A sharp pain spread across my stomach, grabbing me, as sweat beaded up upon my face.

Suddenly, the door flew open and in rushed Sammy and my mom. They came right to me and gave me a hug. "You'll be alright," Sammy said for the hundredth time. "I'm here."

"So am I, honey," my mom said, then hugged me tightly and kissed my cheek.

I smiled at them, then the doctor walked in. "Alright Isabelle let's have a look. Shall we?" He sat down on a stool. Then he examined me, which was rather uncomfortable by this point. "You're doing well," he said as he looked at some papers. "You're moving along well. We'll begin pushing to see if you can do this without the C-section soon."

"Is she going to have it?" Sammy asked.

"I believe so," the doctor replied. "But I won't know for sure until she starts pushing."

Starts pushing, I thought. That scared me. Was it really that time? Could it really be coming now? I was so overwhelmed once again, but this time I fought back the feeling. Suddenly, another wave of pain grabbed my stomach, ripping through me. I clutched my stomach, gasping, trying not to yell.

"Ms. Bell," the nurse said. "You'll need to relax and get ready to push."

I was in shock, but I knew I had to do it. As I started to push, the doctor gave me directions. "Push, push," he said as I screamed out in pain. "Rest," he said, then, "Push, push!" And right then I felt it. I felt the baby come out.

It was such a relief to have it out, but my mind was filled with questions once again. Was it all right? Was it a boy or a girl? Then I looked down to see the doctor holding the most beautiful baby I had ever seen.

"Congratulations, Isabelle. It's a girl," he said as he placed my baby girl within my arms. She was amazing. So beautiful. I looked into her eyes and I didn't know anything else existed in the world.

Later that morning after I got into my room again, I lay on the bed, holding my new baby. She was so precious. Sammy went to eat with my mom, dad and brother. I was alone with my baby and it was magical. As I rocked her back and forth, I looked up to see the old lady once again. This time she didn't startle me. I knew she was there for us. Down deep within my heart, I knew that I was the only one who saw her.

"Who are you?" I asked sincerely.

"I am her angel," she replied pointing to my baby girl. "I was sent to watch over her until she was in your arms." I looked down at my baby as tears gently flowed from my eyes, then I looked back up to the old lady.

"What's your name?" I asked.

"Samantha," she replied, then smiled a sweet smile and she was gone.

As I lay on the bed staring at where she had been, Sammy, my mom and my brother, Mike, walked into the room.

"Hi, honey," my mom said, kissing me on my forehead. "How you feeling?"

"Great," I replied as a stray tear of joy streamed down my face.

"Did you name her yet?" Mike asked.

"Yes," I said looking at all of them. "Her name is Samantha."

MY GUARDIAN ANGEL
By: Callie Cool

Tears were still running down my cheeks as I slowly walked out of the hospital with Dad; my step mom, Kathy; and Cory, my twin brother, after seeing my Grandma Sherry for the last time, or at least that's what my family said. The doctor told us that she had no longer than 48 hours to live, or maybe, just maybe a little bit longer, but no longer than a week at the most. Grandma Sherry was always a tough fighter, having fought arthritis for over twelve years which made her handicapped. But this time, she was losing.

Before heading to the Indianapolis Heart Hospital about twenty minutes away from the house, I had begged dad not to make me go. We both knew that Grandma Sherry didn't want us to see her like this, to see her life slowly fade away. I wanted to keep that promise, but it looked like I would be breaking that promise.

"Ali, this is going to be the last time that you might see your Grandma Sherry. If you don't go and say good-bye, then you might regret it later. Wouldn't you come and see me if I was on my death bed?" Dad said impatiently.

"Yeah, I would but Grandma Sherry wouldn't want us to see her dying like this. And this isn't about you. It's about grandma and what she wants before she dies!" I yelled, irritated. Sitting at the kitchen table, I placed my head into my hands and let out a long frustrated sigh, trying to get hold of myself.

"Don't you dare talk to me like that, young lady! We're going to the hospital and that's final!" he snapped, then left the kitchen.

My heart dropped to the pit of my stomach as we pulled into the hospital parking lot. *What will she look like? How will I react when we leave? Will she be awake talking when I walk into her room? Or will she be asleep?* My head started to spin with all the questions running through my head. I slowly got out of the car and followed my family toward the entrance.

True to his word, Dad dragged me into her room where my other family members were. A nurse with long brown hair and a tall, tanned body stood by the sink. My body froze in shock and tears ran down my face like a horrible rain storm. *What's going on? Is everything okay? Is Grandma okay?* I wondered as my body fought the urge of collapsing onto the floor in front of everyone. Spotting a seat in the corner by the window, I dragged my feet over to it and plopped into it just before my legs gave out. Everyone looked at me, concerned. I looked up at them with tears in my eyes.

"Do you want a Kleenex or something, dear?" The nurse asked sweetly with soft, hazel eyes, watching me cry.

I shook my head no.

She nodded then held a small sponge under the water and handing it to Grandpa. "Here, put this in your wife's mouth so it can stay moist," she said, drying her hands on a paper towel. Then she grabbed a Kleenex box, and handed it to me. "Just in case," she said with a smile. I grabbed the box from her hand and placed it on my lap. The nurse looked around the room checking to see if she'd forgotten anything, then left the room.

When I was able to move again, I slowly rose to me feet and walked over to the hospital bed were Grandma lay sleeping. She didn't move a muscle, except for her chest rising and falling as she breathed in and out.

"Will she wake up?" I asked, not caring who heard me.

"No," someone answered behind me softly in a deep, male voice. I looked up to see my Uncle Stan looking down at me from across the room, leaning against the wall. He stood up straight and walked over to me, then wrapped his arm around my shoulder and pulled me to his side. "The doctor gave her some medicine that makes her sleep deeply. That way she can pass peacefully."

I nodded my head against his chest as we both looked down at her. Uncle Stan was my favorite uncle. I always loved that he was always there for me when I needed him, someone that I could trust. Wrapped in his arms was like when I wrapped my little hand around his finger when I was a child. Even though I was close to everyone in my family, I was the closest to him.

The woman in the bed didn't look like Grandma Sherry with her red, rosy cheeks, gray puffy hair, and crippled hands. This woman was now a complete stranger whose hair was half gone and skin was very pale and fragile.

I gently wrapped my shaky hand around her fragile, crippled hand as more tears cheated and rolled down my face even faster than before. "Can she hear me?" I asked.

"Yeah, she can hear you, sweetie," Uncle Stan said.

I nodded. "I love you, Grandma," I whispered and stepped back away from the bed and Uncle Stan. I walked across the room and sat in the chair in the corner of the room I sat there for a couple of hours watching grandma take slow deep breaths. *Does she even know that we're here?* I wondered to myself.

"Come one, Ali. Let's eat some lunch, then we can come back," Uncle Stan said, waiting in the doorway. I nodded and followed him, my brother, and my cousin, Aaron, out into the waiting room where Kentucky Fried Chicken was waiting for us. I sat down in a deep red couch next to Cory and slowly nibbled on the chicken and cole slaw, as the image of Grandma Sherry slowly dying around the corner from me replayed within my mind.

After eating, we talked about random things to get the image out of our minds. Then we went back to the room with the rest of the family. I walked over to my chair and sat down looking at everyone in the room, then back at Grandma Sherry. A hand touched my shoulder lightly. I looked up to see Grandpa smiling down at me, trying very hard not to cry.

"You okay Ali?" He whispered then wiped his eyes with a Kleenex he held in his hands.

I shrugged. "Yeah, I guess so. Will she ever wake up to talk to me? I miss hearing her voice and her laugh," I said.

Grandpa slowly closed his eyes and shook his head even though I already knew the answer.

"No. I know, I miss hearing her voice, too."

I nodded in understanding and turned my attention back to Grandma Sherry who had her mouth slightly open, snoring softly.

"Mike ..." she moaned. Grandpa patted my head gently before going to the small counter and dipped the small sponge in water and dabbed it in her mouth. I perked up a little when I saw her move her head and bit down on the sponge gently moistening her mouth.

Is she waking up? I wondered to myself.

I got up and stood next to her, took her hand into mine and gently squeezed it. Cory came to stand beside me and smiled weakly. It looked like he had been crying, as well. His eyes were red and his cheeks were wet. He gently patted my shoulder with his hand and touched Grandma Sherry's hand before walking away.

After being at the hospital all day, it was time to go home. I grabbed my things and said my goodbyes to everyone. I leaned down to give Grandma a kiss on her cheek. "I love you, Grandma," I said, "You'll always be in my heart." Then I walked out of the room and looked back once more. That was my last time I saw my grandmother.

On our way to drop me off at my mother's house, I smirked at the fun memories I had of grandma and me when I was a little toddler. I will never forget the sleepovers we had, staying up all night — or at least she did. I'd usually fall asleep on the couch or on the floor watching Disney movies. Memories ran through my mind of going shopping at the mall with Grandma, looking at jewelry and going to the Disney Store and a pet store. Also, I remembered that we always called her a pack rat since her bedroom was filled with nothing but shopping bags with things in them that hadn't been opened for a long time.

"You okay, Ali?" Cory asked as his crystal blue eyes filled with concern.

I smiled weakly. "Yeah, I'm just thinking about the good memories I had with Grandma Sherry."

He nodded, understanding, then went back into his little book land, reading the *Eragon* series.

When I was dropped off, I said my good-byes and climbed into my mom's van. I told her what had happened this past week and then broke down into tears again when I told her about my visit to Grandma at the hospital. She knew I didn't want to be there to see Grandma dying. I cried so hard that mom had to pull off the interstate into a McDonald's to calm me down. She cradled me within her arms as I cried into her shirt. When I finally calmed down, we were back on the road heading home.

At home, tears slowly ran down my face once more as I looked at Grandma's picture of her and Mom. Mom was six weeks pregnant with me and Cory. Looking at the picture, I missed Grandma already.

"Ali? You okay, sweetie?" Mom asked, slowly opening my bedroom door to check on me.

I grabbed a Kleenex and wiped away my tears and blew my nose. I gently laid the picture back onto the night stand next to me. "Yeah, I guess," I replied, letting out a heavy sigh. "Will this get any easier? Letting her go?"

Mom walked over to my bed and sat down next to me, then wrapped her arms around me in comfort. I lay my head on her shoulder and let the tears soak her shirt. She rubbed my arms and gently rocked me back and forth. "It will, sweetie. It will. The first few years are usually the hardest, but after that, it'll get easier."

"Promise?" I asked looking deep into her crystal blue eyes.

"I promise. She loved you very much. You were here little Tinker Bell," she said, pulling back to look into my eyes. "She would be so proud of you, being so strong with this tough situation you're going through." Mom got up and kissed my head, then left me in my room, turning out my bedroom light behind her.

I lay in my bed for what seemed like hours wide awake, not even a bit tired. Was it because I'm still depressed about Grandma Sherry? Giving up on my sleep, I got out of bed and walked down the hall to the living room and popped in a movie. I grabbed a pillow and a blanket and curled up in a ball on the couch.

I must have fallen back to sleep because I woke up to mom covering me with a blanket, then she gently kissed my head. "Mom ..." I moaned, hugging the blanket close to my body.

"Shush ... go back to sleep. Everything's fine. Go back to sleep," she cooed, then turned off the movie and TV before going back to bed.

It didn't take me long to fall back to sleep on the couch. I woke the next morning to mom talking on the phone. It wasn't good because she had tears in her eyes. After hanging up, she sat down on the couch with me and told me that Grandma Sherry passed away early in the morning. I cried all day after hearing about Grandma's death. Especially since the next day was my birthday.

I was absolutely miserable on my birthday. I tried my hardest to act happy, but everyone knew I wasn't. Every year for my birthday, she would send me a birthday card that had fairy dust on the envelope to make it sparkle. When I opened the card to read it, fairy dust would fly everywhere! Mom really hated it when Cory and I opened the cards in the car before going inside the house. I laugh at the memory, then frowned, realizing that I would never get one of those cards again for my birthday, unless Grandpa sent it. But that wouldn't be the same.

The day of Grandma Sherry's funeral was really stressful. All of my family members from my father's side came for the week for the funeral. Talk about a full house! I played out back most of the time either tossing a football around or playing Crochet while everyone else was inside in the air conditioning.

On the way to the funeral, my whole family stopped at Starbucks to get a bite to eat since we didn't have time to eat at home. I got a huge blueberry muffin and a big cup of chocolate milk since I'm not a fan of coffee.

Once at the grave site, I saw the green tent above rows of white chairs and a brownish gold casket. In the distance was a field filled with cows grazing on the grass and a big white barn behind them. Their tails swished back and forth shooing away the flies.

Tears rolled down my cheeks before we stepped out of the car. I slowly walked to the casket where grandma was and ran my shaky hand over it, wondering what she looked like since we didn't have a visitation. It was her wish. Grandma didn't want her family crying over her; she wanted us to remember the way she was, always smiling and laughing. Her tombstone was dark silver with her name written across it and a fairy holding a handful of flowers next to her name. On the back had my dads, and uncles and aunts names on it in cursive writing.

"What is she wearing?" I asked when I felt a hand resting on my shoulder, Uncle Stan.

"A lacy, white dress," he answered softly, trying to hold back the tears himself. "She looks like an angel. Pink cheeks and red rosy lips." Then he pulled me into his arms for a hug. I buried my face into his shirt and soaked it with my tears, tightening my hold on him as he gently rubbed my back.

"Can everyone take their seats, please, so that we can get started?" the minister asked.

I let go of Uncle Stan and took a seat in the front row next to my Aunt Terri and Grandpa. Everyone else said their last words of their conversations they were having with one another before taking their seats, as well. "Thank you. We're all here today to say goodbye to a wonderful woman, Sharon (Sherry) Lee Cool, who went home to the Lord Jesus Christ on the eighth of August," the minister said.

The minister said a few more words, than prayed before inviting my grandpa to stand up to say a few words. Then it was my turn.

Stay calm, stay calm, I told myself over and again as I slowly rose from my seat and stood next to the casket, and began talking as if I was speaking to her.

"Gosh, I miss you, Grandma. I'll always remember the fun times we used to have together, going to the mall looking at girlie stuff, staying up late until I fell asleep on the couch or in your arms watching Disney movies, or telling fairy stories. But most importantly, I'll always remember that you were the first one to hold me when I was born, and that you came up with my middle name, Tatiana. You'll always be in my heart, Grandma. I may be small, but I have a big heart, a big heart like yours. I always have and always will. I miss you, my guardian angel," I said, then kissed my fingertips and pressed them onto the casket before turning my attention to the crying audience and taking my seat.

Many hands touched my shoulder, telling me what a beautiful speech I had made. I smiled and thanked them all.

Aunt Terri then stepped to the casket carrying a small basket with little baggies of purple, white, and pink glitter. "Before we go, I would like for all the kids to come up, take a baggy of glitter and sprinkle some onto the casket if they want. We all know how much she loved glitter or what she called fairy dust."

All the kids, including me, got up and took a baggy, then walked over to the casket and sprinkled some of the fairy dust on it. One of my younger cousins dumped all the glitter on it, than cried for another. Unfortunately for him, there were no more baggies.

I pinched a little bit of my glitter and let it fall gracefully out of my fingers and down onto the casket, then zipped the baggy up and put it in my pocket so that I won't lose it. I didn't put all the glitter onto the casket. I wanted to keep some to remember this day and Grandma.

Before leaving the cemetery to eat at a church, I watched from a distance as Grandma's body was slowly lowered into the ground beside her father's grave. Grandpa wanted to bury her by her family's grave and by the church that she used to go to when she was a little girl.

The church all of us were going to go eat at was about ten minutes away from the cemetery, or that's what my grandpa told me. My heart dropped to my stomach as tears poured down my already wet face silently saying "good bye" and "I love you" to Grandma's grave.

As we drove away, within my head I could hear her say, "I love you, Tink. You'll always be my little TinkerBell." I never really knew why she called me that, but deep down I knew that it meant something very special to her. I wanted so badly to tell her how much I missed her already, but I couldn't.

I laughed as my father tried to find his way to the church, but he ended up getting lost, so it took us longer to get there than everyone else. We all hooped and hollered when we finally found the church, after twenty minutes or so. The church looked old with white wooden siding, and it looked very small with a big stained-glass window above the brown door. The cross on the top of the roof sparkled in the sunlight, giving us a friendly welcome.

I followed the sound of people laughing and talking just downstairs leading to the basement where everyone was standing in a big line to get their food. I followed dad, Cory, and Kathy to place our things on a table in the back corner before going over to stand in line with everyone else. Once I filled my plate with roast beef, corn, mashed potatoes, and a few cookies, I went back to my seat.

"Hey, sweetie!" Grandpa interrupted me saying a silent prayer.

"Hi, Grandpa!" I said as I took a bite of roast beef.

He set his plate down next to mine and sat down on the chair beside me. "I have something for you before you leave to go back home," he said.

I raised my eyebrows, confused, and covered my mouth with my hand, "What do you mean?" I asked, swallowing my full mouth of food.

"It's something that your Grandma Sherry wanted me to give you before she passed," he replied with a smile.

I nodded and returned the smile. We ate in silence while we finished eating our meal. I shoved the last bite of corn into my mouth, then threw away my trash as Grandpa did the same. Grandpa waved me over to stand next to him by a black piano with Cory and my cousins. My heart beat fast and hard as I slowly walked over to him, wondering what he was up to.

"Now," Grandpa began as I drew near, "Before you kids leave here to head back home, I wanted to give you each a yellow rose in remembrance of your Grandma Sherry. Your Grandma Sherry loved yellow roses. It was her favorite flower. So when you kids go home, I want you to either scrapbook it or put it in a vase of water until it dies then scrapbook it." Then he handed a rose to each of us. I carefully held mine in my hands, trying not to get pricked by the small thorns. Everyone nodded in agreement and said "thank you" before heading back to their seats, admiring their yellow roses. I was just turning around to head over back to my table when Grandpa stopped me.

"Ali, I want to give you a couple more things that belonged to your Grandma Sherry. She kept them in a little shopping bag in our bedroom with the other shopping bags," he explained softly, kneeling down on the ground, eyelevel.

Grandpa dug his hand into his pant pocket and pulled out a little dark blue box and handed it to me. I carefully opened it and looked inside and gasped as I looked at the small, golden ring with a tiny, golden Tinkerbell blowing a kiss. There was also a small, golden teddy bear with a silver diamond ribbon around its neck and bright pink eyes. I carefully held the ring with my little fingers, trying not to drop it, and slid it onto my right middle finger. I held out my hand to examine it, leaving the little bear in the bag.

"It's kind of big," I admitted.

"You'll grow into it one day. Don't worry," Grandpa promised with a smile.

I smile up at him and give him a hug, and said, "Thank you, Grandpa. They're pretty. I'll take good care of them."

"You're welcome, baby girl," Grandpa said, hugging me back. He squeezed me once more then walked away. I watched him leave, then took out the little bear to examine it. Flipping it around carefully within my fingers, I noticed a small opening around its body. I carefully opened it and saw

Angels Among Us 53

some kind of hard orange cream inside. My eyebrows rose up in confusion. *What on earth is this stuff?* I wondered, then raised the bear up to my nose and sniffed it. A sweet familiar smell filled my nose making my heart jump.

Why does this smell so familiar? I thought to myself, then it hit me. It's the same perfume that Grandma Sherry put on her wrists. Smiling, I rubbed some of the perfume onto my finger and rubbed it onto my wrists. Happy tears rolled down my cheeks as I let all the memories come flooding back.

I smiled looking down at my new ring and bear, feeling Grandma Sherry smiling down at me. I held out my ring and bear close to my heart, knowing that my guardian angel would always be in my heart ... forever and always.

In Loving Memory of
Sharon Lee Cool (Grandma Sherry)
1939-2007

HIDDEN
By: Sara Drake

Just when you really thought you knew who you were, something happens and you discover your real true identity. I grew up in a small town on the outskirts of London called Esher. My childhood and teenage years were quite straightforward. I was brought up in a middle-class family by my mum and dad, along with my older adopted brother, Jake, to have to contend with.

Mum had a lot of problems with conceiving naturally, so she gave up all hope of having a child. After they had adopted Jake, they had assumed in time that they would just adopt a sibling for him, but God had other plans in store. So when she discovered that she was pregnant with me, she was overjoyed.

As I was growing up, she would always say that she believed that she had been blessed by God and that I was her little miracle. Mum and Dad were of Spanish decent and had very dark features, so my golden blonde hair and bright green eyes were the only strange things to them about me. Strangers who didn't know often asked if I was the adopted one. It didn't bother me, but Mum would seem a little upset.

As I grew, not much went on — just your normal day to day family life. I did really well in school and wanted to go into journalism when I'd finished college. My mum often said what a sweet-natured person I was, though genuinely speaking, I was quite shy and felt awkward around people that I didn't know very well. Occasionally I felt like a outsider, but could never pinpoint the reason why. That was until was till I was about seventeen. As then my life took a traumatic leap into something very out of the ordinary. I will never forget that fateful day, when it was revealed that I would be running for the rest of my life from demons that were intent on trying to destroy me.

I often wondered to myself, *why?* Why would God not have enough power to be able to really protect us? But I guess that this evil has becoming just too strong! Man has given the Devil far too much power, that our Father is now sadly losing the battle for Heaven and Earth. So to save his angels from being destroyed, he had to make us all hidden — hidden inside a human body and to be just like one of you.

Although if I had known this much earlier, it would have been of great benefit, as then I could have saved her.

My name is Vincent, but I am also known in Heaven as Ecanus, the Angel of Writing. I continued to fight for the great cause, but I seriously feared that we are on the very sad road to defeat. It could even be that humans are really the ones who will decide our destiny.

On that particular day, I was out with Alisha. She was the most amazing girl who had finally agreed to a date with me, after I'd pestered her constantly for the last eight months or so. She was just something out of this world — far too beautiful for a proper description that would do her true justice. But I'll just try and give you a brief idea of what I saw.

She had very long thick and wavy, crimson red hair, with the bluest, big eyes that you'd ever seen. They sparkled like bright topaz gems and the deep blue sea. She had an enchanting smile with deep red, plump lips that would just melt the heart of even the grumpiest person. At the time when she had suddenly walked into the classroom, I thought that my instant attraction to her was just due to her sheer beauty. But as I discovered later on, it was very likely because she was just one of us.

Naturally, of course, I would love her, as she was Heaven sent, too. She was friendly to me from the get go and would laugh at my half-hearted attempts at humor. In truth, I didn't believe for a moment that she would see me as anything other than a friend, but when I noticed that she wouldn't give the time of day to the popular guys, I started to believe that maybe I had a chance. First, we went out to eat some lunch at the pizza bar. As I looked starry eyed into hers, we chatted away. I was trying so hard to look cool and not the nerd that other people said I was.

Most of my life up to the point, my head was lost in some book either learning about ancient places or reading about some mythical beings. I just loved writing, too, and often spent hours coming up with some new stories of dragons and heroes saving the day. Unfortunately, being a hero in this reality is much harder than in any of those stories I had written about.

After we had dinner, I took her ice skating. It was something she said she had always wanted to do. She laughed at the amount of times that I fell over, landing hard on my ass. But she herself glided with perfection, just as if it was second nature to her, even though she swore again to me that she had never been ice skating before. There was a lot about her that I didn't know, as if she was hiding secrets. All anyone knew about her was that she moved here from Canada eight months ago. After her parents had tragically died, she was now living here in England with her aunt and uncle. And she would completely freeze up if any of my questions steered in that direction. Her eyes would moist over and she quickly looked away, saying it was not something she couldn't talk about right at the moment. So I decided not to mention it and just let her tell me in her own time.

After I had fallen down for the hundredth time, she reached down and took one of my hands to pull me back up, laughing as she did. Our eyes suddenly met and we shared a special moment. It was strange, like somehow I had known her for all of time. She smiled so sweetly at me before our lips locked and we lightly kissed, but then she quickly pulled away looking panic stricken.

"What's wrong?" I asked, concerned.

"We need to leave. I think that they've found me!" she replied, nervously scanning the rink in every direction.

"Who?" I asked, as she grabbed my hand. We sped across the ice with her trying to keep me from tumbling down again.

"I'll tell you when we are safe. You need to know the truth about yourself now anyway," she cried, pulling me along as we quickly left the ice.

In the sitting area, we took our skates off and hurriedly tried to put our shoes back on. But it was all too late. Someone suddenly grabbed me from behind. Clutching my throat tightly, they pulled me up against them.

I struggled, clawing at his arm, but I was never built for any real strength. My dad always said that I was such a puny kid and how he had hoped that I'd butch out as I got older, but sadly that never happened. Alisha though on the other hand, seemed like she had suddenly turned into Xena the princess warrior.

From where this strength arose, I didn't know. She quickly rammed into us, pinning me and the guy up against the brick wall. Her eyes were also now glowing white. She then snapped his arm that was still around my neck, just as if it was nothing more than a twig. He screamed loudly as he released me. Alisha, then quickly grabbed hold of me and screamed, "Run, Vincent, quickly!"

We fled as fast as we could, running fast down the road that backed right off from the Ice skating rink. I almost tripped, but just as I thought I was going to fall flat on my face, I found myself rising quickly into the air.

Panic filled my entire being and my heart raced as I saw that the ground disappearing beneath my feet. Trying to make some sense of the crazy situation, I could hear what sounded like the beating of big wings. As I craned my neck up and to the side of me, I saw massive white, feathered wings. But more shockingly, I suddenly realized that the wings belonged to Alisha!

She flew swiftly until we were several blocks away, then we quickly descended into an alleyway. Touching down with a slight bump on the ground, I was relieved to be back on solid ground. She set me down as her huge wings folded quickly back up. They seemed to completely disappear, as if they had never existed. I looked totally dumbstruck at her, unable to understand. She put her hand lightly up to my pale face and rubbed my cheek.

"We need to have a serious talk, Vincent," she said.

I tried to open my mouth to speak, but no sound came out except what could only be described as a little croaking noise.

"I know this is really hard to accept, but you will understand everything in due time. I promise you," she said as she smiled, looking straight into my bewildered eyes.

I frowned, still trying to believe any of this. She was just about to say something, then out of nowhere, a group of four nasty looking guys appeared behind me. Turning around, the first thing that I saw was that their faces seemed almost contorted or deformed. Alisha quickly pushed in front of me, trying to protect me. But before I knew, something happened: the one thing that I would prevent if I could go back in time.

The four guys all joined hands, as a bright, red light appeared in each of their eyes. Suddenly, a laser beam shot from out of each of them, fusing together in the middle, forming one single lightning bolt. It hit her full on and she shook very violently before falling down to the ground. I looked on in horror at her charred remains, just before I felt it.

There was an overwhelming, strange feeling that was brewing deep within my stomach. As it rose further up to the surface, two huge white wings sprouted from my back. A fire radiated from within me and I became hotter and hotter until I nearly exploded, engulfing everything in sight, including the four guys. Within seconds, they turned into nothing but dust. As the feeling started to lesson, I began to cool down and my wings retracted back and completely vanished. *What the bloody hell is going on?* I thought nervously to myself.

I was overwhelmed with disbelief and grief at what had just happened. My mind was racing. What did this mean? In a daze, I walked aimlessly away, trying to understand. It was really late as I crossed over a small river bridge and, for a moment, I thought of throwing myself in. But suddenly from behind came a deep voice, "You don't really want to do that, Ecanus. You would be letting them win the easy way."

I quickly turned around to see a tall, dark-haired guy about twenty or so standing beside me, looking over the rails.

"What did you just call me?" I asked, clearly shocked.

He turned to face me and replied with a smile, "I called you Ecanus, because that is your true name."

"Who are you? And what do you know about what just happened?" I shouted angrily, having no idea what was going on.

"My name is Gabriel. I am an angel just like you and as Charmiene was, too," he said as he placed a gentle hand upon my shoulder, then squeezed it lightly. A sad look radiated within his brown eyes.

"When you say Charmiene you mean Alisha, don't you?" I asked, my voice suddenly catching.

"Yes. Sadly, we have lost yet another angel in this terrible war. But now that you have awoken, we have gained as we have also lost. We finally have some hope now, my brother," he said.

It took a while for me to understand any of this. I needed more answers. Looking confused, I asked, "Who were the guys that killed Alisha? And if I'm really an angel, then why am I here on earth? Also, why didn't I already know that I am an angel?" I paused for a moment, then continued, "How did Alisha know what I am?"

Gabriel looked up at the stars.

"We are sadly losing the battle for Heaven and Earth, Vincent," Gabriel began. "Hell and the Devil are winning. The devil and his many demons have become very strong, all due to the evil corruption of man. Demons have taken out so many of heaven's angels that they are no longer safe now in heaven. Heaven is mostly in ruins, as the devil has penetrated into its holy barriers. But to fully succeed and become the king of heaven and earth, he needs to get to God who is still protected by some of the light that exists within his angels. For him to win, he needs to eradicate every single angel. Only then will he be able to enter into God's realm and destroy him. So God had no other choice but to hide all of his remaining angels. His only available option was to send us to Earth in human form. So you and I, and the rest of us were born as humans. To try and protect us as long as possible, we also had no memory of what we once were. Even with these human bodies, we still send our protective light up to our Father." He stopped talking for a moment, even more sad than before.

"They were demons that you and Alisha faced. And now they know who and what you are. Now you will be in danger and you will need always to be ready to fight. Like a few other angels, Alisha could sense an angel within a human. After she had been discovered by the demons in Canada, she fled to safety here. She could have sensed you, even over a great distance," Gabriel said.

"So what was she doing? Waiting for the best time to reveal who and what I am to me?" I asked, confused.

"Not exactly, the longer you were kept in the dark, the better. She would only reveal such things if it was truly necessary for your wellbeing. And even then, she would have only been trying to keep watch over you. But I fear she grew too close to you, and was not being vigilant enough, as a result. She wasn't looking out for her own safety," he replied, looking down at the ground.

I paced back and forth on the bridge, trying to make sense of everything, but it was all spinning out of control inside my head. I felt physically sick as I gripped the hard steel rails of the bridge. After finally composing myself, I asked him, "So, what now?"

"Now you must learn how to harness your angel powers. The only place where you're safe on earth is inside a church, the only place where there can be no true evil. This is what demons live on and how they become strong. There you will be able to learn how to help influence humans on a good path. This severely weakens the devil. But we have a huge fight ahead of us. Never before has evil had such a stronghold over them," Gabriel said, looking away.

Sadly, I realized what this all meant. I would have to sacrifice so much now and I could never go back home or have a normal life, as my family would be in danger. I also learned from Gabriel that this was how Alisha had lost her own parents.

Quickly, Gabriel led me to a church, and there I met with two other angels and learned how to fully use my powers. Each angel possesses different powers and mine was blowing up demons! The other angels were pleased that I was no longer a sleeper angel, and would often want me to be by their side when they dared venture out of the safety of the church. But sometimes I would weep in despair, as I stood alone in the church, thinking about my parents or poor Alisha. Sometimes I wondered if I could really go on, but deep down I knew that I must survive, as there is a lot depending upon me. But the real way of winning this war is that humans must realize the true error of their ways, for now they are what really determines theirs, ours and even God's own fate.

ANGEL 101
By: Stephanie Greenhalgh

I watched the rain pour down in a steady stream through the window. I've never really been a fan of the treadmill, but when a good rain blows into town, exercising on one is a must. Running clears my head. As my mileage adds up on the screen in front of me, I can't help but let my mind drift over the past few weeks.

To say they have been strange is a gross understatement. I found out a few weeks ago that I'm a Human Angel, or HA for short. Most of the time, a person has to die to become an angel, but I'm special. I am one of a handful of Human Angels. They are rare. I'm rare. I couldn't help but smile. I love that I'm unique.

Several weeks ago, I was stalked — that's a story all its own — but at the end of it all, my Guardian Angel, or GA, died saving my life. When this happened, his angel essence found its way right into me, making me an HA. I have some special powers, although I'm not real sure what they are or how they work yet. According to Angel Law, I have people to protect and guard called Specifics, or Specs for short. Honestly, I'm muddling my way through this whole angel thing; it didn't exactly come with directions. I like to think of it as Angel 101.

I grinned at my own creativity. Before I have time to resume my thought processes, my timer buzzes and my treadmill slowed. Pleased that I got in my five miles despite the downpour, I glanced at the clock. I had about forty minutes before my Spec arrived, so I headed back to the locker rooms to change.

Freshly showered, I dried my long-layered chestnut hair and admired the freshly streaked blonde highlights. My dark brown eyes studied my fair complexion carefully as I applied a touch of powder, bronzer, a quick coat of mascara, and finished with a quick dash of lip gloss. It was humid in Vegas today due to the rain this morning, so I opted for a short pink pair of runner shorts and a black tank. I slid my feet into my black and gray Nikes and pulled my hair up in a cute, easy bun on the top of my head.

I checked my reflection in the full-length mirror before walking out. I turned right and then left, admiring my toned runner's legs. All my recent work had paid off. Most days, I run through Red Rock Canyon with my dog, but the treadmill serves its purpose on rainy days.

Feeling better after an intense sweat session and a shower, I headed to the front desk to wait for my Spec. Her name was Sarah. I've known her for a few weeks. She's a dowdy mother of three and apparently in need of protection from a Big Bad something, only I don't know have any idea what this Big Bad is or how to protect her at the moment. I got her information via a carrier peacock. Yes, I said a carrier peacock. It's an angel thing. They fly around all over the place, but you have to be an angel to see them. It's kind of cool, but still a little unsettling to see things others don't. Sometimes, I think I'm crazy and need to be institutionalized, but I know in my soul this is all really happening. It's been a transition period on my part; it would help if I knew more But since Human Angels are so uncommon, there is very little known about them. And Guardian Angels are no help. I'm still alive, so I'm left to my own cunning and ingenuity to figure things out.

There are many things that are new to me. Since I had absolutely no idea how to engage my Spec, I decided to use my human part to help my angel part. I'm a personal trainer, so I called and told her she won six months of free training. It took some coaxing, but finally I convinced her that one of her friends must have entered her and I was already paid, so she might as well enjoy it.

Finally, Sarah came for her first session and I wasn't sure what to make of her. She was a tad overweight, dressed in a frumpy manner, and looked heavier than she was. She had long, mousy brown hair, which she always wore in a braid down her back. She had plain brown eyes and didn't wear a stitch of make-up. And to make matters worse, she showed up on the first day wearing Crocs with socks!

Since I had absolutely no idea how I was supposed to help her, I treated her like any other client, with a simple goal in mind: health and a positive attitude. After a few weeks, I'm pleased to say she morphed into a new Sarah. She's more outgoing and has lost some pounds. She's even started wearing a little mascara and blush to highlight her eyes and stunning check bones.

Needless to say, I'm pleased with the progress I've made with Sarah the person, but I'm still at a loss as to what to do with Sarah the Spec. She cancelled her last three sessions at the last minute with minimal explanation, so I haven't seen her in a week. I was starting to worry about her.

The sun shining through the glass doors caught my eye as a little blonde whisked through the double glass doors. She was smiling and waving at me. I didn't recognize her and glanced behind me to see who she was waving to, but there was no one there. I turned back around and she was standing right in front of me, grinning. The perky little blonde was my sweet, mousy Sarah. Whoa! She had on some tight black yoga pants and a bright green sports bra under a gray tank top. She had chopped her hair into a sexy, shaggy blonde bob. She also sported a perfect French manicure. What a transformation! She smiled brightly and hugged me. I couldn't help but get swept up into her excitement.

"Wow, Sarah! You look amazing! I love the hair and the new workout wardrobe!" I grabbed her hand and admired her new nails. A smile plastered to her face, Sarah could hardly contain herself.

"Oh, Avery! Daryl came home last weekend from his latest sales convention. He made a huge sale and spoiled us all. I got this fantastic makeover and he bought Jeremy a used car as a belated sixteenth birthday gift! He even got the younger kids new clothes and gifts. It's been a great week! And I'm so sorry about cancelling, but we've been busy doing family things," she squealed, bouncing up and down.

"That's great, Sarah. I'm so glad to hear some of your financial worries have been taken care of," I said, genuinely happy for her. I know how hard her husband's struggling sales business had been on the family recently, especially on her oldest son, Jeremy. He had a meager sixteenth birthday two weeks before. She'd mentioned how heartbreaking it had been the last time I'd seen her. This good news still didn't help me with the Spec part of Sarah, but at least things were improving in her life. Hopefully, I didn't have to worry about her so much.

"Come on. Let's get started. I want to introduce you to yoga today. I think you'll really enjoy it, plus you're dressed perfectly for it," I said giving her my signature lopsided grin. We headed through the gym toward the back rooms where they hold the athletic classes.

Near the end of our workout, my phone buzzed. Normally, I don't answer my phone or check text messages during sessions, but I had been waiting for a reply from the girl that saved my life last month. In my haste for more information about my new situation, I looked down to check the message.

Suddenly, the room vibrated. My equilibrium was thrown off, so I immediately tried to steady myself. I looked up as several screws popped out of the wall. The large speaker mounted on the wall teetered and tottered then plummeted to the ground toward my Spec. I panicked and dropped the phone — the text message forgotten. Stunned, I brought my hands to my temples. At that very moment, the heavy speaker zigged while Sarah zagged and it landed with a crash just inches from my Spec. I exhaled loudly. *Holy crap! Did I do that?* I wondered. Thankful for whatever had happened, I bolted toward my Spec.

"Sarah, are you alright?" I shouted, kneeling down to help her.

"Oh, my goodness," Sarah said with a shaky voice. "That thing almost landed on my head!"

"Yeah, you were lucky. It missed you by inches," I said, trying not to let my own voice quiver as I reached down to help her up.

She exhaled steadily. "Boy, my Guardian Angel must've been looking out for me today." Sarah's unsteady voice turned into a low laugh, even though terror still filled her eyes.

A nervous laugh escaped my lips. "Yeah, I guess."

Sarah looked at me seriously, and asked, "You don't believe in Guardian Angels?"

Taken aback, I was at a brief loss for words. I never expected to have this conversation with anyone. "Um ... no ... it's just ... well, I guess I never really thought about it," I said honestly and, in truth, I hadn't ever thought about it until last month.

"I see," Sarah said curtly. "I believe in Guardian Angels and I always have, Avery. My mom used to tell me that one watched over me. It's funny ... she even named him Nate. She said he was handsome and had blue eyes." Sarah laughed at the memory.

My stomach dropped. Nate and I have an interesting and complicated relationship. Not only is he my former Guardian Angel, he's also the love of my life. We are currently living together. I needed a moment to process all the pieces of the puzzle that were suddenly falling into place. "Um … let's get you to the juice bar," I replied, changing the subject.

She nodded and limped a bit. When she'd slid sideways, her ankle had slammed down on a free weight. I quickly deposited her on a stool and went to get her an ice pack. "Hold tight," I said before I got in line.

As I waited, I thought about Nate. I fell in love with him long before I knew he was my Guardian Angel. We dated for over a year before he abruptly disappeared from my life. Then last month, he showed up around the same time as my stalker. He was part of a little team that saved me. It was Nate's "angel death" that actually saved my life. It was at that moment I inherited his angel essence, which turned me into the HA. I guess it made sense that I acquired his Spec, as well.

Once his guardianship ended, he had been given a second chance as payment for all the good he had done as a Guardian Angel, or GA. He had been sent back to Earth to resume the human life that had been cut short decades ago. Anger brewed in my eyes. He had some serious explaining to do. Why hadn't he told me that Sarah was his Spec? It might have been helpful! Why would he have kept that from me? As I neared the counter, I made a mental note to confront him the moment I got home.

I ordered a bag of ice and a pomegranate smoothie loaded with protein and antioxidants for Sarah. I made my way back to the table and she was grinning down at her phone.

"Well, I'm glad to see a smile after that incident," I said, handing her the drink. Then I placed the ice on her right ankle that was now puffy and turning a dark purple. She winced slightly when I applied the ice, then took a sip of her smoothie.

"I just texted Jeremy and asked him if he could come pick me up. I don't think I can drive with this ankle and, in all honesty, I should probably get to a Quick Care and get my ankle looked at sooner rather than later. He said he was close and would be here soon," she said before taking another sip of her drink.

"Put your arm around me and I'll help you get to the front of the building," I said. Then we hobbled together toward the double glass doors. I idly wondered if that was the Big Bad the message from the carrier peacock alluded to. Was that what I was supposed to protect her from?

"That's Jeremy's car parked outside," Sarah said with a smile. Her love for her son lit up her face.

I pushed open the doors and Sarah hopped through with most of her weight on me. I grabbed the door handle and it vibrated. Suddenly I felt uneasy, queasy and disoriented all at once. Sarah seemed unfazed as she smiled, thanked me and eased herself into the vehicle. I could barely hear over the buzzing. The color drained from my face and I tried to steady myself on the car, but that only made everything worse. Then I saw it, Jeremy's eyes. They glowed red when he lowered his sunglasses and smirked at me. My world whirled and twirled around me. I hadn't saved Sarah from the Big Bad after all. It was right in front of me, living in her son.

I felt helpless. Functioning on autopilot, I pushed the car door away. Completely oblivious, Sarah pulled the door closed and waved through the window. As the evil in the car sped off, my physical world calmed down and returned to normal, but my mind swirled frantically in a million different directions. I just sent my Spec home with the Big Bad and I had no idea what to do. I wanted to cry, to scream, to throw a temper tantrum. I needed help, now! Suddenly, I thought of Nate. He was my only hope.

I ran inside and informed the young girl manning the front desk that I had an emergency to attend to. She sweetly offered to cancel the rest of my clients for the day. Within seconds, I was in my car, swerving in and out of traffic to get to my condo. Traffic was definitely one of the pitfalls of being a HA.

"Nate!" I cried, bursting through the door.

"Hey, babe. Where's the fire?" he asked casually, leaning against the counter in the spacious kitchen eating a bowl of something, barefoot.

Nate took my breath away. He stood beside the counter, tall and lean in nothing but a pair of basketball shorts. His ripped abs and sculpted chest were shaded lightly with dark brown hair. Now, he's a golf pro and believed that a fit body produced a better swing, so he prided himself on his toned, muscular physic.

Nate's ocean blue eyes danced when he saw me, brushing his shaggy, brown hair out of his eyes. But the laughter in his eyes quickly faded when he realized I was on the verge of hysterics. "Whoa, babe. What the hell is going on? Are you okay?" he asked urgently, setting down his meal. He embraced me quickly after checking me out for cuts and bruises.

I stammered, barely able to sort out everything that had happened. "Sarah, your old Spec … is mine now. I saved her from a falling speaker … her son is bad. I couldn't breathe … he had red eyes … I sent her home with the Big Bad. Why didn't you tell me I had your Spec?" Tears streamed down my cheeks as I fell into Nate's arms, hoping he could somehow make all this okay.

"Avery, I need you to be strong," Nate said, then grabbed my face and looked into my eyes. "I'm sorry. I couldn't tell you about my Spec until you found out on your own. It was one of the restrictions of me being sent back. But we can't dwell on that now. We need to focus on Sarah."

I closed my eyes. My inner strength stopped the flow of my tears as I slowly breathed in and out, trying to calm myself. He's right. He's going to help me. I can do this. I have to think about Sarah. "Okay," I replied, then opened my eyes to look into his.

"Good," he softly said, loosening his grip on my shoulders. "Now, tell me everything from start to finish." I relayed all of the events since the moment I laid eyes on Sarah today, detail by detail, ending with the rumbling of my world and seeing Jeremy's red eyes and sinister smirk.

Nate leaned back against the counter and brought his right hand up to the slight stubble on his chin. "Hmmm ... I think Jeremy must be a vessel for something more menacing. He's fine in there for now, but we need to figure out what's taken over his body before we can do anything," Nate said.

"*WHAT?* I'm not going to let anything happen to Sarah! Tell me what you know about Human Angels ... about me!" I demanded. Nate dropped his hands from his chin, looking at me questioningly. I closed my eyes to focus my thoughts. "She's not your Spec anymore, Nate. I have to save her. I saved her from that speaker. I know I did. Now, tell me about me ... about the stuff I can do ... please," I pleaded in a softer, more controlled voice.

"Honestly, Ave, I don't know. I've never known a Human Angel before. But I know Guardian Angels can do just about anything to save their Spec, including giving up their own angel life. But you are different and I'm not excited to have you rush off to give your life."

I looked at him evenly, then replied, "You gave your angel life for me."

He couldn't hold my gaze, lowering his eyes. "That's different."

I turned to face him and grabbed his hands, then looked into his clear blue eyes. "Nate, please help me save her."

"I don't know how anymore, Ave. I'm sorry," he said sadly. "I know that most guardians have the power to protect. You should be able to shield her from whatever is living in Jeremy, but what is going to save you?"

"I have to try, don't I? I have to trust that this has all been given to me for a reason, right?" I asked.

He looked at me in a new way before he responded. "You're right, Avery. Go to her. You'll know what to do. It's inside you now." Then he leaned down to rest his forehead against mine. "Please, be careful. And when you feel overcome with evil, think of this," he whispered before cupping my chin into the palm of his hand and kissed me passionately.

I leaned into his kiss as my lips hungrily found his. I knew he would make it all better and I planned to thank him properly for it, but right now I had a Spec to save. "I love you. And don't worry, we'll finish this later. I've gotta run."

"Go ... and come home soon," Nate whispered intensely, brushing my hand across his lips. I couldn't help but smile as I grabbed my keys, then walked backward toward the door. I winked at Nate and blew him a kiss as he shook his head. He smiled and caught my kiss before the door closed.

I drove like a madwoman, weaving in and out of traffic. Thankfully, I programmed Sarah's address into my GPS shortly after my carrier peacock delivered the info, having a suspicion I might need it one day.

I stopped in front of Sarah's small-single story home in a regular track neighborhood in Vegas and sighed with dark despair, for the whole house radiated evil. Pain came from the house and immediately I knew that Sarah was in trouble. It hurt deep in my gut, like someone was sucking out my insides. Taking several deep breaths, I thought about Nate and the pain lessened. I smiled, thinking about our vacation to Hawaii last year. Suddenly, the pain was gone and I felt strong. My body radiated with positive energy, so I knew it was time. Resigned and focused on the mission, I got out of my car and moved toward the house.

Stealthily, I made my way to the back of the house and ducked into some bushes. I carefully peered through the window. Shocked and horrified, I was completely knocked off guard by what I saw.

A figure hovered about two feet off the ground, as a black cloak rippled around him. His face was hidden underneath the cloak, but his long boney hands stuck out and pointed to two other figures on their knees in front of it. Greenish smoke emanated from the figures on the floor, and went into the hands of Black Cloak.

Suddenly, I knew the figures were Sarah and Jeremy. Black Cloak was sucking their souls right out of their bodies. Then another person standing behind Black Cloak caught my eye. Fear tormented his face, and I knew this had to be Sarah's husband, Daryl.

"You said you only needed to use Jeremy as a vessel. You promised you'd leave him alone once you got Sarah's soul, since she has the soul of an angel and will one day be a Guardian Angel. You said that her soul was more than enough to cover the debt for my losses at the casino," Daryl pleaded.

Well, I didn't expect that. Her own husband sold her out for his gambling debt. Jerk. Now, I was really ticked off, but before I could react, a sharp pain in my gut seized me again. I doubled over as Sarah's pain sliced through me.

"Fool!" a dark, sinister voice boomed. "He's the spawn of an angel. I didn't realize he would be quite so tasty. You owe me your life. Would you rather I took that?" Black Cloak asked as his boney fingers sucked Jeremy's soul from his body. The boy coughed slightly in his unconscious state and Black Cloak moaned hungrily.

"No," Daryl whimpered and wet himself.

"You're lucky I'm not taking it now. Shut up while I finish my delicious meal," Black Cloak said in an evil voice, then laughed.

Now I was really ticked! Daryl was a gutless turd who sold the souls of his wife and son to pay for his gambling debt. And they were nothing more than a meal? I idly wondered if he cared at all about Sarah. Or was he just so stupid he didn't think a deal with Black Cloak would be a bad thing? I had to do something, but the stabbing in my gut returned. My time was running out.

Nate's words popped into my head, *when you feel overcome with evil, think of this.* And the thought of his kiss flashed across my trembling lips. Suddenly, I stood in the middle of the room between Black Cloak and my Spec as positive energy pulsed through my body. I was a powerful and courageous Human Angel!

My arrival broke the connection and the soul sucking ceased. Black Cloak froze for a brief moment as his beady red eyes emanated from under his cloak. His wicked voice boomed, "Stupid angel! You can't stop me! Now get out of my way!" he yelled, then sent a stream of smoky darkness at me. Instinctively, I lifted my hand, deflecting his evilness back toward him. Surprised, Black Cloak jolted back.

"I don't think so. Not today and not ever!" My voice wasn't my own. It was deeper and louder as it bellowed through the room. I brought my hands up above my head in a circular motion and a shower of golden droplets sprouted from my fingertips. They sprinkled down, surrounding my unconscious Spec, her son and me. Frustrated, Black Cloak shot his black stream of nastiness at us again, but it ricocheted, striking him in the elbow and singeing his cloak.

"A Human Angel?" The wicked figure flared at a confused and horrified Daryl. "If I can't have them, then your life is mine! But I just may keep you around to torture you for a bit. That might lessen the blow of the pain of losing out on two angels," Black Cloak grumbled as shackles appeared around Daryl's arms and legs. "I think I should keep you as my pet for a few decades," Black Cloak said, chuckling at the idea.

"Help me," Daryl whimpered, as his eyes met mine. I just shrugged, knowing that I couldn't help him even if I wanted to. And honestly, I wasn't sure I wanted to help him.

"She can't," Black Cloak's deep voice bellowed idly as my eyes shot toward him. He continued as if talking to himself. "Her golden droplets only protect innocents. You, my friend, are no innocent. Therefore, an angel can't protect you. You lost your Guardian Angel a long time ago. You're so far gone even a Human Angel, the most powerful of all angels, can't even save you," he said, laughing evilly. "It's going to be fun to have a pet again. It's been at least a century."

There was a pop in the room and then he and Daryl disappeared. I knew I had won. I wasn't entirely sure how, but at this point I didn't care. Jeremy and Sarah were safe and I was still alive. Plus, I gained some great information. I couldn't wait to get home and tell Nate everything. I closed my eyes and exhaled deeply at the thought, and my lopsided grin flickered across my face.

Sarah stirred, shifting the attention of my thoughts. "What the heck?" she asked, trying to sit up as she brought her hand up to her temple. "Avery? What are you doing here? What's going on? Where's Daryl? He brought that man … er … thing into the house." Her voice trailed off as she looked at me. I studied her carefully, having no idea what to do now. Big surprise!

"Oh my gosh," Sarah gasped. "You're my Guardian Angel. No wonder you looked so surprised when I mentioned angels earlier today." She spoke slowly, piecing bits of information together. "You saved us from something terrible. Something Daryl did."

I nodded. I wasn't sure how much I was supposed to tell her, so I just kept quiet. "I'm sorry, but I don't think Daryl's coming back," I said gently. I thought she should at least know that. They had been together since they were teenagers.

"What?" Sarah asked. I had obviously interrupted her train of thought. "Yeah, I knew he wasn't coming back, thank goodness. He was such a loser. I stayed with him for the kids. Maybe that's what earned me a spot in the Angelhood." She laughed still lost in her own thought. "He's always been a gambler. His intentions used to be good, but then he got so far in the hole. I should have known the last windfall was too good to be true," she said sadly. "I feel honored to have a Human Angel looking after me and my kids, though. Thank you, Avery."

I looked at her oddly. How did she know about all this? My befuddlement must have been obvious, because she laughed a little, wrapped her arm around my shoulder and sat me down.

"Avery, I come from a long line of angels, so I know a little bit about them ... more than the average human. I know that one day I will become a Guardian Angel, the natural way. I also know that Human Angels are rare and have a Spec only once. I supposed I will conveniently forget you," she said sadly. I must have looked horrified because she went on to explain further. "It's dangerous for most humans to see their Guardian Angels. The memories of you will be wiped clean, so seeing you won't trigger a memory of my Guardian Angel. You will be reassigned to the next person who needs you, and I'll be assigned a new guardian, one that I won't be able to see. Human Angels are very powerful, but they can only protect a person once," she explained. "I will always be grateful to you for saving my son's life."

"You knew all this time I was a Human Angel?" I asked. Of all the information I had just received, this is what tumbled from my mouth first.

"No," Sarah said, somewhat taken aback by my question. "I had a hunch when the speaker missed me earlier today, and then I hoped you were an angel when Daryl showed up with that monster after dinner tonight." Sarah smiled, shrugging and laughing.

I laughed along with her. It felt good to laugh. Jeremy started to stir and that was my cue to leave, so Sarah and I hugged, parting ways. This session of Angel 101 had been very informative, but I was ready to get home to my sexy golf pro.

The moment I walked into our home, I knew Nate was up to something. Candles were lit, and rose petals covered the floor. I followed the trail to the bathroom. There was my handsome guy in the tub filled with bubbles with a rose in his mouth, a glass of wine in each hand and an expectant look on his face. He nodded to the empty end of the tub.

A smile crossed my face as my lips curled slightly. I quickly shed my clothes and slid into the tub opposite him. I moved closer and took my designated glass of wine, took a sip, then set it down. Nate's eyebrows shot up in anticipation as his lips curved into a sly smile. I laughed and took the other glass. He frowned, looking at me quizzically. I took a sip from his glass and set it down, too. I held his gaze and shifted until my face was in front of his. He leaned in, and I removed the rose from his mouth, then dropped it carelessly into the tub.

"How'd it go? Are you safe? Wanna talk about it?" his husky voice whispered in my ear.

"Fine. Yes. No," I answered.

Then he reached his hand behind my head and crushed his lips to mine.

The End

AN OLD MAN'S TALE
By: Beth Hoyer

The old man sat by the fireplace with a fire roaring away, bringing warmth into the room. He sat in an armchair patiently waiting while glancing out the window. Outside, the sun was setting. Noises of people coming into the room from eating dinner rushed to his ears as they chattered away. He eyed his children that sat in sofas, complaining loudly to their spouses about finding their youngest children seated in front of their father next to the fireplace. The old man frowned, listening to his children talk until they became silent. His grandchildren gazed at the fire, daydreaming.

The old man spoke loudly, "Grandchildren, I have a story to tell you. Do you care to listen to it?"

His grandchildren shifted their attention from the fireplace to him. They bobbed their heads while focusing on him attentively. The old man began his tale:

I didn't know that I had a Guardian Angel who guards me from harm and that makes me feel safe until my mother told me a story about Guardian Angels, after a scary nightmare that woke me when I was age five years old. I couldn't sleep in the dark alone, despite my Father hooking up a nightlight for me in my bedroom. The nightmare was of something I couldn't explain, but it scared me enough to keep me from sleeping for nights on end. I wound up too scared to sleep alone in my room and tried to go to my parents' room next to mine, but the dark hallway scared me, too. I turned on the nightlight in my room and it illuminated the hallway enough so that I could go to my parents' room. I opened the door and would sneak into my parent's bed, where they slept, unaware that I was there until morning. My parents weren't happy to find me in their bed nearly every morning. And despite multiple punishments and trying to give me rewards in an attempt to change my behavior, I still kept sneaking into their bed at night.

One night I found the door wouldn't open, even though I tried the doorknob repeatedly. I threw a crying fit and banged onto the door, but it was ignored, despite how much noises I made and how loud I was. I was forced to go back to my room to keep the lights on until daylight when I fell asleep.

In the morning, Mother attempted to wake me, but I protested that I wanted to sleep. She insisted that I go outside to play, despite the hot sun shining overhead. When I did go out, I sat at the base of a tree and slept until my mother called me to come inside when it was time for meals. I found that sleeping at the base of the tree wasn't good because bugs crawled all over me like a rug. After that, I forced myself to stay awake for hours.

Then one night before bed, Mother told me, "Travis, you have a Guardian Angel that protects you from harm, helps you sleep, and is always guarding you. Next time you get scared, tell your Guardian Angel to help you and help will be given."

I was confused with what Mother as saying, but I knew that she said something important. That night, she put me in bed, turned off the light and took the nightlight with her. I wound up scared again as light flashed outside, glaring through my window, casting odd shadows around my room. Mysterious loud noises made me nervous and refused to go away, despite my loud pleas of, "Go away your scaring me!" One night, I was too scared to get up from bed so I said, "Guardian Angel help me! I'm scared!"

Suddenly, I saw a glowing light of a man with short, sun-colored hair and large, white wings jutting from his back. He wore some dress covering him from the waist down while baring part of his chest. He glowed like the sun, eyeing me with the same look that my parents gave me whenever they said that they loved me. He gently leaned forward and touched my forehead. It as a gentle caress like my mother gave me when I was sick. His presence soothed me. Soon, I closed my eyes and fell asleep.

I awoke the next morning with my mother insisting that I get up and go outside to play. The sun was shining brightly again, but this time, I didn't feel tired as I went out. I'd had a good night's sleep, thanks to the vigilant watch of my Guardian Angel. That day, I played with the neighborhood's kids near a river running across the street from my house and had lots of fun.

My Guardian Angel protected me at night whenever I was scared. He appeared to me after I screamed for him to come after a nightmare. He also protected me during storms, when I was scared because of the flashing lights. Later, I learned that it was lightning and the noises were from thunder. When storms hit during the day, I clung to Mother in fear. Then she told me that the storm was a part of nature. Soon, I got over my fear of the storms, but the darkness of night still scared me from time to time. Again, I called for my Guardian Angel, and he always appeared to comfort me until I fell asleep.

When I was teenager, my Guardian Angel came in different forms to protect me. Once day, I was out walking along a river on the way home from high school when the ground gave way abruptly and I fell into the river. Swollen from too many continuous days of rain, the river was rushing quickly past, making it hard for me to swim. The water slammed me against multiple objects, such as hidden rocks and tree limbs. It carried me toward the falls, past a deadly pile of rocks. Suddenly, a small whirlpool appeared. People had been rumored to disappear into it, once they were caught within its grip.

I tried to swim toward the shore. "Help me!" I yelled, but no one was around.

The next thing I knew, a strong, muscular arm wrapped around my waist and pulled me with an ironclad grip toward the shore and deposited me onto the river bank. I looked up to find a man with a familiar face and familiar curly blonde hair that reminded me of my Guardian Angel. But instead of wings, he was wearing jeans, hiking boots, and a red plaid shirt which showed a bit of his muscular chest and his sleeves were rolled up. I stared at the man, assuming it was my Guardian Angel. I was shocked when he pointed a finger in the opposite direction away from the river, then made a shooing gesture. Quickly, I scrambled up the river bank. At the top, I found that I was on the other side of the river. I turned around to find him, but he was nowhere in sight.

I quickly walked home and told my mother what happened. "I was saved by my Guardian Angel! When I fell into the river, he pulled me out."

My mother gave a chuckle, sounding like she was proud of me and said, "What did I tell you regarding your Guardian Angel?"

I replied, "My Guardian Angel is always there for me to protect me from harm, even when I don't ask for it."

Mother nodded her head and shooed me out of the kitchen, insisting that I change out of my wet clothes and do my homework while she cooked dinner.

I didn't know that my Guardian Angel had the ability to talk to me until I came home from college one night during a rainstorm. I took a bus, then walked home wet and on a holiday. When I arrived at the door, it was locked and my parents weren't home. There was no way of getting inside from the rainy weather.

Suddenly, my Guardian Angel appeared by my side. He was sitting on the front steps and said, "Go to your neighbor's house and stay there out of the rainy weather."

I obeyed and went to Mr. and Mrs. Harris' house. They were always friendly to me over the years.

Mrs. Harris arrived at the door after I rang her doorbell. I told her, "My parents aren't home for me to get inside and I don't have a key. May I stay here and wait for them until they come home?"

Mrs. Harris let me inside. I sat next to their fireplace, warming up by the fire. I stared at the fire and paced the floor until the doorbell rang. Tired, I sat down in an armchair by my Guardian Angel. No one could see him but me. When Mr. Harris answered the door, a male police officer as standing on the porch. He walked into the room with a grim look on his face. Eyeing me, he asked, "Are you Travis Jones?"

I nodded, so the policeman added, "I'm sorry, but your parents were in a car accident. The car crashed into a tree, killing them instantly. I'm sorry to have to tell you this, son."

I went numb with shock. My Guardian Angel hugged me when the policeman added, "Your neighbor Mr. Harris left a message on your parents' answering machine saying that you were at their house. That's how I found you. After arriving at their house, no one answered the door. I thought that maybe your parents didn't have any family because there was no information in the car or on their person. Again, I'm sorry to be the bearer of bad news."

The days that followed were a blur, but my Guardian Angel stayed by my side, comforting me with hugs and hand squeezes while still remaining unseen by people. He stayed by my side through the sale of the house and its contents. I didn't want to live there anymore with the memories of my parents flooding into my mind. It hurt each time I remembered things about my parents. Memories were triggered by anything and at any time.

Soon, I began drinking too much and forgot about my Guardian Angel. I forgot my reason for going to college. too.

But my Guardian Angel never left me. Sometimes I would see a man hanging around and I forgot who he as in my drunken state. No one else saw him. Oftentimes, I pointed him out to people while I was drunk and they thought I was crazy, seeing nothing.

One night I was drunk and the bar I was in kicked me out for inappropriate behavior. I walked out to a busy road where traffic was zooming by in both directions. I remember thinking to myself, "Life isn't worth living. I have no purpose in life and I don't do anything but drink. I may as well throw myself into traffic and hope a car kills me."

Then a young male around my own age wearing the clothes of a lumberjack came into view and blocked my way He forced me to turn around in the direction of my small college dorm room, despite my resistance. But I tried to step around him, heading toward the road.

The young man said to me, "Don't throw your life away for nothing. You have a purpose, whether you're aware of it or not. So turn around and go to your room … now."

At first, I refused to listen to the young man until he added, "Don't make the same mistake I've seen many people make by throwing away their lives, not recognizing that they had a purpose. Don't do this. It's a mistake."

Suddenly, I sobered up a bit and said, "Who are you, anyway? Why are you telling me this?"

He glowed like sunlight in response, showing his white wings on his back. Then he folded his arms across his chest, sobering me up instantly. Immediately, I recognized that he was my Guardian Angel. Then he jabbed a finger in the direction of my dorm room in the opposite direction of the heavy traffic. I obeyed, walking in the direction that he pointed. But he was always behind me whenever I looked over my shoulder, glowing away. He stopped and stood with his arms folded each time I glanced in his direction.

I finally reached my room and fell into bed. I woke the next morning and said to myself, "It must have been a dream or I must have been hallucinating in my drunken state. I don't have a Guardian Angel, anyway."

Instantly, my Guardian Angel appeared in my room, glowing with his wings clearly visible, glaring at me with his arms folded. Then he said, "What were you just saying about Guardian Angels?"

I clamped my mouth shut in response. Suddenly, the urge to drink left me and I started focusing on my studies instead. I caught a glimpse of my Guardian Angel from time to time, blocking my way to bars when the urge hit, telling me the same old thing, "Don't waste your life drinking. Your life has a purpose, whether you recognize it or not. And I aim to see that you live to recognize that purpose … period."

I forced myself to listen to my Guardian Angel and avoided hanging out with people who habitually had drinking parties on the weekends. I also threw myself into my studies, and decided to transfer to a major university to become a doctor. After three years, I managed to graduate from that college and transferred to yet another college. There, I threw myself into my studies again. I still saw my Guardian Angel giving me glares upon occasion, showing himself to me whenever I was tempted to drink. But he shook his head and I forced myself not to drink. As a result, I managed to graduate from that college, as well, and became a doctor.

Over the years, I found that my Guardian Angel remained by my side, even when I married your Grandma Julia, may God rest her soul. I became a father to a young daughter, Angela, who had nightmares and problems sleeping at night, as well.

After finding that my daughter, Angela, had snuck into bed with my wife and me one night, my Guardian Angel said to me, "Tell your daughter that a Guardian Angel protects her, like your mother told you when you was her age."

I obeyed and carried my protesting daughter back to her own bedroom. Once she as tucked safely into her own bed, she whined, "Daddy, I want to sleep with you and Mommy. I'm scared."

I quietly shushed her and then spoke to her, recalling the words my mother said to me so many years before, "Angela, you have a Guardian Angel that protects you from harm. Your angel is always guarding you, even when you're scared and need protection. When you're scared, call upon your Guardian Angel for help and help will be given. My Mother told me of my Guardian Angel when I was your age. So I called on mine to protect me whenever I was scared, and he comforted me. I know what you're going through, Angela, so call upon your Guardian Angel and you'll receive protection. I promise. Now, go back to sleep."

Angela gazed off to a far corner of the room with a peaceful look on her face. Out of the corner of my eye, I saw a shimmering light. Then I knew that it was Angela's Guardian Angel doing what I told her, giving her peace and protection. I gently kissed my daughter on the forehead and then left the room, turning off the light to the hallway. The door was ajar, but I saw a familiar glow coming from her bedroom. I smiled in response and went back to bed where my wife was sleeping and saw my Guardian Angel standing next to my bed. He gave me a nod of approval. That night, I closed my eyes and slept peacefully, knowing that he would be there for me and my family, protecting us for as long as we lived.

After his story, the old man, Travis, paused and said, "Well, children, what is the lesson that you learned from this story?"

He eyed his grandchildren and his own four children, his eyes narrowing, ignoring their spouses sitting next to them. His children cleared their throats loudly.

He looked at his grandchildren when the oldest, ten-year-old boy Travis — named after him — spoke loudly, "The lesson is that we should depend upon our Guardian Angels to protect us from harm and comfort us when we're scared. That's what I keep telling my baby sisters, but they're too stupid to know that Guardian Angels exist and that they'll guard us forever."

The grandchildren began arguing amongst themselves about who was and wasn't stupid until he clapped his hands loudly, getting their attention and said firmly, "No one is stupid. It's just that you must know to ask your Guardian Angel for help at all times. I've been telling all of you this for years."

He heard multiple groans from the adults. Travis, his grandson, spoke up again, "Alright, Grandpa, we get it. There's Guardian Angels guarding us from harm. They even help us when we're scared. Besides, whatever Grandpa says about Guardian Angels is the truth, isn't it, baby sisters and cousins?"

Scattered agreements resounded among his grandchildren. The old man sat back in his chair eyeing them, listening to his grandson talk about how to communicate with Guardian Angels. The elder Travis sighed and felt a gentle squeeze on his shoulder. When he turned around, he spotted his familiar Guardian Angel with a hint of a smile lighting his face, for the message of Guardian Angels was finally given to the next generations.

THE CHRISTMAS WISH
By: Theresa Oliver

The cold bit through the rags wrapped around Ella's feet as she trudged through the snow. The eight-year-old girl kept to the shadows, so as not to be seen. Huddled outside hidden at a corner of a house, a twinge pulled at her heart as she took in the heartwarming scene in the house across the street.

It was New England, 1912.

In the house across the street, a family sang carols in front of their Christmas tree, flickering with the light of a hundred candles. *Oh little town of Bethlehem* ... the family sang as Ella watched, shivering outside in the shadows. The sweet voices of the children filled the air, harmonizing with their father's bass and mother's soprano voices. When the chorus finished, the father swung the littlest girl high up into the air, and set her upon his shoulders, then danced around the room as the family laughed.

The little girl wasn't much younger than Ella.

A tear slid slowly down Ella's cheek as she shivered in the cold. She took a deep breath and let it out with a sigh, then wiped the tear from her cheek and headed down the street, trying to find a warm place to stay for the night. As she passed the New England row houses, the sounds of cheery, holiday celebrations rushed out to meet her, making her miss having a family now more than ever. Not so much *her* family, but a family to care for and to care for her ... especially around the holidays.

She ran away from home six months before from an abusive father, who missed her mother terribly since her sudden death the year before. Her mother died of influenza, slowly withering, becoming weaker each day. When it became too much for her father to bear, he turned to ale to deaden the pain, leaving Ella completely and utterly alone.

Then the beatings started.

One night after her father had passed out drunk, she slipped on her worn shoes and took the only thing that she had that belonged to her mother: a dark blue cloak. It was ten sizes too big and dragged the ground as she walked, sliding across the snow behind her, but it was her only protection from the harshness of the bitter, cold night. Within a few months, her shoes were worn out, so she wrapped her feet in discarded rags, throwing her shoes away. Now, she wished she had her holey shoes again.

Then Ella passed another window where no Christmas decorations hung and no music filled the air. The only light in the house came from a dimly lit fireplace across the room. To Ella, it looked warm ... inviting. Looking both ways down the dark cobblestone street, she hurried across to get a better look. Placing her little hands onto the window ceil, she lifted herself onto her tiptoes to peer through the thick glass panes.

Inside, a woman slowly rocked back and forth in an old, wooden rocking chair. The furniture within the room was sparse, except for a small dining room table setting near another window in the kitchen. Upon closer inspection, tears were slowly sliding down the woman's face. Ella's eyebrows pulled together as she wondered what could make the woman so unhappy, momentarily forgetting her own pain.

Then the woman rocked back and forth, revealing a sleeping boy within her arms.

Ella gasped and ran quickly down the street as tears rolled swiftly down her cheeks, wondering what was wrong with the boy. Blinded by tears, she came to an old, abandoned house ... or at least it appeared to be so.

The house was dark, as dark as the black iron fence surrounding it. Slowly, she looked back and forth down the street, but no one as paying attention. In fact, the cobblestone street showed very little signs of life on this Christmas Eve. Ever so gently, she pushed the gate, testing it. It opened with a loud creak.

Ella was too tired and cold to question her good fortune, so with one last look over her shoulder, she darted through the rod iron gate. She timidly walked up the wooden stairs, each creaking as she placed a tiny foot on each step. On the porch, she placed her hand on the ornate doorknob, twisted it, and the door opened.

Ella didn't understand it, but she as too tired and hungry to question.

Timidly, she ventured through the house, padding along the floor in her rag-covered feet as she pulled the cloak tightly around her. But already, she was beginning to warm. She slowly walked through the house, admiring the ornate furniture and wall hangings. Ella looked up at the high ceilings with little cherubs dancing in clouds painted high above as she walked through the dining room. She stopped a moment to take in its beauty, but her stomach growled loudly, forcing her down the hallway on a quest for food.

Within minutes, she knew she went in the wrong direction, for she was in a series of rooms. She passed room after room and was about to turn the other way when she came to a library. Slowly, Ella walked in. Her mouth opened in awe, taking in the rows and rows of books that lined the shelves from ceiling to floor. She wished she knew how to read as her hands trailed along the books. Then, on a shelf, she came to an ornate, heart-shaped box.

The jewels sparkled on the box, catching her eye. She gasped, having never seen anything so precious in her entire life. Slowly, she reached out a hand to touch it. The jewels were of every color of the rainbow, but were not overly done. Carefully, she trailed her hand along the stones of red, purple, blue and gold, admiring their color and sheen.

Then suddenly, it began to glow from within.

She stepped back. Her eyes widened, as the glow slowly filled the room, seeping from under the lid. Ella looked around, wondering if someone outside the house would see this strange glow coming from inside the house, fearing that someone would come to investigate. But she was captivated by this strange box, so her curiosity won out instead.

The box glowed a bright golden color, much like warm candlelight, but much, much brighter. And as she stepped closer, the glow brightened from between the cracks of the lid.

Ella bravely reached out a hand to touch the box. Immediately, she was filled with warmth and love. Carefully, she took the delicate box into her tiny hands and sat down with it on the floor. Slowly, she opened the lid.

Suddenly, a light even more brilliant than before filled every crevice of the room and a woman stood before her.

"How did you get in here?" Ella asked, confused. But upon closer inspection, she realized it wasn't a woman at all … but an angel.

Enormous, iridescent wings protruded from the angel's back, filling the room, stretching from ceiling to floor. For a moment, Ella wondered how her wings could fit into the room, but the angel seemed to fit comfortably. The angel's golden, wavy hair flowed passed her shoulders, falling in lovely curls just above her waist. Her blue eyes smiled kindly at Ella, the way her mother used to look at her before she died, filled with so much love.

"Who are you?" Ella managed to get out, stepping back in awe. Immediately, she fell to her knees.

"Rise, little one," the angel spoke. "You are not to worship me. That honor belongs only to God."

"God?" Ella asked, taken aback. She had heard of him, but didn't know much, really. To Ella, He was a kind man who lived in the sky, removed from His children on Earth.

"Yes, God," the angel smiled at Ella lovingly. "I have a message for you, Ella, from God."

"From God?" Ella repeated, dumbfounded.

The angel's smile broadened. "Yes, from God, Ella. He wants you to know that He loves you. God loves you, Ella."

"He loves me?" Ella asked, then something occurred to her. "But how can He love me? He's in Heaven, after all. How does He even know who I am?" After all, Ella knew that The Most High must have lots of people to look after. He must be too busy to even think of her.

"Ella, God is not some being who lives in Heaven, completely removed from us. He's with us and knows all of His children. And yes, Ella, He knows and loves you, too," the angel said. "In fact, He sent me to you to grant you a Christmas wish."

"A wish?" Ella asked.

"Not just any wish, Ella. A Christmas wish."

"A Christmas wish?" Ella asked, even more confused than before.

The angel laughed, admiringly. "You see, little one, a Christmas wish is very special. If you make a wish on Christmas Eve, God will grant it to you." Then the angel added, "But the wish must be pure. It must come from your heart."

Ella nodded, understanding.

The angel sat down on the floor before the little girl, and Ella sat down, too. "So, what will you wish for, Ella?" the angel asked with the kindest, most loving eyes Ella had ever seen.

Ella thought of all the things she could wish for: food, shelter, shoes, a family, warmth, love ... but then Ella though of something. "That woman ... rocking the boy ... what is wrong with him?"

"Well, let's go see," the angel said, holding out a hand to Ella as she rose to her feet. "Shall we?"

Ella nodded, concerned, not wanting to leave the warmth of the house.

As if reading her mind, the angel smiled and said, "Worry not, dear Ella. As long as you are with me, you will never be cold."

Ella nodded, smiling, then took the angel's hand.

"Hold on tight!" the angel said as excitement lit up her face.

Ella squealed when suddenly flashes of bright light in all the colors of the jewel box surrounded them. Then the angel closed her eyes. They moved at the speed of light and within the blink of an eye, they were standing in the parlor of another house.

"How did you *do* that?" Ella asked, looking up at the angel with wide eyes.

The angel shrugged, then replied, "It's just something we can do."

Ella nodded, then noticed their surroundings. The house was dimly lit with only the glow of a small fire coming within the fireplace that illuminated the room. Beside the hearth, a few wooden sticks lay in the coal bucket. Ella knew immediately that the owner of this home was not rich. There was hardly enough sticks to last through the night. No lovely paintings adorned these walls, and no flying cherubs adorned the ceiling of this dwelling.

As Ella's eyes looked around the room, they fell upon a woman slowly rocking a boy.

Ella gasped, realizing it was the woman and child she had seen earlier that night. "Can't they see us?" Ella asked, taking a step back, but the angel held her hand firmly.

"Fear not, dear Ella," the angel said with a gentle smile. "They cannot see us." Then the angel sighed. "In fact, she probably couldn't see us even if we wanted her to."

"How so?" Ella asked, confused.

The angel took a deep breath as her perfect eyebrows pulled together. "She hasn't spoken to God in years."

"Why?" Ella wondered, astonished. No matter how bad things had been in her own life, she still spoke to God occasionally. She always wondered if He heard, but now she knew He did.

"Well," the angel began, "her son fell ill last year and she just stopped praying, blaming God for what happened to her son."

Ella was truly shocked. "Doesn't she know that you are supposed to pray when things get tough?"

The angel shrugged with a smile. "I guess she forgot."

Ella smiled, then thought of something. Letting go of the angel's hand, Ella crossed the room and stood before the woman.

Sensing that someone was there, the woman asked into the empty room, "Who's there?" Silence greeted her as she looked around, never seeing the angel and Ella standing with her. The boy stirred, so the woman resumed her rocking as tears rolled slowly down her cheeks.

Ella knelt down before the boy cradled within his mother's arms. His skin was pale and she knew death was near. "Will he live?" she asked the golden angel.

The angel looked down sadly, then replied, "He probably won't make it through the night."

Ella nodded as tears rolled slowly down her own cheeks. "But why?" she asked. But before the angel could answer, she had a thought and whispered into the woman's ear, "You know that if you make a wish on Christmas … a Christmas wish … it will come true."

"Ella …" the angel warned.

Hearing Ella's words as her own thoughts within her mind, the woman said, "Please, God! Please help my son. I know that things happen for a reason, but if you can hear me, please grant me this one Christmas wish." The woman paused, wanting to word it correctly, then continued, "Lord, I'm not asking this for me, but for him. He's a very special boy. Please let him have the opportunity to leave his mark upon the world." Tears coursed down her cheeks as she added, "If you are to take one life this night, let it be mine. But please, let my son live."

Then the woman cradled her son to her cheek and sobbed uncontrollably. Ella reached out a hand to gently touch the woman on the head. Suddenly, a feeling of warmth and love filled the woman, and she knew that it was the love of God. The woman gasped, feeling hope for the first time in years.

A hand touched Ella on her shoulder, and she looked around to see that it was the angel, looking upon her with a look of love. And Ella knew that it was the love of God, the same love that radiated within them both. "It's time," the angel said. Ella nodded and stood.

Ella slipped her hand unto the angel's and the angel closed her eyes. Within a flash, the bright, colorful lights surrounded them in every shade of the box and a second later, they were back in the library of the abandoned house. The jewel encrusted angel box lay upon the floor. Ella walked over and picked it up. The angel sat upon the floor and Ella curled up within her lap, carefully holding the box. The angel wrapped her arms around the little girl, and curled her wings around her in protection, then she gently pushed a strand of hair out of her eyes.

"I know what I want," Ella whispered as her eyes began to close.

"What, little one?" the angel asked as a tear rolled down her cheek.

"My Christmas wish," Ella said. "I want the boy to live … for his mother."

The angel bowed her head, gently stroking the little girl's face.

Then Ella looked up to Heaven. "Please, God. Please let the boy live. This is my Christmas wish," Ella said as she slowly closed her eyes.

Tears rolled down the angel's face as she said, "Ella, what about a wish for you? Don't you want anything for yourself?"

"Yes," Ella said, then looked into the angel's kind eyes. "I want to see my mother again." Then Ella realized that God loved her unconditionally. For the love radiating within the angel's eyes was the love of God.

Moved, the angel said, "And you will, little Ella. You will." Then she stroked a strand of hair one last time gently away from her face. "I promise."

And Ella just went to sleep, safe within the arms of an angel, holding tightly to the jewel encrusted angel box as the angel rocked her gently back and forth, with tears in her own eyes.

Sometime in the night, the angel stood and gently took Ella's hand. Ella opened her eyes and everything glowed around them. "It's time," the angel said with a smile.

Ella nodded, feeling more love and happiness than she had ever felt before. Without hesitation, she took the hand of the angel and stood, leaving her body behind. Together, they walked until they came to the Stairs of Heaven. Ella looked up and saw the Pearly White Gates at the top.

"Are you ready?" the angel asked with a smile. Ella nodded, then the angel added, "I'm very proud of you, Ella."

Ella nodded.

Then another voice responded as the Gates of Heaven opened, "I'm proud of you, too." And when she looked up, she saw God. He was very nice looking and powerful, but gentle and filled with love and light. "And there is another person here that I'm sure is proud of you, too," God said.

"Yes, I am," another voice said.

But it as a voice that Ella would know anywhere. "Mommy!" Ella yelled as tears fell onto her cheeks. Ella ran quickly up the Stairs of Heaven straight into her mother's waiting arms.

Her mother kissed her, wrapping her arms around her daughter, filling Ella with more love than she had ever felt before ... the love of God. And together, they walked through the Gates of Heaven into Paradise.

***

"It's really a shame," the police officer said, looking down at the lifeless body of the little girl lying on the floor of the abandoned house.

"I'm sorry, sir," another man said with a worried look on his face. "But I came home this morning and found the poor little thing laying there. I called you immediately."

"I understand," the police officer said, placing a gentle hand on the man's shoulder. "These things happen." Then he added. "It makes you wonder, though. How could this little thing have died alone?"

But an angel with golden wavy hair looked on with a smile, knowing that Ella wasn't alone at all.

***

The glowing embers of the fire died in the fireplace as the woman rocked her sleeping son back and forth within her arms. Pulling him closer to her chest, she wrapped her own cloak around her sleeping son. Then she fell asleep some time during the night with her son cradled within her arms.

"Mommy?" a little voice asked.

The woman woke, disoriented, thinking that she was dreaming.

"Mommy, wake up! It's Christmas morning!" the voice said again.

And at that moment, the woman knew that what she had heard was real. She wasn't dreaming at all. Her eyes flew open wide to see her son, sitting up in her lap, smiling with bright eyes. And within his eyes, his mother realized she saw the love of God.

"Oh, my boy, my boy!" she said, wrapping him within her arms as tears streamed swiftly down her cheeks. "Son, you're alive!" Then she remembered the Christmas wish she had made the night before on Christmas Eve. "It's a Christmas miracle!"

"No, it was a Christmas wish," a golden angel with wavy blonde hair whispered into the mother's ear, smiling, remembering Ella.

"Yes, the Christmas wish!" the mother said, never seeing the angel standing before her. Then her eyes looked up to Heaven. "Thank you, God. Thank you for giving me back my son."

And at that moment, the angel touched the mother and then the son, infusing them both with the love of God and renewed strength.

"I'm hungry, Mommy," the little boy said, as his mother hugged him tightly to her chest.

Then her tears of joy turned to sorrow, remembering that she had no food. Suddenly, she smelled something coming from the kitchen. "Could it be?" the mother asked. Her voice trailed off as her son excitedly jumped from her lap. "Careful, honey ..."

But within an instant, the boy ran into the kitchen and back, announcing loudly, "Mommy! Come quick! Look what Santa brought!"

"What on Earth?" the woman wondered, realizing that the miracles on this day were not stopping. When she walked into the kitchen, a full buffet was spread across the dining room table: fresh goose, stuffing, cranberry sauce, corn, potatoes and more. Long, tapered candles were lit upon the table along with three plates were set. "My goodness!" the mother exclaimed, but out of the window, she saw a man shivering outside in the cold street.

Concerned, she turned her attention to her son and said, "Son, go ahead and eat. I'll be right back."

Leaving her son in the kitchen with a plate of food, she opened the door as a rush of cold wind and snow blew into the house. "Sir, would you like to come in? Where do you live?"

On his knees in the snow, the man looked up into the woman's eyes. The look in his eyes broke the woman's heart, as tears streamed don't his cheeks. "No, I don't live around here, Ma'am," he replied, then he looked back down at something he was holding.

"Please ..." the woman begged, reaching out for the man, "come in and let's talk." Then she paused for a moment, remembering the banquet awaiting them on the table. She also remembered that three plates had been set upon the table. Then, she understood. "It's Christmas. Please come in."

The man nodded, still clutching something within his hands. Upon closer inspection, the woman saw that the man was holding a jewel encrusted, very ornate box.

Cautiously, the woman asked, "What do you have here, sir?" The woman reached for it, but the man pulled it back, clutching it to his chest as tears streamed down his cheeks.

The man cleared his throat. "This was my little girl's ... or at least, I think it was," he paused as the woman waited for him to explain. Her heart sank at the implications of his words, remembering her own son and how close she had come to losing him. The man continued in a soft voice, "She was holding it when they found her this morning."

"Oh, I'm so sorry," the woman said, then she remembered the rocking chair. "Please ... sit down."

Lifelessly, the man did as she asked and made his way to the chair. He sat down and slowly rocked the box back and forth, clutching it to his chest, remembering his daughter.

"What happened?" the woman gently asked.

Looking off into the distance but not seeing anything in the room, the man began, "She was found this morning in an empty house. The police think she froze to death. When the owner of the house came home, she as holding this box, so he gave it to me." He paused, remembering past events, as fresh, anguished tears streamed down his cheeks. "Her mother died last year and I ... I ... I beat my little girl because of it. I couldn't stand to look at her because she looked so much like her mother." The man paused. The woman waited, listening. "Well, she ran away a few months ago. And who could blame her? After she left, I looked for her, but couldn't find her. And when the cold weather set in, I worried about her." He looked at the ornate box, running his hand along the top of the variously colored jewels. "It turns out that my worries were justified." Then he began to sob and shouted, "What have I done? My little girl is gone!" Then he sobbed uncontrollably as the woman wrapped her arms around him, letting him cry on her shoulder.

After a while, she pulled back and looked into his eyes, then said, "Sir, God will forgive you."

The man laughed without humor. "God? Will forgive me? How can you say that after all that I've done?"

The woman's eyes filled with concern as she replied, "I just know. Believe me. Last night I made a Christmas wish ..." her voice trailed off as she recalled her tale, then she finished with, "God forgave me, and He will also forgive you, too."

The man looked down at the jewel encrusted box again. "If only it could be true ..." Then he looked into the woman's eyes and saw the love of God radiating within them.

Then he felt something touch his shoulder from behind him. And for a split second, time was suspended. He looked around and Ella was standing beside him with tears in her eyes, standing beside a golden angel with wavy long blonde hair and giant wings. But his attention was only for his daughter, glowing with the love of God.

"Oh, Ella!" he said, then wrapped her within his arms and pulled her to his chest, crying into her hair. "Oh, Ella, I'm so sorry, baby. I love you so much. I looked for you, honey ..."

"Shush," Ella said, as a smile lit her lips. "I know, Daddy. I love you, too, and I forgive you. Please ... be happy." He nodded, and an instant later, she was gone.

"Sir, Sir?" a voice asked in the distance as he slowly regained consciousness.

He opened his eyes and his daughter was gone, but he knew that God had worked a miracle.

"Sir, are you alright?" the woman asked, as concern filled her eyes. "You passed out for a few minutes. Can I get you something?"

"No," the man shook his head, as he clutched the box tightly to his chest, remembering his daughter and her special gift. Not the gift of the box, but the gift of love and forgiveness. "I'm fine."

A moment later, the boy rushed into the room. "Hey, Mister. Are you hungry? We have lots of food! Santa left it!" he announced, already tugging at the man's hand.

"Here, let me take that for you," the woman gently said, carefully edging the box from his hands. But this time, the man let the jewel encrusted box go. Then the woman walked over to the mantle above the fireplace. "I'll just place it here until you are ready to leave."

The man nodded, and, somehow, he knew that his daughter had led him to this place, to this house, and to this family. He smiled, knowing he had just been given a second chance, and that he wouldn't be leaving for a long time to come.

***

Angels Among Us   *101*

The jewel encrusted box set on the mantle for many years. Soon, Ella's father married the woman and was a wonderful father to the boy. And, over the years, he came to forgive himself, just as he knew both Ella and God had forgiven him. And when it as his time to leave the Earth, Ella was waiting to greet him at the Gates of Heaven.

The boy grew into a man and performed many great deeds within his life, never knowing the sacrifice that Ella had made for him and his mother. As a man, he had a soft spot for the homeless, because of the story of his stepsister — the man he came to know as his father's daughter, Ella. Over the course of his life, he built several homeless shelters and helped many families as Ella and the golden angel looked on, helping him along the way, whispering into his ear when needed.

Taking in the accomplishments of the sickly boy who had grown into a man, the golden angel knew that Ella's sacrifice was not in vain, recalling the words from the Bible: "There is no greater love than to give one's life for a friend."

AN ANGEL GROWS UP
By: Jennifer Paquette

Angel of God, my guardian dear
to whom God's love commits me here.
Ever this day/night be at my side
to light, to guard, to rule and guide.
Amen
-Traditional Catholic prayer to one's Guardian Angel

Ten stubby toes curled over the edge of the downy cloud as it floated listlessly across the azure sky. The tiny figure's gold skirt billowed in front of her. She quickly gathered it back to her legs, her sweaty fists bunching the delicate fabric. She knew she was stalling as she gave a sideways glance to her Elder Sister, Sylvie. She wrinkled her pug nose and defiantly pushed back a flyaway strand of flaxen hair.

"I don't want to go," she mewled for the tenth time that hour. "I want to stay with you. Can't I just be your helper?"

Her violet eyes pleaded and she even managed to squeeze out a fat tear as she tugged at the bodice of her dress. The fabric was so itchy and the gold sparkles were all over the place. She wished she still had the soft, white robe she wore for all of her seven years as an Angel-In-Training. Thinking of her comforting, old clothes made more tears fall.

"Stop crying, silly. You'll ruin your beautiful new dress!" Sylvie chided. Sylvie's dress was all sparkly and silver and full of bursting moonbeams. She looked so beautiful that Little Sister felt she could never look that pretty.

"It's time. You have to go. I've chosen just the right home for you and if you don't go now, you'll miss it," Sylvie said, giving her a gentle push. Little Sister turned instead and grabbed the silvery skirts of her Elder Sister.

"I'll go, but I'll never be able to do what it takes to be a Guardian Angel! I can't even take care of my dress without ruining it," she said with a sniff, then wiped her nose with the back of her hand and onto her skirt. Her hand was now sticky with gold flecks stuck all over it. She hid it behind her back.

"Sshhh, little one. You'll surprise yourself. You'll see. Just don't try too hard. And make sure you listen to the one you were chosen to protect. Remember, you're not there to do their will; you're there to guide them to do what's right." Sylvie stroked her baby sister's hair and lightly kissed the top of her head. "Now go. I'll be watching over you," she said gently, then turned Little Sister around and gave her a final hug.

"Okay, I'll do my best to make you proud!" Little Sister said, smiling through her tears. Then she gave Sylvie's hand one last squeeze, uncurled her toes and jumped.

***

"Eeek!" she squeaked, as she landed with a soft thud in the funny smelling dark room. She fell on something hard and bumpy. Then she scampered to her knees to feel behind her to see what it was. She rubbed her hands along the floor until she found the culprit and held it up in front of her face. It was a little plastic man, boxy in shape, with a sword in his tiny fist.

"You hurt big for someone so small," she whispered to the little plastic man. She looked around her, sniffed, and wrinkled her nose. She couldn't quite place the smell, but sensed a bit of innocent sweetness underneath. She quietly stood up and stared out the window. It was nighttime, but the room was awash in hundreds of lights from big buildings, and not moonlight as she as accustomed to. "Wow," she gasped, "so many lights ... where on earth am I?"

Suddenly there was a grunt behind her and she whirled around. Peering into the shadows, she saw a small, huddled form lying in a bed across the room. She tiptoed closer and stepped on another sharp object.

"Gosh, drat, darn!" she said, not even bothering to whisper now. She wiggled the culprit from her toes and held it up. This one was just a rectangle with protruding circular bumps.

"Hey, who are you?" The voice from the bed asked, thick and muffled with sleep. "And what are you doing with my Legos?"

She stared blankly at the little figure sitting up in the bed. Creases from sleep lined one side of a chubby face. Then she noticed the tousled brown hair, large blue eyes and slightly protruding ears. Her eyes drifted downward to his soft pajamas with colorful trucks parading across.

Oh no, she thought. A BOY!

She cleared her throat and frantically whispered, "It's just a dream. Go back to sleep!" But instead of obeying her, the little boy scrambled out of bed and padded over to where she stood. They were about the same height. She couldn't tell if he was really awake or not, since all he did was hold out his hand and waited until she put the Lego piece into his moist little palm. He closed his fingers protectively around the toy, turned around and marched back to his bed. He curled up like a caterpillar, bringing his hands under his chin. After a few seconds, he opened one eye lazily and mumbled, "Nice dress." Then went back to sleep.

* * *

Only until she could hear the soft snoring of the little boy did she realize she had been holding her breath. She slowly exhaled and let everything sink in. A *boy* ... how could her sister do this to her? It was bad enough that she didn't want to come here in the first place, knowing nothing about being a Guardian Angel — she barely passed her instruction classes — and most of all, she knew *absolutely nothing* about boys! What a disaster. Tears welled up within her eyes and she slumped in despair. She would never get her fluttery Guardian Wings and pretty tiara with a *BOY*.

She sniffed and brushed her tears away. She knew no one was going to come and help her. Sylvie made that very clear. She took a deep breath and decided to concentrate on the Rules of becoming a Guardian Angel and how in the world she was going to achieve them. There were four rules and once they were all met to the Committee's satisfaction, could she get her wings and tiara. She sighed and focused on the first rule as she listened to the gentle, rhythmic breathing of her little boy in the background.

Rule One: Acknowledge and Name

Oh dear, she thought, already stumped. Did he actually acknowledge me or was he sleepwalking? How was she to get to know him? She couldn't do anything until he named her. He *did* say she had a nice dress ... did that count? She wondered what Sylvie would say.

Tears sprang to her eyes. Why couldn't she control her crying? She would never make it to Guardian Angel this way.

Suddenly, a sliver of light appeared under the bedroom door and seconds later the door opened, flooding the room with light. She sat absolutely still in the shadows and watched as the tall figure moved silently into the room and sat on the edge of the bed. The figure began to stroke the head of the little boy. He smiled even before he opened his eyes.

"Hi, Mommy."

"I thought I heard you, Peter. Is everything okay? Did you have a bad dream?" his mother asked.

"Actually, I had two dreams. The first one was about a clown with a big red smile and he scared me. He was throwing rice at me … so much rice that it was filling up my room and I couldn't breathe."

"It was just a dream, honey. There are no clowns and no rice in here that I can see," his mother said, her voice low and silky, like warm honey.

"My next dream had a little girl in it. She was wearing a gold dress and playing with my Legos, but she didn't scare me," he said, rubbing his eyes.

She smiled in the darkness. He was kind of cute.

"Who was she, Mommy?"

"Well, maybe she was there to protect you from the clown," his mother suggested.

"You mean, like an angel?"

She almost jumped for joy and screamed with glee.

"Sure, Pete. I believe in angels, don't you?"

Now the little boy was wide awake as he sat up excitedly. "Can she be my very own angel?"

"Of course she can. Now, get under those covers and get some sleep. School tomorrow, remember?" His mother's voice was firm, but kind.

"I'm going to name her … Goldie," he murmured. Clouds of sleep were already taking him.

"Goldie," his mother said as she kissed his forehead and closed the door quietly.

"Goldie," the little angel repeated, hugging her knees tight, smiling. Rule One accomplished! Maybe this wouldn't be so bad after all.

Rule Two: Guide, Don't Grant

"What are you going to do with all those black things?" Goldie asked, looking at the Legos sprawled across the floor.

Goldie and Peter were sitting on his bedroom floor early one morning before school. Goldie was scrunched in a corner, watching Peter deftly assemble piles of black, plastic Legos into the middle of the room. His disheveled brown hair fell into his eyes, which were still puffy from sleep and allergies. He began to pick up random pieces and fit them together with soft clicks. Goldie scowled as Peter ignored her question. She had said it nicely, why wasn't he answering her?

She pounded her chubby fists onto the floor and asked again, a little louder this time. All of a sudden, the pots and pans that were clanging in the kitchen quieted down. Soft footsteps grew louder and then the bedroom door squeaked open. Peter's mom poked her head in, squinting in the light of the tiny room.

"Pete? Who are you talking to this early? You don't have to be up for another hour."

"No one, Mommy. Just playing with my Legos," Peter replied without looking up.

His mother frowned, "Okay, but remember you have a multiplication quiz today and you should rest." She paused, then continued, "I'll call you when your breakfast is ready."

After the door shut, Peter looked up at Goldie angrily. "Can't you just keep quiet? Why do you have to talk so much? Can't you see I'm in the middle of making a Batmobile?" He bent over the black pieces again and feverishly locked a few more pieces into place. He picked up two mismatched wheels and looked at them in disgust.

"If you were really my Guardian Angel, you would grant me the actual Lego set from Toys-R-Us instead of making me figure out my own with the random pieces I have." Peter looked like he was about to cry. He continued in a broken voice, "It's $25 and my mom and dad said it's too much money for a toy," he said, staring at Goldie. "But *you* could get it for me, right?"

Goldie stared at Peter and mused at the range of emotions that had passed over his determined little face within a matter of minutes. She scrunched her face as she thought about how she *wanted* to help Peter and how she was *supposed* to help him. She remembered Rule Two: Guide, Don't Grant. Did this apply to little boys who wanted a toy? She sighed. If it was her, she would have done the same thing, except she would have wanted Angel Barbie.

The morning light began to brighten the bedroom and Goldie looked around as a thought formed in her head. She spoke tentatively. "You know, Peter," she began, "it smells kind of funny in here. Maybe if you picked up your clothes and put some of the really smelly stuff in the laundry without your mom nagging you, then your parents might rethink the whole Lego thing."

Peter stared at Goldie wide eyed. He didn't say anything, so she continued, "Yeah, and you could offer to do a chore or two. When I'm home, I have to clean the cloud-webs from my room and shine all the stupid tiaras for the Elders. It's disgusting, but if I do a really good job, sometimes I get to stay up late." Goldie stopped. She had said enough. It was up to Peter to make the next move. She hoped she didn't overdo it on the guiding part.

Suddenly Peter jumped up and kicked his small, bare foot through the pile of black Legos. They scattered across the floor, some sliding under the bed. His chin jutted out and tears squeezed from his luminous blue eyes, "You're a terrible Guardian Angel! You can't do any magic. You just say the same dumb things as my parents. I hate you!" he yelled as he ran out of the room.

Goldie wanted to curl up and cry, but she knew she had to stay with her little boy throughout the day. She sighed, hoping that he didn't expect her to help him with his multiplication quiz. She was awful with numbers.

Rule Three: Believe

Everything, even the math quiz, was going fine until the kids came in from recess. Albert, who had the desk next to Peter's, left his eyeglasses on his desk when he went out to play. When he came back, they were smashed.

"Peter, can I speak to you for a minute?" Mr. Taramanto asked. He pulled him aside as the children lined up to go to Art, their last period class. Peter had noticed Al's broken glasses and felt really bad. He wondered if they had fallen or if someone did it on purpose. Al was the smallest kid in the class and sometimes did stuff to get attention.

"Yes, Mr. T?" Pete asked, thinking that maybe it was about the quiz. Pete thought he did really well, even though he was tired and his allergies had his brain all stuffy.

"Peter, do you know how Albert's glasses were broken? You were one of the first ones in from recess. Perhaps you saw something?" Mr. T's hooked nose seemed to point at him accusingly.

Peter stepped back and opened his mouth in surprise. Did Mr. T think *he* broke Albert's glasses? That was crazy!

"Mr. Taramanto, I didn't ..."

"That's enough, Peter. We'll need to see how much those glasses cost and then I'm going to call your parents. Now get to Art. You're late."

This day stinks! Peter thought angrily. First, the fight with Goldie — whom he hadn't seen since this morning — and now being blamed for stupid Albert's broken glasses. He ran to his Art class and gave Albert a mean look when he got there. Albert, who now really couldn't see anything, just stared with wide owl eyes.

Peter loved Art class. It was a special way to make his feelings have certain colors and strokes. Today, they were working with watercolors. Peter used a thick brush and only chose the color red. His thoughts raced while he painted.

First of all, he missed Goldie. He figured she was around … somewhere … just laying low. He felt bad that he yelled at her. As his brush glided over the paper, he realized she was only trying to help. She really couldn't solve all of his problems. Now he had a big problem and asking Goldie to fix Al's glasses or make Mr. T. blame someone else seemed silly and childish. What would Goldie say now?

Suddenly, he saw a quick flick of pink in the corner of his picture. He painted a swirl next to it. Then a pink splotch appeared. He smiled and looked up and Goldie was there with paintbrush in hand, as pink paint dripped from its tip. Her lips curled up slowly. "How was the math quiz?"

It was good to see her. "Fine," Pete whispered. "But I have a bigger problem now."

"I know," she whispered back. "What are you going to do?" She knew it was a big leap, but Peter had to figure some things out on his own. If he gave the wrong answer, she'd try to help him. But she was hoping that wouldn't be the case. She felt he was ready.

"Well, I think I should forget trying to talk to Mr. T. He's already made up his mind," Peter said, looking so sad that Goldie just wanted to give him a hug. Instead, she added a flower with her pink paintbrush.

Peter drew a whirl and curlicue around her flower and continued, "Instead, I'm going to go right home and tell my mother the truth. I wasn't anywhere near Al's glasses. She's my mom. She'll believe me instead of stupid Mr. T." He looked up at Goldie and smiled shyly. "Then I'll go clean up my room."

Goldie's laugh tinkled as she drew a heart on the picture. "Sounds like a plan, Pete."

Rule 4: Accept

"Well Peter, I hope you learned your lesson."

"Yes, Sir," Pete said, lowering his eyes to stare at the floor. He wasn't sure what exactly the lesson was, but all he knew was that his parents believed him when he said he had nothing to do with Albert's glasses. He heard his mother talking low to his father in the kitchen about crazy Mr. Taramanto, so he figured that had something to do with it, too. It also helped that he got a hundred on his math quiz *and* cleaned up his room. He also put two armfuls of dirty clothes in the laundry basket and, best of all, found a Lego wheel under his bed that enabled him to put together a pretty good looking Batmobile.

Goldie was waiting with a big smile when he got back to his room. She was rolling the Batmobile back and forth along the hardwood floor.

"What the heck is that?" Peter asked, pointing to the driver of the Batmobile. His crude, but accurate, Batman was now in the passenger seat. The driver was a white figure with yellow hair and white wings.

"It's a Lego Angel!" Goldie exclaimed. "I made it myself."

Pete laughed and sat down next to her. "Cool. How'd you make the wings? What pieces did you use?" His hands began to filter through the plastic shapes on the floor.

Goldie suddenly sat up and stared solemnly at Peter.

"Pete, do you think I earned my Guardian Angelship yet? How am I supposed to know when it happens?" she asked.

Pete looked up, his hands overflowing with red, blue and green Legos. "Well," he stated matter-of-fact, "isn't it just a matter of me believing in you?"

A big grin spread across Goldie's rosy face. "Hey, that makes sense," she said, scooping up some Legos and examining the shapes. "What shall we make next?"

Goldie and Pete leaned over the colorful collection of Legos as their two small heads lightly touched: one dark, one fair. Their muffled giggles wafted upward and scattered through the air like the first spring raindrops.

High above them in the folds of a large cloud pillow, a baby angel was shining a tiara for Goldie.

fin

DANCING FOR HEAVEN
By: Susan Burdorf

"Hey, Maggie. How are we doing today?" the nurse asked as she lifted the limp wrist of the older woman lying in the hospital bed. She didn't seem at all concerned that the woman didn't answer. She jotted down notes on the chart then replaced it at the end of the bed.

She returned to the side of the bed and patted Maggie's hand. Staring at the monitors a minute longer, she nodded, satisfied that everything was in order. Then her eyes fell on the photograph resting on the small table near the IV pole where Maggie's pill bottles and teeth swam in a glass of cleaning solution.

"Oh, were you a dancer?" she asked, picking up the frame. She was staring a petite but strongly muscled woman in a tutu and wings who smiled back at her.

Maggie, eyes misting, nodded and smiled as she gently reached for the frame.

The nurse handed it to her then tucked the blankets a little more securely around the wasted body of the woman.

"My daughter loves to dance," the nurse said. "Her class is having their Christmas play tonight. Shari's an angel. I can't wait to see her dance on the stage."

When Maggie didn't respond, the woman patted her on the shoulder absentmindedly before leaving the room. Outside in the hall, Maggie could hear the nurses exchanging comments as the next shift came on and her nurse's shift ended. Laughter came from some of the leaving nurses and grumbles came from those still working.

The slap-slap of the rubber soled shoes of the nurses and orderlies passing her doorway lulled her into a sleep where she dreamed of tutus and beautiful music. She remembered the sounds of applause, the dimmed lights, and the sparkling costumes. She also remembered the smiles on every face when a show went well, and the devastation and tears when it did not.

At least, she remembered when they didn't pump her up with drugs. Now, all she remembered was that Friday was sickly-yellow-Jell-o-for-dessert-day; that her children were spread to the four corners of the earth — too busy to bother with their dying mother — and that her once strong body was failing her.

Oh, what she wouldn't give for a chance to dance one more time. She held her hands up in the remembered position and imagined herself as Shari, taking one last pirouette around the hardwood stage before an adoring crowd.

This was her final show and all she could do was moan and press the pump for the pain medicine. It would not heal her, but sure made her *feel* good. She just hoped the nurses would not stick her with another needle.

"This. Is. My. Life," she whispered bitterly to the empty room. She wondered what it would be like to press the pain pump and never stop pressing. Her only answer was the swish-swish of the oxygen machine as it helped her breathe, and the staccato beep-beep of the monitor that read her heartbeats, slow and steady, even they were betraying her, keeping her alive when all she wanted to do was die.

She closed her eyes. Darkness was her only friend these days.

When she opened them again, she saw a figure standing at the edge of her bed that she didn't recognize. She couldn't tell if it was a man or woman. Radiant in a white dress, the figure was almost glowing. *An affect of the drugs,* Maggie wondered?

A doctor?

A nurse?

No, this person was not wearing a stethoscope or other tools of the healthcare trade. Also, he or she never made a move toward her chart hanging at the end of the bed.

Maybe this was a friend she had forgotten? Maggie wondered, smiling at the figure to hide her agitation.

"No, but I wish to be ..." the soft voice said as if reading her mind. The face was wreathed in a smile that reassured and somehow comforted her.

"Are you a hospital volunteer, dearie?" she asked the figure, confused about the reason for the visit.

"Not exactly," the figure said, moving closer. With the slight movement, the back of its gown swayed, causing feathers to peek around the side slightly. Maggie blinked her eyes. Was she seeing things? Perhaps the medication caused hallucinatory side effects that they had not told her about.

"What're you here for?" Maggie asked, concerned that she could not get a good view of the figure. The last rays of the sun filtered through the slats of the window blinds, illuminating the figure in light and shadow that was painful to her eyes. She reached for the button to alert the nurses that she needed help, but the smile on her guest's face stilled her unease. Maggie dropped her hand back on her blanket, leaving the button unpressed.

"What do you miss most?" the figure asked softly, so softly that Maggie had to strain to hear.

"Miss? About what?" Now she was really confused. Looking around, Maggie saw the room as she always saw it: stained, yellow curtain pulled slightly away from the wall to separate her side from the side of the room that held an empty bed; her monitors and IV pole placed near the bed for comfort; and the cracked ceiling tiles overhead. She wiggled her toes just to make sure she was awake and all seemed in order, except that the figure smiling at her, as if it held a great secret that she only had to guess to share.

"About life," the figure said, bobbing its head toward her wasted body.

Okay, she thought trying to hide her rising anxiety, *now I'm scared. What if this is a person who kills old ladies in their beds in a hospital and I'm just lying here making it easy? I can't even scream because then it'll just finish me off quicker.*

She moved her legs as if to get out of bed, just to show this person that she was not such easy prey, when the figure moved to her side and rested a hand on her arm, stopping her.

"Don't," the figure admonished her gently. Where the figure touched her, a soothing warmth burned, taking her by surprise.

She eased her body back into the bed. Looking out the door, she didn't see even one nurse or orderly walk by. Usually they were all over the place and you could never get a minute's peace, but now that she needed someone, there wasn't anyone around.

Come to think of it, it was way too quiet ... as if she was in a place where no one else existed but her and this person.

"Who are you?" she whispered, not afraid anymore, just curious.

"Ah, Magdeline, don't you know?" the figure's smile was broad and sweet and she wished she did know, but she shook her head. How did this person know her name? And why did the voice sound so familiar and yet not?

"No, I don't know who you are," she started to say, then stopped as the face of the person in front of her melted into that of her youthful lover Donald, before it melted back into the face of the anonymous person in front of her.

"I'm here to grant you one wish before you leave this mortal body," the person in front of her spread out its wings and revealed itself to her as an angel.

Maggie stared in astonishment. Somehow she had known this was not a normal visitor.

And she was right.

The monitors started to react to her excitement with loud beeps. Soon, the nurses would rush in and the moment would be lost.

"I haven't been a good person all my life Donald, you know that," she thought back to their last parting. The tears, the recriminations, how he stormed out, vowing never to speak to her again and how he had lived up to his promise. She regretted few things in her life, but hurting Donald had been the worst thing she had ever done. And for what? She remembered a chance to dance in a big city in a big performance hall. When she came back to their tiny flat after her show, he had packed his things and left her. They never spoke again.

And now that she was dying, he was willing to come back to her, to grant her a wish. Oh, how she wished she could wish that night back. She had been so young, so foolish, but she had resolved to never regret anything after that night. Hard work, lots of dance lessons (she could still remember the blisters and the muscle spasms after the lessons) and one lucky break after another, for a time, let her live her dream and Donald became nothing more than a memory.

She found a good man and married him, recognizing that letting him go would have been the second biggest mistake of her life. Together, they built a life, she'd raised three children and taught dance lessons when it became impossible to raise a family and be on the road. When he'd died last year, she had not regretted any part of her life … except for Donald. She still thought about Donald more often than not.

Maggie heard that Donald died a few years back and she wished she could have told him what he really meant to her, and how sorry she was for the way things had ended between them. But regrets had become something she never indulged in. She just carried on until cancer robbed her of the ability to teach dance — let alone live it — and she had ended up here.

It was a week before Christmas and all she wanted to do was find a way to kill herself. Then this angel, her Donald, returned to remind her of what mattered most. She didn't deserve it and Maggie found herself weeping in fear, not of dying, but of dying without having danced one more time with the man of her youth.

The angel she knew as Donald smiled at her, as if knowing what she was thinking. He held out a hand to her that was warm and smooth. She held tightly, wincing when he lifted her from the bed anticipating the pain. Shocked when she felt none, she looked down to see herself as she had been sixty years before. Her body was encased in a pale pink leotard that matched her youthful flexibility. She rolled her shoulders and laughed with joy. Maggie had not felt this good since ... well ... since the last time she and Donald had taken the stage together. Her smile could have warmed the world. Her excitement revealed itself in the tiny, girlish giggle she hid behind her delicate liver-spot-free hand. She flexed her fingers and did a quick pirouette, awed by how her body moved without pain or hesitation. *I haven't forgotten the steps,* she realized in amazement.

Donald smiled back at her in encouragement. She tested out her body by bending and crossing her legs and arms in dance movements long forgotten but now remembered. Her laughter was loud and joyous and her smile, brilliant.

It feels so good to be out of the bed ... to be alive again, Maggie thought. She stopped only when Donald's eyes clouded as he looked back at the bed.

Maggie followed his gaze and saw her tiny body, shriveled and old, laying on the bed. Nurses and a doctor rushed in and surrounded the bed. Maggie watched it all as if it was a film and she was not a participant at all.

"We have to go, my love," Donald said, taking her gently by the arm.

"Go? Go where?" Maggie asked, following him. She was marveling at the swift, pain free movements she could make. She looked at her body and costume with pride.

On her back, she had wings of pale white tipped with gold. Her costume from the production of "Swan Lake" that had been produced off-off-Broadway all those years ago. How kind of Donald to remember her greatest dancing triumph and the very night they had left each other. Bittersweet. Fraught with both love and hate. The whole night had been a blur.

"Donald," she started to say, but he put a finger over her lips to silence her.

"Words don't matter anymore," Donald told Maggie softly. "What matters is your wish. Where would you like to go?"

"I want to dance," Maggie said simply. "Can we go someplace so I can dance?"

"Of course, this is *your* desire," he pointed out the window and it opened, slightly ruffling the curtain with a sudden breeze.

Taking her by the hand, he floated up, carrying her with him. She paused only a second to look behind her and saw the nurses and doctor still working on her still body, before following Donald through the window.

They floated above the street and over the hills surrounding the town before finally coming to rest in front of a school. Cars were parked in the lot and on the grass nearby. People were streaming into the building and the tension in the air was exciting and strong.

Performance night was always like this. There was a special kind of energy that surrounded everything, filling the air like a visible presence.

Maggie noticed immediately that no one could see her. She and Donald walked through them as if they were nothing more than disturbances in the air. The people shivered for a second as they passed, and then smiled with such joy it was as if they had been touched by God.

She found herself wanting to make them smile that way and kept touching people until Donald finally told her to stop. His smile made her feel like a misbehaving child that he was indulging. Well, tonight she felt like a child and she touched one more person out of defiance, then chuckled as he rolled his eyes heavenward.

When she turned, Maggie realized the shoulder she had just touched was that of the kind nurse who had visited her earlier that night. She reached out and hugged her, hoping to give her some peace. She had seemed so upset tonight before she left.

The woman reacted by shivering and then saying to her friend, "Did you feel that? I think there is a draft somewhere around here."

"It's okay Janie." her friend said, squeezing her arm. "Everything will be okay. Shari will be fine. The doctor will take care of whatever it is and she will be fine."

"I hope so," Janie said as she and her friend entered the crowded auditorium and found two seats near the front.

Maggie wanted to follow her into the auditorium. She sensed when she touched her that the woman was having problems. Her first instinct was to help her, but Donald pulled her away.

"You're here to fulfill your wish tonight," he reminded her as he led her to the dressing room where the evening's performers were getting ready to go on stage, "God will take care of her in his own way."

Maggie nodded. Her eyes followed the nurse and her friend until she couldn't see her anymore.

Inside the room were the performers. Second and third graders, and harried moms and teachers were getting ready. It was pandemonium. People scurried to repair torn costumes, put bows in hair, attach wings to little angels, and generally get ready for the show.

Maggie loved the energy. She glanced at Donald and waited for his guidance, but he was gone. It was just her and the performers and the other adults in the room.

One of the children came up to her and stared.

"Who are you?" she asked, turning her head sideways to look at the adult in the angel costume.

Maggie looked at her in surprise, "You can see me?" she whispered to the pale little girl.

"Of course," she said, dismissing the adult's concern with child-like honesty. "You're an angel. Are you here to take me to heaven?"

"Take you to heaven? Why would I do that?" Maggie asked, looking around the room to see if anyone else could see her. But it looked like she was the only one since everyone else was still running around getting ready.

Maggie bent down until she was the same height as the tiny girl. She reached out and patted the little girl on the shoulder, then asked her name.

"I'm Shari," the little girl replied. She looked at Maggie with blue eyes, unafraid.

"Well Shari," Maggie asked her, "aren't you afraid of me?"

"Oh no," Shari said with a big smile, "my mommy told me that the angels come to comfort us and I might be seeing them soon."

"Oh?"

"Yes, I'm sick you see," said Shari with a sad look, "and it's okay, really. I'm just worried about Mommy. I have to go see a doctor tomorrow and he is going to tell me if I'm going to get better." Maggie did not know what to say to that. But before she could say anything, Shari continued, "Are you going to dance with us tonight?"

"Would you like it if I did?" Maggie asked softly.

"Oh yes," said Shari "That would make me very happy."

"Then I will dance with you tonight, and only you and I will know it," Maggie said, giving her a hug. Shari hugged her back. As her small warm body pressed against the angel, instinctively Maggie felt the wings cover the nearly weightless little girl. She was definitely sick. Maggie could feel the blackness eating at her little bones. Without thought she closed her eyes and prayed for the little girl to be okay. Was it her imagination, or did it feel like some of the darkness inside the tiny girl's body was going away? She prayed and hugged her harder, but not too hard. As she did, she could feel the girl's body was fragile and she could, if she was not careful, do more harm than good.

"Your feathers tickle," Shari laughed.

"Shari, come on, we have to get your hair ready," said a tired woman. She came over and took Shari's hand and led her away. She never glanced at Maggie at all.

Maggie straightened, watching them walk away. Shari turned and waved shyly at her and Maggie returned the wave with a big smile of reassurance.

After a few minutes Maggie wandered out of the room and down the hallway to stand behind the stage. The lights were dark and the stage was empty for now. She listened as the stage crew went over their orders one last time from the stage director before they were sent to their positions to wait for the start of the show.

"Is everything ready for the show to start?" asked the nervous teacher from the school whom Maggie took to be the Director of the show.

"Sure is, Ma'am," the stage director said looking at this check off list.

"What did you decide about the angel?" he asked checking off the rest of the list. His pen poised over the last item.

"We're not going to let her fly, it's just too dangerous and the Principal doesn't want to take the chance. I'll let her know just before she goes on stage," the teacher replied.

"She'll be mighty disappointed," the stage director said, shaking his head sadly. "That little girl was really looking forward to flying like a real angel. Said something about it being "practice" for when she really gets to be an angel."

The woman shrugged. The stage director gave the thumbs up to his crew waiting in the wings of the stage. Putting up his hand, he held up four fingers.

Four minutes to show time, Maggie thought with a sigh. Shari would be so disappointed not to get to fly. She wiggled her wings and smiled.

Who said Shari couldn't fly?

A minute later, the children all came out to stand in the wings of the stage. They were whispering and giggling behind their hands as they waited for their chance to go on stage and perform their parts in the play. When Shari got to the front of the line, she smiled at Maggie and wiggled her wings. Maggie wiggled hers back and winked.

Walking carefully around the people sending the children on stage, she walked up to stand next to Shari.

"Do you trust me?" she asked Shari.

Shari nodded, trying to watch the stage for her cue to go on.

"Hold my hand," Maggie instructed her when it was her turn to go out.

Shari looked up at Maggie and then took her hand without hesitation. Shari and Maggie danced out onto the stage. Pirouetting and pointing their toes, Shari and Maggie danced in unison. Young and old, it did not matter. They were a beautiful pair, the people in the audience watched, awestruck as the little girl, smiling brightly, seemed to float on air as she danced. They oohed and aahed when the little girl lifted off the ground to fly toward the ceiling and then gently landed on the stage. Clapping furiously, the audience stood on their feet as Shari took a small bow before gracefully leaving the stage. Looking back, she saw her angel friend, Maggie, had collapsed against part of the scenery as if exhausted.

Shoulders bent, head bowed low, Maggie felt herself weakening. Looking up, she flashed a tiny smile toward Shari and gestured for her to leave. Shari exited the stage and ran down to where her mother was waiting by the side of the stage.

The stage director was staring at his list and listening to an angry play director. The woman kept shouting at him that the angel was not supposed to fly and he kept insisting they had not connected the wire to the harness so he did not know how it happened.

"Did you see her, Mommy? Did you see her?" Shari asked her mother.

"See who, dear? All I saw was you, my little angel. You flew so high!" her mother said gathering her things. Just as she stood, her phone vibrated. Taking it out of her purse, she made a small cry and, clasping her daughter's hand, she practically ran from the auditorium.

Shari looked back toward the stage and her angel friend, Maggie, was gone. All that remained was a pile of small, white feathers.

When they arrived back at the hospital where her mother worked as a nurse, Shari was asked to wait in the room with all the colorful plastic chairs and children's toys. Usually she liked to sit there while she waited for her mother, but tonight, whether because of the play or because she was part of something bigger, she could not sit still.

Wandering around the hallway, she smiled whenever anyone complimented her on her costume, as she was still wearing her wings and tutu. She looked into several rooms and did little pirouettes as she went from patient to patient. She wasn't sure what she was looking for, but when she got to the room where her mother went, she stopped.

Her mother was holding the hand of a tiny, frail woman who was so still Shari was certain she was dead. Her mother was crying and the other nurses and the doctor were patting her on the shoulders, telling her they did what they could to save her.

Shari watched, wide-eyed as a shadow separated itself from the wall and walked toward her. It was Maggie, her angel. She had followed her here.

Maggie, sensing that Shari was watching her, smiled in welcome. Maggie wiggled her wings and laughed when Shari wiggled hers in return. No one else in the room noticed the two angels as they danced around the room. When Shari stopped and whispered, Maggie bent low to hear.

"Are you my special angel?" Shari asked.

"Do you want me to be?" Maggie answered.

"Am I going to be an angel soon?" Shari asked unafraid.

Behind Maggie another angel, a boy angel, appeared and Maggie looked over at him. He shook his head slowly.

"Not yet, little one," Maggie said kindly. She touched the top of Shari's head and pointed to her mother, "Right now you need to help your mother. She needs a hug from *her* special angel."

"Will you dance with me again?" asked Shari.

Maggie looked at the boy angel who pointed up and shook his head again.

"I can't, darling. Why don't you ask your mother to dance with you?" Maggie said. Then she turned to the boy angel and took his hand.

Maggie smiled at Donald and then back to Shari. "Remember to live your life with all the love in your heart, little angel," Maggie said to Shari. Then she bent down and kissed Shari on the forehead before leaving the room through the window.

A breeze ruffled the curtains gently when they left, as if waving good-bye.

ANGEL STORY
By: Dana Piazzi

November 22nd
Sydney, Australia
Susan Whitley

A flash of lightning lit up the house. I sat at the kitchen table with a small packet of papers in front of me. Next to them was a picture of a happy couple on their wedding day. I picked up the picture frame and looked at the couple. Was there a hint of betrayal in his eyes? Some clue to the fact that he couldn't be faithful? What about the bride? Was there a sign of her naivety in her eyes? Worse, was there something wrong with her that made her unlovable? Was she the reason that the marriage fell apart in its fifth year? Was I the reason?

I stood up on shaky legs and walked into the kitchen. I poured a glass of wine and carried it back to the table and set it down beside the divorce papers, waiting to be signed. I looked them over again. It was fairly straight forward. We didn't have children, so there was not going to be a custody battle. The papers called for a 50/50 split of all of our assets. It was a fair deal and I knew I should just sign the papers, but I couldn't. Not without knowing how it came to this.

Patrick had been a friend first, my best friend, in fact. We grew up together with the same interests and friends. Our families had been close since we were babies. In high school, I fell in love with him and I thought he loved me too. I found out that he was having an affair with his secretary for the last four years. Four out of five years of my marriage were a lie. What had I done wrong? I felt wounded through to my soul. I wasn't just losing my husband; I was losing my best friend.

There was no one I could talk to about it, either. He was my confidante. With a lump in my throat and tears in my eyes, I reached into my purse for a pen. It was time to get it over with. I was rummaging through the purse when my purse fell off the table and its contents spilled onto the floor. Tears flowed freely, then. Could you cry over spilled purse? Were there any rules about that? I shoved my things back inside, my hand coming to rest on my bottle of Xanax.

I picked it up with shaking hands. My mind was whirring in directions it shouldn't. I wasn't that depressed, was I? Some voice in my mind whispered *"Yesss! It would be so much easier."* Another voice cried out a resounding *"No!"* It was as if there was an angel and a devil on either shoulder, and I was on the devil's side. It would be so much easier. I put the bottle down on the table trying to fight my weakness, yet my hand remained on the bottle.

With a quick jerk, I picked it back up, flipped off the top, and poured half the bottle into my hands. Yes, that would be enough to do the trick. I wouldn't have to worry about signing any papers and I wouldn't have to worry about living every day without Patrick. I poured some more wine into the glass to swallow down the pills, and raised my hand to my mouth to place some of the pills in my mouth. Suddenly, there was a booming *"No"* that echoed through the house. I dropped the pills as a smoky face suddenly formed in front of my eyes, and dissipated just as quickly.

In that moment, confusion mixed with shame filled my soul, snapping me out of it. I couldn't believe that I was about to take my own life. I knew I was stronger than that. I broke down crying and placed my head into my hands. My body racked with sobs releasing the pain I was holding inside. I felt a slight ruffling of my hair and a warming sensation. I looked up, the tears drying. The rain stopped outside, the sun filtered through the broken clouds, and a rainbow formed in the misty skies.

I didn't question that something strange and phenomenal had just happened. I threw away the pills and poured the wine down the sink. Inside of me something changed, and I knew that the pain would lessen. I knew that I would be okay.

***

November 22nd
London, UK
Roger Easton

"That will be sixty-five pounds," the man said.

I pulled out my wallet and my fingers grazed the bills inside. I had a moment of doubt.

"I don't have all day, do you want it or not?" the dealer said again.

I pulled out the money and gave it to him. In exchange, he handed me a small bag filled with white powder. I shoved it into my inside jacket pocket and walked quickly out of the alleyway.

It was windy out, so I pulled my jacket closer to me to drive away the chills. I had lost so much weight lately. I couldn't eat or sleep because the withdrawal pains were killing me. It had been a month since I last stopped down that alley. I thought I was getting stronger, but this last week was the worst. My parents were so proud of me and helped me out, giving me money for bills and food — money I just gave to a hooded man, who made his living with crime. Which bills wouldn't get paid due to my moment of weakness?

I reached my flat and ran up the stairs to my door. Once inside, I began the process right away. I heated up the powder until it formed a liquid, and then pulled it into the syringe. I sat on the living room floor and grabbed a tourniquet. Just as I was tying it on, I saw the my healed arm when I experienced another pang of doubt.

I had worked so hard to quit this horrible habit. I had hurt my mum and dad more than I like to think of. Yet, here I was, about to fall back into the same trap. Even the pain I suffered for the last month was all for nothing. I had put myself through hell to end up back in the same place I was before. Then I felt another shuddering rack of pain go through my body. I began to shake and feel nauseous, and I barely made it to the kitchen sink in time to throw up bile and saliva.

Why wasn't it getting any better? I cursed, looking up to the heavens. I sat back down next to the waiting needle. I couldn't take the pain anymore and I had to do something. So I picked up the needle and slid it into my vein. My thumb was on the plunger and I closed my eyes as I threw away all the recovery work I had done.

Through my closed eyelids, a light exploded. It was as if I was staring at the sun even through the barrier. I opened my eyes and was blinded. White light surround me to the point that I couldn't even make out my own hands in front of me. I wondered if I had somehow injected myself and overdosed. How else could I explain what was happening? I pulled the syringe out of my arm and threw it onto the floor.

The light grew even brighter and I squeezed my eyes shut once more. *Maybe it wasn't a heavenly light. Maybe it was the fires of hell rising up to meet me,* I considered. But as quickly as it came, the light was doused and I opened my eyes to my living room. The full syringe lay beside me on the floor, but I was feeling like a new person. I didn't feel sick or in pain. I felt hungry, instead. Walking into the kitchen, I opened the refrigerator, wondering if I had any food in there.

I found spaghetti that my mother left when she visited two days ago. I warmed it up and tucked into bed. After eating, I felt so tired, but I had confidence that I would sleep well. I wasn't sure if what I experienced was real or not, but there was definitely a difference in how I felt. I wasn't particularly religious, but I was considering the possibility that a miracle had occurred.

On the way to the bedroom, I picked up the syringe and zip-lock bag from the living room. I went into the bathroom and flushed the powder and liquid down the toilet. But as I watched sixty-five pounds get flushed away, I felt stronger and better than I had in the last five years.

***

November 22nd
Brooklyn, NY
Michelle Stevens

I held the cell phone between my shoulder and my ear as I washed dishes. I had so much to do that I tried to multi-task while talking to my mother, Rose.

"You know, Michelle, you really should go to church today," she reminded me.

"I know, Mom, but I'm very busy and Kyla won't sit still that long," I replied.

Saying her name must have brought my precocious 6 year old into the kitchen. She tugged on my skirt, getting my attention. "Mommy, I wanna go out and play."

I shook my head in response as my mother continued to remind me of the reasons I should go to church. "I know, Mom," I repeated, not listening to her fully. Kyla kept pulling on my skirt.

"Please, Mommy," she begged. I shook my head again with a firm expression on my face.

It was hectic with my mom in one ear and my daughter in another. Also, I still had to clean the house before my husband got home from his business trip. I didn't have time for this.

"Mom, I have to let you go. I have to clean before Rob gets home and Kyla wants to go out. I'll try to make it to church next week. Love you, bye," I said and hung up the phone before I could face any more argument.

It wasn't as if I didn't understand. I believed in God and His Son. I had my own relationship with them. I prayed and thanked them. I just didn't want to worry about Kyla behaving, and finding the time to go to church was just too hard.

I turned my attention to the dishes until I felt a tug on my skirt once more. "Please, I want to play with my new ball," she said with a tear in her eye.

"For the last time, no!" I said, harsher than I should have. "I'm sorry, baby, It'll have to wait until I'm done cleaning up the kitchen." She ran away with a wail, and I heard her banging on her toys in the living room. Knowing she would get over it, I started cleaning the dishes again.

Once all the dishes were dried and put away, I realized Kyla was no longer crying or playing with her toys. I went into the living room to see if she had fallen asleep, but the room was empty. When I came around the corner of the kitchen, the front door was sitting open. I ran toward it in a panic. I reached the screen door just in time to see the new ball bounce out into the street. Kyla ran after it. I screamed her name as I threw open the door. A taxi was bearing down on her. A scream continued to pour from my chest.

Suddenly Kyla was airborne. The taxi hadn't hit her and thrown her into the sky, but it was like she was physically lifted up and then was placed down on the sidewalk in front of our house. The taxi screeched to a halt, and the driver through the car into park. He got out of the car and walked around looking for something — the thing that had saved my baby.

I ran down the steps and fell to my knees in front of my daughter, then wrapped her in my arms and held on for dear life crying and rocking her.

"Mommy, I floated," she said.

"I know," I replied, my eyes shining with tears. Then I remembered that she disobeyed me. "Kyla, you never leave the house without telling me, and don't ever run into the street again." I reprimanded her lightly, too grateful that she was alive to be really angry.

In the street, I saw the taxi driver make the sign of the cross and get back into the car, with no explanation of what had happened. I followed his lead and made the sign of the cross myself. "Thank you, Jesus," I whispered to the open air.

"Mommy," Kyla said.

"Yes?"

"I think we should go to church."

I laughed out loud. I was right back at the beginning, but I agreed. "Let's go get ready. We can still make it if we leave now." After all, I had a lot to be thankful for today.

***

November 22nd
San Diego, CA
Sara Sharpe

It was late evening in the hospital and not many people were around who weren't doctors or nurses. Every night, though, I came and sat down next to the incubator holding my premature son, Matthew. Every night I prayed for him to get stronger and healthier. I wanted to take him home so badly. It was torture every night, leaving him to go home. I couldn't do it for long. I stayed with him during the day. Then when my husband fell asleep, I headed back to the hospital.

It was hard. My husband didn't understand. He loved our son, but he didn't feel the same separation that I felt. I had just had my baby taken out eleven weeks earlier than he should have been born. I didn't have him at home to hold and to bond with. I was in a constant state of loss whenever I wasn't at the hospital.

So far, things had been going pretty well. They gave him a shot to make his lungs stronger, and he was off the oxygen. He had one transfusion so far, but they assured me that it was pretty routine. Now, it was just a waiting game. I just had to wait for Matthew to get bigger and to be able to drink his bottle and breathe at the same time.

I pulled out my rosary, prepared to say my nightly prayers for him, and I was on the fourth decade when his alarm started beeping. It wasn't the first time. Monitor alarms frequently went off throughout the NICU. Usually, it was nothing severe. I moved aside as the nurse came to his incubator. She looked at the alarm and then at Matthew.

"Mrs. Sharpe, I'm afraid you're going to have to move out of the way," she said.

That didn't sound good. They've never asked me to move away before. I took a step back, and then a second alarm went off at his station. I was jostled as several more nurses and a doctor rushed past me toward my infant son. I stood back as the incubator was opened and they started working with him.

I couldn't see what was happening and I didn't know what was going on. I wanted to ask them what was wrong, but I didn't want to distract them from keeping him safe and alive. So I kept backing up to give them room until I bumped into the wall. I put my hand over my mouth to stifle a sob, and my shoulders shook with my cries. Minutes felt like hours as they kept working on my son. I saw the doctor drag a hand across his forehead and his shoulders slumped a little. What did that mean? Was there no hope? I should be there with my son in his last moments, if that was what this was.

I stepped forward, but was stopped when I saw a golden form step behind the doctor and place its hand on the doctor's shoulder. I saw his shoulders raise and he bent over

Matthew again. The figure place his hand on top of the doctor's and guided it as he worked. A gasp escaped my throat as I watched what couldn't be happening. It couldn't be real.

One of the nurses moved out of the way and I got a view of my son and the doctor stitching his tiny chest back together. The golden being touched Matthew's head and heart and I saw a subtle glow surround him. Suddenly, the monitors stopped beeping. I fell to my knees, wondering if I was witnessing something divine, or if I had lost my sanity. The doctor turned around and smiled at me. "Everything is going to be okay," he said.

Tears of relief fell slowly down my cheeks. I cried in happiness with the release of tension and fear. Then the golden figure came toward me and touched my head. Immediately, the tears dried up and I was filled with an amazing feeling of light and hope. There was the hint of wings behind the figure, and then I knew for certain. I was in the presence of an angel. No one else noticed him and I wondered if he was choosing to show himself to me or if in my despair, I was able to see the impossible. The angel picked up the rosary from the floor and dropped it into my hand. I looked up into the golden light and then before my eyes, it faded and the being was gone.

The doctor closed the top of the incubator and I moved closer to see my baby. "It was touch and go for a minute, but your son will be fine, ma'am," he said with a smile. "One of the valves in his heart was weakened and wasn't pumping blood properly. There will be someone in here to give him another transfusion in a few minutes." He shook my hand and walked away. I reached in and touched my baby for a second and then backed away.

They didn't allow parents in the room when they were giving a transfusion, so I decided to go home for the night. When I got home, Steve was up. "I woke up about an hour ago, feeling like something was really wrong. Is everything okay?" he asked me.

I nodded and threw myself into his arms. I told him about the alarms and the emergency surgery that the doctors performed. I left out the part about the angel, I didn't think my Atheist husband would believe me if I tried to tell him, not sure if I had imagined it myself.

Steve wrapped his arms around me as we lay down in bed together.

"I prayed tonight," he said. I looked at him in surprise. "I just felt like I needed to," he answered my questioning eyes. "I think it was a miracle."

I kept my mouth shut and nodded in agreement as a single tear slipped out of my eye. It seemed that there was no shortage of miracles that night.

***

Cyril

An Angel's job is never done. With several charges all over the world, I work non-stop. Most of the time, the interventions are just a blur. Then a quick lead in the right direction and off to the next call I go. In most cases, not a soul knew I had come and gone, not to mention influenced a decision or changed a step that would have had dire consequences for my charge. It was better that way. People didn't take kindly to interference.

Not that what I did was always interfering. I didn't take away free will. God knew I couldn't do anything as encompassing as that. A little help in the right direction was just the protocol. To be honest, there was so much work to be done and it happened so quickly that I was just going through the motions when doing my job. I didn't know who these people really were, just that they were about to walk into a dangerous situation or maybe make a bad decision. And most of the time, my actions did not change all that much. I just needed to keep God's children on the right path, or near it.

Every once in a while, I was touched by a call for help. Sometimes, I was pulled in deeper and I felt changed when helping the person. Usually in those instances they felt me, as well. I knew it happened four times in the last rotation of the Earth. I felt burned by the experiences and the desperate calls shook me to my core.

In Sydney, the woman who was thinking of ending her life was so strong in most situations. I knew that suicide was not in her nature, but that some negative being was preying on her weakness. I tried subtle mental influences and felt her start to strengthen, only to pull away. With one touch of her head, she gathered her resolve and the evil influence faded away.

In London, my charge was not just in danger of slipping into a former bad habit. I was gifted with the knowledge that this would be his last foray into drugs. He was about to overdose. I had to pull out all the stops by letting my true light shine, but I was rewarded with seeing him flush the illegal substances into the toilet. The warmth and strength I fed into him wouldn't last forever, but it should carry him through a good while until he was strong enough to kick the habit for good.

It was rare to have one interaction such as these, but two really threw me off. I was late to my next call in New York. Almost too late. There was nothing for me to do but a drastic action. I had to pick the girl up and fly her over the car. I exposed myself to three different people, at least. I watched as the parties looked around. They couldn't see me, but moving the girl had definitely not gone unnoticed. They knew someone or something had stepped in.

My last call for the day was the hardest. I rolled my shoulders thinking of the harrowing situation. No Guardian Angel wants to lose a human at such a young age. In truth, the child should not have even been born yet. He needed extra protection. When the alarms went off I felt the life seeping out of the newborn, so I rushed into the situation and helped guide the doctor's hand as he performed the risky, emergency surgery. Afterwards, I touched the baby's head to infuse him with some of my strength. I felt relieved when the monitors stopped their shrill cries.

I looked over at the mother and was surprised to see her staring back at me in astonishment. She was not my charge and I had been keeping myself hidden from mortal view. But sure enough, she knew I was there. I could only discount it to the stress and tiredness I could see in her face. She was almost in another state of existence. I looked down at the rosary lying on the floor and picked it up. I handed it to the distraught women, and even though she was not in a critical state, I infused her with a little strength, as well. She looked like she needed it.

I knew that these people would soon forget what happened, or try to reason it out — to find an explanation other than divine help. It was the way of the world. I also knew that it would take me a long time to forget these souls that somehow changed me that day and brought me closer to humanity for a little while. But it would be hard to forget four heightened situations in one day, and the fact that I had faced so much exposure. I wondered as the new day began and I heard a cry for help in China, was this just a strange day or a sign to come? What was happening in the world?

A DIVINE JOURNEY
By: Nikki Shah

We all gathered round into a glowing group of individual energies of light ranging from many different colors found within the spectrum. That is how we recognized each other. We did not have names; we were pure energies of light. We each had our own signature that was unique only to ourselves and no one else. Only when it was time for us to fulfill our duty as a guardian angel did we give ourselves names. The name that I chose for myself was Maya.

"Your training is now complete," our spiritual master informed us. "Everything is in place and souls have been allocated to the unborn children. By the time you reach the earth they would have already entered their new world. Some you will recognize you as energies from our realm that you may have seen before or even know. In their lifetime, they will not remember anything of our world as they begin their time on earth. You will know when you reach the earth's atmosphere which direction to go to find the soul you are to be guardian of. You are specifically linked to them and you all know what to do when you find them." He paused, then continued, "You will make contact and help nurture and guide your soul toward their destined path. This will all be revealed once the connection between the two of you has been established and activated. Sometimes a destined path is not always followed, but it is your duty to do what you can to help support these souls throughout this life cycle."

"How are you feeling, Maya?" asked Sarah. We were partners throughout our training. Sarah was more experienced than me. I have a lot to thank her for; the lessons of experience she passed down to me were invaluable.

"A little nervous," I replied. "What if we get surrounded by the dark energies?"

"I will be right by your side and don't worry, think positive. Stay strong and concentrate on your protective shield. Remember to surround yourself with the impenetrable light of our creator. That is all you can do until you actually come into contact with a lower or darker energy. You will know what to do. Tap into your higher source and focus on the outcome you desire."

This was my first time. I never did anything like this before. I had a few lives on earth with different experiences and learned from every life that I have lived. In comparison to some of the others in the group, I was young and inexperienced when it came to acting as someone's guardian angel, but I had excelled in training much to the annoyance of some of the more experienced guardians. Some were happy for my success and natural ability to perform each task asked of me, but some were just not interested and made me feel like an outcast. They thought it was beginner's luck that would eventually run out, taunting me that they may have to be sent to take over as guardian to the soul I was allocated to. I ignored those taunts, as I knew deep down in the center of the light shining deep within me that this was not going to happen. Not on my watch.

A few of the other angels in the group had been guardian angels numerous times before and the more experienced angels were guardians to more than one soul on earth. Through each cycle they went through as a Guardian Angel, each angel returned home to our astral plane after escorting their passed soul back to where they needed to be, depending on the outcome of their personal experience on Earth. The angels all had to attend debriefing sessions to share experiences and remain updated on any new techniques that have been developed along the way.

As we all prepared to leave our realm and commence our descent down to earth, I had to admit that something felt off about the timing of our departure. I also knew that as a group our energy was powerful and it was almost impossible to penetrate our protective shield of light. It was only once we reached the Earth's atmosphere that we were open to the possibility of coming into contact with darker energies that are there to interfere with the path of light and love and try to prevent us from doing what we were sent to achieve. Encountering dark forces didn't happen often on descent, but lately they had become aware of a new approach and realized that if they can stop a guardian angel from making contact with a human from the beginning of their life, then they had more of a chance of corrupting that human's soul. This was going to be the hardest part of our journey and it was imperative that we did not fail in making that initial contact.

We had not yet taken on our angel form as yet that would materialize once we were through the earth's atmosphere. As l looked around at the other angels, I could see that I was not the only one who was nervous. There were exchanges of good luck and some of the more experienced were reminding others of the techniques to use in the event of an emergency situation. We all knew what that meant. Their confidence was reassuring.

Our conversations were interrupted by the well-known voice of our spiritual master. "It is time, my Guardian Angels. Go forth and fulfill your journey and remember your training. Upon your descent and transformation please try to remain as close to your partner as possible. I will be watching over you until you make the connection with your allocated soul. There after I will look in from time to time to see how you are progressing."

Our master always had a way with words. We each stood with our partners, strong collectively as a group. Then suddenly our master's energy became brighter and began rising and as his light ascended. The biggest constellation of stars surrounded us one by one, encasing us within their disguise. The stars emitted such bright light that no dark energy would even consider us to be a group of guardian angels. We all held our positions for a moment to ensure that we were all in a group. Then we slowly began our descent down to earth. Before we hit the atmosphere, there was a massive outburst of stars shooting away from us in all directions.

Suddenly, we were catapulted into the atmosphere at different entry points around the earth. Sarah and I remained close. Following her lead, how could we fail? Our energy had been condensed into a ball of light. I found this to be slightly uncomfortable, but it was bearable. Our inner lights began to glow brightly and rotated as we were propelled across the sky carried by the momentum of the velocity at which we were travelling. To our kind already on earth, our entry into this world looked like a meteor shower sprinkling across the sky. During this time, we are not visible to the human eye.

I looked across at Sarah as we continued spinning, and it was at that moment that she broke away from me slightly. Her inner glow expanded, becoming brighter by the millisecond. I could see that within her cocoon of light she was embracing the transformation, taking on her form as an angel. It was time for me to do the same. I concentrated on my own inner energy allowing it to expand and to give me the protection I needed to begin my transfiguration. I felt a tremendous surge of powerful energy running through me and I could feel my appearance adapting to the change that was happening within. My wings sprouted out of my back. I gasped as the pulsating energy electrified me, spreading into my wings as they lengthened and expanded to their full capacity. Then at the last moment, I was overwhelmed with a sense of freedom as the power of my wings kicked in and I took flight across the skies.

It was a wonderful feeling, to feel the air around me supporting my flight. I looked down at myself and admired my new look. I then felt a sharp pain inside of me and I immediately searched the skies for Sarah. We made eye contact and I could see she was under attack, as dark energies were surrounding her beautiful illuminating glow of yellow that was clearly her signature. I sensed a shift in the atmosphere. It felt cold, dark, and everything inside of me was telling me to fly away; to find the my allocated soul and make contact, but I just couldn't leave her there to be consumed by the lower energies whose purpose was to prevent us from fulfilling our mission. Sarah suddenly stopped. Then looked the lower energies face on and closed her eyes.

What is she doing? I asked myself as I slowed down, never taking my eyes from her. Then the purest, brightest, light pulsated out of her and dissolved the dark energies around her. I was in awe of what was happening before me. I should have had a little more faith in Sarah's capability to deal with a situation like this. She flew away and spoke to me via our mind connection and told me to find the human and make contact. I nodded and we separated into the direction of our destined targets descending through the clouds along the way.

I should have been paying attention to my own safety, for at that same moment I felt a heavy weight on my right wing. I looked to the right and could see what was beginning to absorb my energy. I had heard so much about interceptions, but nothing could prepare me for the shock and the sense of losing control that I was feeling. I panicked and began evasive maneuvers, trying to shake off the heaviness that was consuming me. Three quarters of my right wing was changing color from the bright turquoise energy that was mine into a murky tainted shade of grey. I could feel my wing becoming heavier as the darkness penetrated my feathers along my wingspan. It started to make me feel dizzy and confused. I tried to remember my training and the words of encouragement Sarah had given me, but I couldn't concentrate. I closed my eyes and focused, trying to look deep within to find my own inner strength and light to fight off the darkness. I visualized myself surrounded by the purest, whitest light, but as soon as the light travelled along my wing erasing the lower energy, it dissipated just as fast, for the darkness was already having an effect on me. I began to slow down and in my mind I called out to my spiritual master.

"Master, I need help! I am being consumed by the dark energies! There are too many of them!" I heard nothing in response to my call for help. "Can you hear me?" Still, there was nothing. I continued flying through the sky to get away, but all my efforts were in vain until I spotted a cloud shining brightly. I don't know why, but all I knew is that I had to get to this cloud as quickly as I could. By this time, the energy in both of my wings was being dominated and it took all the inner strength I had to pull away and I clumsily fell into the cloud that I was aiming for. I was enveloped with a warm feeling of finding refuge away from the lower energies. They were trying their best to get me, reaching and swiping at the cloud. Every time they made contact with the light their energy diminished and became weak, preventing any further attempts to get me. I stayed there for what felt like a very long time and I thought this was it. I have failed. I will return to my world a failure. I felt disorientated and didn't know where I was supposed to go, or even which human I had to find to make contact with. My energy was drained so I decided to descend to the earth's surface to find my bearings and decide what to do next.

The lower energies I had absorbed left me feeling lost, confused. I had no idea where I was supposed to be. I was flying around for quite a while trying to see if I could at least sense where I should be going, but nothing came to me. The sun was shining as I flew lower over some treetops. I could hear the sound of birds singling and it was music to my ears. I passed some houses with some really beautiful gardens and there was one garden in particular that caught my eye. I was tired and drained, so I decided this would be a good place to stop for a while and rest.

I landed gently on the ground and contracted my wings. I was in the middle of the most beautiful garden I had ever seen. I knew I could stay here for a while unnoticed as the humans aren't able to see guardian angels or any kind of angels for that matter.

I sat down by the blue overlapping fencing next to a big apple tree toward the back of the garden. I thought this would be out of the way in case any dark forces were still trying to locate me. The smell of the ripening fruit hanging from the branches tickled my senses as I inhaled the refreshing scent.

"Hello?"

I looked up to find a young girl with brown hair walking toward me, dressed in a pretty flowery dress with some lovely red-patent leather shoes, holding daisies in her hand. I remained still, trying not to make eye contact.

"Hello! Can you hear me?" she asked as she approached me.

Of course! I thought to myself. The older humans couldn't see me, but the younger ones can. The young girl couldn't have been more than five years old. Young children on earth are highly sensitive, naturally open and attuned to the spiritual world around them.

"Hello, little one," I said, making eye contact.

"Are you a bird?" she asked

I smiled; the imagination of a child was something rather special. "Do you think I am a bird?"

"No, but you have wings like one," she said, pointing at my wings. "Can you fly like a bird?"

"You are very curious aren't you? What is your name?"

"My name is Louise and I am five years old!" she replied, proudly holding up a hand to show me her age with her outstretched fingers.

"Hello, Louise, it is very nice to meet you. My name is Maya," I replied.

"What are you?" She asked

"I am a Guardian Angel."

"An Angel?" she gasped. "Angels are messengers of God."

"They certainly are," I replied, then added, "We also watch over you everyday to make sure that you are happy and safe."

"Do you think I have a Guardian Angel?" she inquired curiously.

"I am sure you do," I reassured.

"Are you someone's angel?"

"Not yet. I am a little lost and can't find the person I am supposed to be looking after," I said.

"Oh no!" she cupped her hands over her mouth.

"Louise! Lunch will be ready soon," a female voice called out into the garden.

"Okay, Mum. Coming!" answered Louise. "That's my Mum. I need to go and eat my lunch soon. Would you like some too?"

"That's lovely of you to ask, but I need to ..." I was interrupted by the sound of a crying baby. "Is that a baby I hear crying?" I asked.

"Yes!" she answered, then added, "That's my sister, Yasmin. She's new. My Mummy had a baby."

"Really? That's wonderful! Congratulations on becoming a big sister!"

Louise giggled. "Will you still be here after I finish eating my lunch?"

"Maybe, I have lot's to do today. But if I am not here, is it okay if I come and see you soon?" I asked.

"That would be nice," said Louise as she handed me one of the daisies she was holding in her hands. "This is for you," she added, then ran into the house. As I watched her run into the house I could hear the distant cries of her baby sister and could see her mother comforting the child in her arms, trying to calm her down.

I turned my focus back to the garden around me. The life energy surrounding the plants, flowers, and small insects were calling out to me. I looked down to the daisy in my hand and bent down to touch the pink petal of a flower beside me hidden in the grass. I touched one of the petals and felt an amazing surge of energy jolt me. *WOW! Now that's what I am talking about,* I thought to myself. Then I touched the base of the apple tree I was sitting next to. There it was again; another surge of energy. With every contact I made with the life surrounding me, it made me feel better. It was a wonderful feeling and it felt so good to feel back in control again. I could feel my energy replenish itself. I could also feel all my other responsibilities beginning to kick in, too.

As soon as I felt strong enough I pushed off the ground, I took flight once again.

This time I could sense the inner light of the human I was to make contact with and I knew exactly which direction I to needed go. Following my inner guidance, I flew over the fields, passing some small towns and caught sight of a beautiful house of God and stopped to admire its wonderful architecture. I could hear the angelic voices of a choir, as I looked through one of the decorated stained glass windows. I could see that they were rehearsing their hymns. I was enjoying the moment and found myself humming along to the familiar sound of one of the songs when I heard a cry for help. I immediately stopped humming and flew high above the church steeple and looked around. I could see a pure white light glowing in the distance, drawing me toward it.

Suddenly, I could hear a young voice in my mind. "Help!*" There it was again,* I thought, "I'm scared and alone.*"

"I am here, Little One. Help is on its way. Don't be afraid," I reassured and flew toward the white glow in the distance.

I was there in less than a few seconds. The glow was coming from within a house, from one of the rooms upstairs. I flew up to the window and hovered outside as I glanced into the room. The walls of the room were decorated with a blue-sky effect. Drawings of birds flying around with the sun shining and beams of light filtering through the clouds were painted on the walls. Below the sky was the outline of a town below. As I looked at the room, it reminded me of my journey here to earth and my transition to become a Guardian Angel. Inside the room was a baby boy lying in a cot with an angel mobile hanging above it, moving as the air passed by. This was most definitively my human soul. His inner light was glowing brightly. He wriggled around, looking a little distressed, like he was about to cry. Without hesitation, I was by the side of the young child, surrounding him in a soft, pink energy of love to help calm him down. He looked up at me with his dark brown eyes, and as our eyes made contact, I smiled and brushed my hand along the side of his cheek.

"It's okay, little one. I am here now. You have nothing to be afraid of."

The child communicated with me through his mind again. "My mother left the room. I don't like being alone."

"Joshua, you are not alone. It's okay. I am here now. I am your guardian angel." As soon as I informed the child of this, his light began to glow even more brightly than before. It started off small near his heart, then began to slowly spread, travelling out along to his arms, hands to his fingertips, then down his body to his legs, feet, and right to his toes. It was at this moment that Joshua's inner light was at its strongest.

I closed my eyes, still able to see his energy glowing and concentrated on my own energy. I surrounded myself and Joshua with my own inner light of turquoise energy. We were illuminating light, love, and peace. It was a precious moment to be able to experience. I then raised my right hand and placed my thumb on his forehead between his eyes, just above his eyebrows. As I made contact with his mind's eye, Joshua's life flashed before my eyes. I saw his life as he is now, in the present, and his life as he grows into an adult in the future, too. It was quite empowering to be able to see into a human this way. It gave me a great insight to how a human's life operates from a spiritual point of view. It was amazing. Joshua just looked at me and although he was not sure what was going on, he wasn't crying and seemed happy, content and safe.

The connection has been made and the spiritual bond I now have with Joshua will become stronger with every moment we are together.

"It is done. I am now your Guardian Angel. I am here to help, comfort and protect you for as long as you need me," I declared.

Once those words were spoken, Joshua closed his eyes and fell asleep. It was very peaceful watching him sleep. I stayed with him, watching over him throughout the night to make sure that no harm came to him. It had been quite an eventful night for us both, but this is where I will remain, by his side. For I am now officially a Guardian Angel.

CHRISTMAS
By: Kim Stevens

The mist gently swirled across the ground like small waves. The delicate notes of a harp wafted in the gentle air. The gold trim glittered while hundreds of jewels sparkled on nearby buildings. The sun was warm, catching crystals hanging in windows, sending rainbows dancing across every surface.

This, unfortunately, was lost on Baier. He leaned a shoulder on a nearby dwelling and sighed heavily. He folded his arms across his broad chest while watching a human soul being prepared for travel.

Baier's wings twitched in irritation. The scene before him bored him, as he'd seen it countless times before. On occasion, he had even been the angel to coach the souls and teach them right from wrong. It was a pointless job.

Baier knew humans were stubborn creatures and couldn't fend off temptation.

"Weak, pitiless ..." he said, narrowing his eyes.

"Say, what's really on your mind," a sweet voice asked behind him.

Baier turned, all disgust gone from his face. "What brings you out on this fine day?" He let his arms drop to his sides as he stood up to his full height.

"I wanted to speak to you," Nevaeh replied, placing a small, porcelain white hand on his chest.

Her intense aqua-blue eyes looked up at him.

Baier had to clear his throat. "About what?" His wing inched closer to the small angel's wings. They were silvery white, magnificent in Baier's opinion.

"I've noticed you aren't yourself."

He forced a dazzling smile, wishing that she wasn't so perceptive. Baier also knew the effect his smile would have on her. He watched as she swayed under his gaze, her eyes briefly going glassy. Baier knew he had her now.

"Explain, please," his voice was silky smooth.

Nevaeh swallowed then broke eye contact. She was momentarily silent for a minute. Baier chuckled.

"You compelled me, didn't you?" Nevaeh asked accusingly. She went to pull her hand from his chest, but Baier caught it and held onto it.

"You don't need compulsion to capture me," his wing was now linked to hers. Electricity coursed through the connection. "You already have me," he said, his voice low and sultry. He bent his head toward hers and pressed his lips to her soft cheek.

"But you didn't answer my question."

Baier smiled and stood up straight. "Let it be."

Nevaeh was small standing next to him. Her line of sight came just below his chest. Baier could have picked her up with one arm, but what Nevaeh lacked in height she made up for in stubbornness.

Baier saw the set of her jaw and the narrowing of her beautiful eyes. He sighed, released her hand, and leaned a shoulder on the building. A deep red ruby caught his attention so he ran a finger over it. The jewel was set in an off-white concrete exterior wall. Every building had jewels scattered in their walls. Baier thought it was over the top.

"Baier … what's troubling you?" Nevaeh asked, stepping in front of him, severing their wing connection. Baier's silvery-gold wings were now flattened to his back and his shoulders were tense.

"Why do we bother sending them back?" he spits out, watching as the human soul vanished in a bright flash of light. "They never take our advice. They always get tempted …"

"Baier, it's our job to send them back," Nevaeh was watching the scene. "Temptation is a part of a human's life. It's up to them whether they go through with it or not."

"But we're the ones who have to go rescue them." Baier shook his head angrily. "I've had enough of this."

"What do you mean by that?" she looked up at him. "Would you give all this up?"

Baier looked around at the swirling mist and the sparkling jewels.

"Yes," he replied, looking down at the small angel. "Yes, I would give it all up."

Baier sees hurt in Nevaeh's eyes. "Does that include giving up on me?"

He bites his lip. Could he stay for her? Baier couldn't answer. Nevaeh nodded, then looked away. He knew she had found her answer in his eyes.

"I am deeply sorry," Baier said softly, then walked away. He heard Nevaeh sobbing, but he didn't look back.

***

It was Christmas morning and a young woman screamed and cursed at the nurses and the new intern. Sweat beaded on the intern's forehead. It's his first birth and he's as nervous as hell. The intern squeezed his eyes shut, said a little prayer, and then prepared himself for the miracle of birth.

"You're doing great, Beth," the intern shouted over the tirade of curse words. "Another big push …"

"Get it out!" the girl shrieked. "It effin' hurts."

The young intern felt like lecturing her, but that would have earned him a foot to the face.

After a slow, agonizing hour, the baby entered the world safe, healthy and crying.

The intern had a tear in his eye while checking over the baby. "Beautiful," he whispered, taking in the head full of bright red hair, soft white skin and wide emerald eyes.

"Do you have a name for her?" a nurse asked her mother.

"No," the young girl snapped. "I dun wan it."

"It's your baby," he can't help but say. Someone had to be on the infant's side. "Don't you want to see her? Hold her?"

"If I could effing sell her, then I would. But who'd take her?" the new mother shrugged, never setting eyes on her beautiful baby girl.

"Why does this have to happen?" the intern said, slamming his fist down hard on the nurses' desk. His anger was at boiling point, earning him a few puzzled stares. "It's not fair."

"I agree, but getting angry won't help," a nurse told him. "We can't force these girls to take the babies."

"So, what happens to the infant now?" he asked, hanging his head, taking a few deep, calming breaths.

"Welfare has been contacted," the nurse replied, touching the intern's hand. "It's hard, but it's what we do." She pats his fingers before turning back to her paperwork.

The intern walked to the nursery and found the baby's crib near the window. A small pink tag read: "Christmas" Jane Doe.

He placed his hands on the side of the incubator and peered down at the little girl. She stared back at him with knowing green eyes.

"I hope you have a guardian angel, little one," the intern said, then turned and left the nursery.

The little girl's eyes are stared out the window. She gives a gummy smile to Bair, who smiled back. It was a dazzling smile.

Ten years later ...

"Christie, get ya backside back to the table now," yells a man with a spreading bald spot. "Christie ..." he's puffing as he chases ten-year-old Christmas around the four bedroom dump of a house.

Christmas zipped into her room, cowering as the man appeared in the doorway. Her back hit the wall and her knees started to shake.

"Come 'ere, ya little ..." the man said, stalking forward, but suddenly stopped, frozen in the middle of the room.

Christmas' emerald green eyes flew open wide as she tugged on a piece of bright red hair.

"Hey, over here," a soft voice came from outside the window. "Christmas ..."

Her eyes darted to the fly screen window and relief flooded her. Christmas slowly moved against the wall as the screen is popped out. Quickly, she is plucked out of the room and is held in strong, safe arms.

"Baier ..." she said, giggling as she wrapped her thin arms around his neck. "You saved me."

"I'll always save you, Christmas girl." Baier replied, enjoying her child-like laugh as his wings snap open. He held the little girl to his body as he soared into the clear blue sky.

"What was he yelling at you for?" Baier asked as Christmas snuck a peek down at the world below.

"I didn't want to eat my carrots," she replied as her small arms tightened around his neck. "He was going to belt me again."

Baier grimaced at the girl's words as images of her battered and bruised body came flooding back to him. Christmas had a five-page medical record at the local hospital.

"You're safe now," he finally said and met her eyes. "You know I will always look after you."

Christmas's head bobbed up and down, making her red hair bounce around her shoulders.

Baier landed softly on a carpet of pine needles. Scanning the area, he decided it was safe then carried a sleeping Christmas into an abandoned log cabin. Baier had called it home off and on now for the past ten years.

Pulling the covers back, Baier gently lay the little girl down then covered her over. The tiny, sleeping body was almost lost in the king-sized bed. He quickly started a fire, squatting down in front of the hearth. Fire danced around in his crystal blue eyes.

When he had walked out of the pearly white gates of Heaven, Baier finally felt free. He felt guilty for hurting Nevaeh, but he had to leave her — to leave his old life behind — for his own sanity.

The day he fell was the day Baier came across this beautiful, innocent life that now slept in the bed: Christmas Jane Doe.

At ten years old, Christmas knew and saw things that no child or adult should ever go through, having been kicked around foster homes since the day she was born. Baier knew Christmas' birth mother had overdosed two days after giving birth, but Christmas never asked and he never volunteered the information.

She knew what he was. Christmas was the only human he approved to actually see him. He mostly stayed invisible to other humans, but somehow, Christmas could see him either visible or invisible.

Christmas called Baier her best friend. Baier called Christmas his lifesaver.

"Baier …" Christmas moaned, then rolled over in her sleep. Baier rose and went to the bed. Her red hair was spread over the pillow and her small arm was thrown over her face. Baier carefully stretched beside her on top of the covers. He didn't want to wake her. He always enjoyed watching her sleep.

He took it upon himself to sit at the foot of her bed at every foster home she was dumped at, keeping watch and protecting her. And Christmas always knew he was there.

Resting his head on his arm, Baier watched over her until the sun rose the next day.

Her bright green eyes snapped open and looked straight at him, as a huge grin spread over her face.

"You stayed," Christmas said, yawning.

"Of course I did," Baier said, moving a strand of hair away from her face. "How did you sleep?"

"I had a dream," her tiny body wiggled closer to him. "I was a princess and you were on a black horse," Christmas said, looking up at him. "You took me away from the wicked old queen."

Baier smiled then leaned down and kissed her forehead. "It was just a dream," he murmured.

"Baier …" Christmas sat up, pushing the black blankets down. "How did I get my name?" It was a story Baier liked to tell and Christmas liked to hear.

"You were born on Christmas day. Your mother hadn't named you so a nurse wrote 'Christmas' Jane Doe. I guess it stuck."

Christmas looked over her shoulder and met his clear blue eyes. Baier thought she looked sad.

"Why didn't my mother take me? Why didn't she want me?" her voice made Baier's heart ache. This was a new question.

He sat up, crossing his legs, then scooped the small girl in his arms, placing her on his lap. "Your mother was very young. Just a few years older than yourself," he said, stroking Christmas' hair. "She was alone and in trouble. She couldn't look after you and decided to leave you at the hospital." Baier didn't go into detail.

"I'm glad she left me at the hospital," Christmas finally said, then looked into his face. "If she didn't, then I wouldn't have found you." She rested her head on his broad chest. "You saved me, Baier," she whispered.

Baier wrapped his arms around her. She was too mature for a ten year old. He knew she was an old soul from the day he set eyes on her.

After enjoying a breakfast of canned baked beans, Christmas and Baier went exploring. Baier knew the area well and kept a protective eye on Christmas. He watched as she picked up a pinecone, running her fingers over the rough edges before something else caught her eye.

Baier sat on a fallen log while Christmas ran through trees, laughing and squealing.

"I could stay like this forever," Baier said under his breath, smiling.

"Why are you smiling like that?" Christmas ran up to him, bumping into his legs.

"What would you say if we just stayed here?"

"Stay here?" she asked, confused.

Baier nodded. "Yes. We could live here. We wouldn't have to go back to civilization," he saw that Christmas was unsure about his idea. "Christmas, you wouldn't have anymore foster homes." He didn't want to sound like he was begging, but it was hard.

Christmas silently stepped back. Baier saw her bite her lower lip.

"It was just a thought," Baier said, forcing a smile. He didn't want to pressure her into anything. He stood, then flexed his wings.

"I'm going to take flight. Please don't stray from the cabin." Baier's wings stretched out to their full length. It usually brightened Christmas up, but she just nodded then headed back to their hide out.

Baier's thoughts were troubled as he circled over the cabin and surrounding woods. His eyes darted around, but he didn't actually see anything. He was picturing Christmas's face, filled with shock and surprise when he brought up them living in the wilderness. Did she want to go back to those horrible people? Or maybe she didn't want to live with him? The latter suddenly made Baier feel sad.

After running scenarios through his head, Baier shot higher into the sky. Up here, with the wind blowing through his feathers, he felt invincible. He looked down and saw that the cabin was now a small pin point in the middle of an ocean of green trees.

Baier sighed then pulled his wings in making him fall toward the earth. Before his feet hit the ground, he snapped out his wings, landing softly on the pine needled floor.

The forest was quiet as he headed to the log cabin. His wings were held against his back as he entered.

Christmas was sitting in front of the fire with a blanket wrapped around her. She looked up at his approach. Baier silently sat beside her, keeping his eyes on the crackling flames. A moment later Christmas climbed into his lap.

"I think I should go back." she said in a low voice.

Baier felt a protest building up inside him so he bit his tongue and swallowed hard.

"It's your decision, Christmas," he finally said, "but you won't be alone."

The little girl cuddled into him. "I know, Baier."

Baier glared at the dirty-white paint peeling off the old wooden house. The yard was covered in knee-high weeds and broken, forgotten toys. He'd spent many hours prowling the layout. There were four small bedrooms in the back, a tiny kitchen, and a combined lounge and dining area at the front. It was crowded with nine occupants. Sadly this was Christmas's foster house.

"Are you positive about this?" Baier looked down at Christmas who was leaning her arms onto the chain-wire fence.

"Yeah," she plucked a delicate white flower from a vine tangled in the fence. "I'll be okay." Silently she walked away; following a rutted drive then looked over her shoulder.

Baier saw that Christmas looked unsure so he forced a smile. He had to be strong for her. Christmas was a few feet away from the front door when it suddenly flew open. The little girl froze as her foster father, Ed, came stumbling out. He turned, drained the last of his beer, and threw the can into the yard.

"Doris, guess who I found," he bellowed, smirking down at Christmas. "C'mon in, Christie." He moved to the side giving Christmas room to enter the house.

Christmas peeked toward the road and saw Baier beyond the fence.

"What'cha lookin' at?" Ed asked, squinting, but couldn't see what she saw.

"Nothing," Christmas mumbled. A secret smile flicked over her lips knowing she could only see Baier. She felt slightly stronger entering the house.

Christmas screwed up her nose as a sour stench hit her. It was a mix of stale beer and body odor. She missed the clean air and the cabin immediately.

"Look who came crawlin' back," taunted a skinny kid, Dylan, as he flopped onto a stained couch. He had mousy brown hair, freckles and a mean streak.

"Get yer feet off the couch, Dylan," Doris ordered, coming from the kitchen. She pulled off pink rubber gloves as her beady piggy eyes glared at Christmas.

"Where'd ya go, girlie?" Ed asked, pushing Christmas's shoulder. She had to take a step forward to keep her balance. "Don't lie to me now."

Christmas glanced at Dylan, but he was smirking, taking pleasure in her unease.

"I went to a friend's place," Christmas turned to face her foster father. She pushed back her shoulders and stood straight.

Ed scoffed, "Friends? You don't have friends!" his hand shot out, grabbing her arm. "You ran away, so you have to be punished."

"Dylan, go get the other kids," Doris barked. "They need to know what happens when they break the rules."

Christmas listened as the older boy hurried off. Ed pulled his belt off then shoved her to the middle of the room. She didn't shrink back, but stood defiantly, acting strong. Inside, Christmas was screaming for Baier.

"Gather round, kiddies," Doris urged the other kids to move forward. Christmas could feel the fear in the air. A little girl, Ariel, sobbed quietly.

"Turn 'round," Ed ordered, then snapped the belt.

Christmas didn't make a sound. The belt stung with each blow and the other kids gasped, frightened. Christmas closed her eyes and pictured Baier's face with each sting of her foster father's belt.

"Punishment is done," Ed announced then replaced the belt around his waist. "Get outta my sight, girlie."

Christmas painfully made her way to her room. She had the lower bunk and muffled a cry into her pillow as tears streamed from her eyes.

Like a ghost, Ariel walked into the room and knelt beside Christmas' bed. Her small hands gently touched her foster sister's arm.

"You okay?" the five-year-old whispered.

Christmas managed a small nod. "I'm fine," she lied. "Don't be scared, okay?"

"Why did you come back?" Ariel asked, her eyes were wide.

It was a good question. Christmas had been safe with Baier and now she was hurting all over.

"Ariel," a boy hissed from the open door. "Come away." he shared similarities with Ariel with the same black hair, brown eyes and a dimple on their left cheek.

"But Shawn ..." Ariel whined.

"I'm okay," Christmas reassured the young girl. "Go."

Ariel hesitated then stood, leaving the room. The pain slowly faded and Christmas drifted in and out of sleep.

Christmas' eyes snapped open when a loud roar boomed through the small house. The room was dark and silence filled her ears.

She slowly and painfully moved off the bed and shuffled to the door. Peering out from her bedroom door, Christmas noticed that the house was empty. Staying near the wall she stepped carefully toward the front of the house. Her eyes widened in horror as she took in the smashed furniture. The couch was upended on the 60" LCD TV; Ed's most prized possession. The dining room table and chairs were now firewood pieces. Christmas noticed a huge hole in the wall where a family portrait used to hang. The kids had always hated that photo.

Christmas shivered as she edged out of the front door, taking in the sight. It wasn't the cold air that sent chills up her spine. It was seeing Baier looming over Ed and Doris. The other kids were nowhere to be seen. Christmas stepped onto the grass and started to move closer to the angel, but his words made her freeze.

"You do not deserve to breathe," he sneered. "You're the lowest of the low. You're nothing but money hungry, heartless creatures." His voice was low and deadly. "I should destroy you ..."

"Baier," Christmas was stunned at the sound of her own voice. It sounded ... strong.

"Go back inside, Christmas," Baier ordered, keeping eye contact with her foster parents.

"No, I'm not leaving," she replied, moving closer to Baier. "Please don't hurt them."

Christmas gasped when Baier looked at her. His crystal blue eyes were now black and dangerous.

"They need to be punished," he seethed. Ed opened his mouth, but quickly closed it when Baier captured his gaze again. Christmas then noticed that her foster parents' faces were slack and dazed. This was a new side of Baier that Christmas hadn't seen.

"They hurt you, Christmas. They need to pay."

Christmas moved to his side and reached out and touched his arm, tight with tension.

"Not physical pain ..." she glanced at Ed's dazed expression, "scare them." Christmas looked up at Baier. "Scare them badly so no more kids get hurt."

The angel gave a silent nod then moved closer to the two pathetic adults. "Meet me down the street," he told Christmas, keeping his eyes on Ed and Doris.

Christmas turned to hurry away, but all she could manage was a stiff march. Her body was being severely stabbed by pain and she had to stop a few times for it to ebb. She felt like fainting.

The sky was turning dark as evening took charge. Christmas saw a twinkling star in the distance then heard soft footfalls behind her on the ground.

"They will never harm another child," Baier said softly. "Christmas, I'm sorry ..."

"Baier ..." his name passed her lips as Christmas started to fall and everything went black.

"Christmas, girl ... hey, are you awake?" Baier gently stroked her forehead as her eyes fluttered open.

"Baier," Christmas said hoarsely. She tried to move, but Baier stopped her.

"Don't move," he said. Then he leaned over and kissed her forehead. "Go back to sleep."

"Sophie, you saw her injuries. She has more hospital visits than you and I put together," Baier's voice brought Christmas out of her deep sleep. She slowly opened her eyes, but the room is empty.

"I'm sorry, Baier, but Edward and Doris Carls are Christmas' foster parents." The female voice belonged to Christmas' case worker, Sophie.

Baier sighed, exasperated. "You've got to be kidding me? Please tell me you aren't going to send her back to them!"

Christmas slowly sat up, wincing from the pain. Through the door she could see Sophie looking up at Baier, and he didn't look happy.

"I've reviewed her case," Sophie finally said. "And I'll find her another foster family."

"No," Baier shook his head. "She's a ten-year-old girl and this is her thirteenth placement. Do your job, Sophie."

Sophie stiffen and crossed her arms over her chest. Christmas knew she had to interrupt their fight.

"Baier …" Christmas' voice was soft, but it claimed his attention. Baier entered the hospital room and walked straight to her side.

"Christmas …" he said. He raised his hands over her, and then lowered them to his sides. "Sophie's here."

"Hello, Christmas," the case worker said with a tight smile. "How do you feel?"

"Stiff and sore," she replied, looking from Sophie to Baier. "Do I have to go back?"

"Good question," Baier remarked, looking over at Sophie.

"Well, ah…" Sophie answered, biting her lip, avoiding their eyes.

"Sophie has another foster home for you, Christmas," Baier said through clenched teeth.

"Another one?" she looks at Sophie. "Can't I stay with Baier? He's the only family I have." The woman's eyes met Christmas'.

"He's not biological family and he's not your legal guardian."

Christmas bowed her head and took her time speaking. "Where am I going now?" when she looked up she sees Baier fighting to control his anger. Christmas reached out her hand and took his larger one into hers. This seemed to calm him instantly.

"It's a nice elderly couple. They live in a cottage and couldn't have their own children," Sophie replied. "They've had almost forty foster children."

"Are they like Ed and Doris?"

"No, Christmas, they aren't."

Christmas' things were transferred to the new foster house that day and Christmas soon followed the next morning. She stood in the sun, taking in the rose covered cottage; freshly cut lawn and well cared for garden beds. It looked like something out of a fairytale.

"You don't have to stay, Christmas girl," Baier said from beside her. "We can go away …"

"No, I think this will work," she said, glancing up at Baier who was taking everything in. "You'll stay with me, though, won't you?"

The angel smiled at her, then stroked her cheek. "I will always be with you," he said, looking up when the cottage door opened.

Christmas faced her new foster parents, wondering if this would be the last one for her. They hurried forward, wearing huge grins. Christmas could feel Baier beside her, but knew he couldn't be seen by the couple.

"Christmas?" the elderly man asked. "I'm George. This is my wife, Elizabeth. Please, come in."

A few years later …

Baier settled into the metal chair, enjoying the bustle of the busy mall. People shoved, children played, and Christmas carols played through hidden speakers. He crossed his arms over his chest while watching a little boy battle with his frustrated mother over a dinosaur shaped doughnut. Baier smiled when the child won.

"What are you grinning at?" a female voice asked from beside him.

Baier looked up, his smile growing. "A battle between mother and son," he replied, jerking his chin toward the small child. "He won."

The girl sat while adjusting her bright red ponytail. "How long have you been waiting?"

"Not long," he said, sitting up in his seat. "Are you ready?"

Christmas nodded then wearily smiled. "I'm so looking forward to escaping to the cabin this weekend." Her emerald green eyes looked tired. "This week of early mornings is killing me." She stifled a yawn.

"Why don't we leave right now?" Baier asked.

"Sounds great ..."

Christmas had grown into a lovely young woman. In two days she would be twenty. Baier felt he had been given a gift to watch as this abandoned infant and child finally found her way in life. He also gave credit to George and Elizabeth, Christmas' late foster parents. Sadly, they died several years ago, leaving their home to their "daughter," Christmas.

After collecting Christmas' bag, Baier held her tightly to his body while his wings snapped open. Christmas gasped in his ear while she wrapped her arms around his neck. Her warm fingers caressed his feathers as they soared above the world, just her and him.

"You're silent," Baier said, glancing at her. "Is everything alright, Christmas girl?"

A small smile came to her lips at the old pet name. "I'm just tired," Christmas replied, nuzzling her face into his neck. "I hope time slows for the next couple of days."

Baier didn't answer. He didn't mean to tune out, but a reoccurring thought filled his mind. Baier had something to decide. If he made the decision it would change not only his life, but also Christmas' life, too. He hoped she wouldn't be angry or disappointed with him.

His feet lightly crunched on a carpet of pine needles as he landed smoothly. He scanned the area before heading to the cabin, carrying Christmas and her duffle bag. She had fallen asleep during their flight.

Baier gently laid her on the bed, then covered her with the blankets. It reminded him of when Christmas was ten. It felt like yesterday to him. Christmas rolled onto her side mumbling, "Would you like fries with that?"

Baier started a fire, watching as the flames grew bigger, warming the cabin. Folding his arms over his chest, he glanced out the window and was surprised to see small snowflakes drifting to the ground. It hadn't snowed in this area for years and it suddenly struck Baier. It wasn't going to snow; he was being summoned.

Baier left a note stating he was taking flight and would be back before night fall. He watched as Christmas' chest rose and fell under the covers before pulling his eyes away and leaving the warmth of the cabin.

Soaring over the earth filled Baier with adrenaline. Nothing could touch him up here. Taking one last look down, Baier batted his wings taking him to the place that he had escaped from many years ago.

The pearly white gates opened silently for him, revealing swirling mist, off-white buildings with glittering jewels and the soft notes of a harp. Baier missed the cheesy Christmas carols that had been playing in the mall. He'd give anything to hear a car horn blaring in the distance.

"You must be a mirage," a sweet voice caresses his skin like a lover's hand.

"Mirage I am not," Baier said, his crystal blue eyes taking in the petite angel with silvery-white wings.

"Baier, what brings you back?" Nevaeh asked curiously, her aqua blue eyes guarded.

"I came to see Him … is He free?" Baier asked. He saw the hurt in her eyes and knew Nevaeh would never forgive him for breaking her heart. When he left Heaven, he left her, too. "How are you, Nevaeh?" He stepped forward.

"I'm fine, thank you," she replied, her wings twitching. "I see earth has treated you well."

Baier shrugged. "I can't complain."

Nevaeh studied him for a moment, then answered, "He's not here, but He knew you'd be joining us." She walked away, expecting Baier to follow. "What can I help you with?"

Baier saw an angel zipping and zagging through buildings. The large pearl colored wings disturbed the mist.

"A child spirit," Nevaeh told him. "They are very mischievous."

Suddenly, the image of Christmas as a child flashed in Baier's mind bringing a smile to his face.

"Yes, they can be," he met her eyes. "What do you know?"

"I know everything," she replied, avoiding his eyes. "How is Christmas? It's her birthday soon."

"Yes, it is. She's well." Baier saw the pearl-winged angel guiding a small child soul to the other side of the compound. He could hear the small boy firing questions at his guardian.

"What brought you here, Baier?" Nevaeh asked, looking up at him. A part of him still felt something for her, but most of him belonged to Christmas.

"I ..." he swallowed, suddenly nervous. "How can one become...human?"

Nevaeh's eyes darken and her face showed the emotions running through her: furious anger, sadness, betrayal, shock and understanding. Her wings flared out as she wrestled for composure. Baier's wings react and stretch to their full height and length. It took him a moment to reign them back in.

"Mortal?" Nevaeh spat out. "May I ask why?"

Baier sighed heavily. "You already know my reason." He said in a near whisper. "I never wanted to hurt you, Nevaeh."

She looked away. Her chin trembling slightly.

"You will always be special to me, but ..." Baier's words trail off.

"But?" Nevaeh asked, turning to him. A little spark of hope filled her aqua eyes.

Baier took a breath. "But you can do better than me."

The hope was quickly replaced by utter shock. Nevaeh opened her mouth, but then closed it, speechless.

He gave her a few moments to process everything, then said, "Nevaeh, how can one become mortal?"

"Ahh," she replied, thinking. She closed her eyes for a second then opened them. "True love's kiss ..."

"Excuse me?" Baier said with a frown, unsure if he heard her correctly.

Nevaeh looked him in the eye. Her feet are off the ground while her wings beat silently behind her. "True love's kiss can change you into a mortal." Her voice was all business.

Baier couldn't help but smile. "Really? Like in the fairytales?" He soon regreted his words when Nevaeh punched his shoulder with her small fist. "Sorry."

"She must be something special," Nevaeh stated, lightly landing on her feet. "For you to turn into a mortal."

Baier nodded. He didn't need words, as Nevaeh knew him too well.

"Good luck, Baier," she said as her eyes met his briefly, then walked away.

Baier passed once again through the pearly white gates of Heaven, his old home. He let himself fall for most of his descent then spread his wings for a soft landing upon the Earth. His mind was spinning with the knowledge of becoming a human as he entered the cabin.

"Where did you disappear to?" Christmas asked, cuddled up in front of the fire with a closed book in her hands. She smiled as he sat beside her.

"I went to Heaven," he muttered, watching the flames dance.

Christmas was silent so he looked at her. Her cheeks were pink from the fire's warmth and her green eyes were wide and questioning.

"I found out how to become mortal ... a human," Baier spoke slowly so each word wouldn't be lost on Christmas.

"How?" she finally asked in a whisper.

"A true love's kiss ..."

Christmas raised her eyebrows. "Like in a fairytale?"

Baier chuckled as he held her hand. It was warm, small and very lovely. "I want your permission, Christmas girl."

"Why my permission?" she asked, surprised.

"Because I love you," he blurted out. Baier's eyes locked with Christmas' for a long time, as he held her hand. "I know this is strange ... you don't have to answer ... I'd understand ..." his words are cut off when she pressed her lips to his.

Her lips were soft and tender. Baier melted into the kiss, into Christmas, when a bolt of agonizing pain shot from his toes to the top of his head.

"Argh!" he screamed, gripping his head. Baier squeezed his eyes shut while his body quivered in pain.

"Baier ..." Christmas' voice was frantic. She moved closer to him, placing her hand on his back. "Baier, what's wrong?"

Baier could hear the fear in Christmas' voice, but the pain pounding in his head made it impossible to do anything to comfort her.

Somehow, Baier lay down on the smooth, wooden floor, curling up into a ball, clamping his hands over his head. A blanket was draped over his shaking form and a pillow slid under his head.

"Please be okay," Christmas whispered, kneeling close to Baier's back. "Please, Baier, don't leave me." She leaned closer to his head. "I love you."

Baier didn't know how long it took for the pain to subside, but after a while, he slowly he opened his eyes. The fire crackled a few feet away. He wiggled his toes and then his fingers. His body felt ... new.

Baier took a deep breath, feeling his lungs expand then deflate. A rhythmic thumping in his chest startled him. Baier quickly sat up, pushing the blanket off, then pulled his shirt off. He looked down at his chest, then rubs a hand over the smooth skin.

"Baier ..." a small voice came from behind him. He looked around to see Christmas crossing the room to him, scared and cautious.

"I ... I feel something in my chest," Baier said. It was his turn to be scared.

Christmas knelt beside him. "Let me feel." She raised her arm and placed her hand on the spot where his hand was. He watched her carefully and was confused when she smiled.

"What is it? Is it bad?" his asked, his voice shaky.

"Baier," Christmas said, her emerald green eyes catching his. "It's your heart beating." A smile brightened her face. "You're human."

The End

TAINTED WINGS
By: Melissa Somoza

Prologue

"Now war arose in heaven, Michael and his angels fighting against the dragon. And the dragon and his angels fought back, but he was defeated, and there was no longer any place for them in heaven. And the great dragon was thrown down, that ancient serpent, who is called the devil and Satan, the deceiver of the whole world — he was thrown down to the earth, and his angels were thrown down with him."

-Revelation 12: 7-9

Many years ago, there was complete peace in Heaven. Everything was right and everyone was content with worshipping the Throne. My brother and I were Archangels, the highest of all the angels. We are the right and left hand of God. I am Gabrielle and my brother is the great Michael. There was another Archangel who was close to God, as well. He was a picture of pure beauty and was quite a magnificent creature. His name is Lucifer, our Morning Star. Lucifer was highly trusted by God, but eventually Lucifer grew tired of serving the Throne. He began to question our purpose. Why weren't we all equal? Why should God be the most important being in Heaven?

It was the highest sin to rebel against the order and will of God, but that was exactly what Lucifer did. He became prideful, believing that he deserved more than already he had. All of Heaven was in an upheaval. Some angels were part of the rebellion while others were completely loyal to the Throne and in complete shock.

Lucifer and his followers approached the Throne and urged that all — mainly himself — should be equal to God.

He claimed that angels needed no law, that they should be free to follow their own will. Faithful angels wept to hear the words of Lucifer and the peace was disturbed. Until Lucifer rebelled, there had been perfect order and harmonious action in Heaven.

Upon hearing this commotion, God declared that the defiant should remain in Heaven no longer. He banished the rebellious and Lucifer. Cast out of Heaven like a bolt of lightning, Lucifer was stripped of his beauty and his position.

This became known as The Fall.

After being cast out of Heaven, Lucifer sought revenge. He was enraged at being thrown down from the heights of Heaven and losing everything. His malice and hatred began to manifest and Lucifer started to do everything in his power to seek retribution.

His first attempt was with God's creation of man when he tempted Adam and Eve to sin.

The Fallen planned a war against Heaven, trying to take over and take down the Throne. God sent my brother, Michael, and I down to stop them. As God's right and left hand, we were given unbeatable power — more than any angel or Archangel in Heaven. So He sent us down, not to return until we destroyed Lucifer once and for all.

One night while we were checking out the area for The Fallen, Michael mysteriously disappeared, leaving me completely alone on Earth.

For the past sixty years, I have been fighting angels on my own and continually searching for Michael. I've walked alone for far too long.

Chapter One

My wings beat up and down, the soft feathers propelling me through the night sky. They glowed brightly, showing what little Glory I had left. These days, there wasn't much. I had never in all my years heard of a depressed angel, but now, I was depressed and alone. There was no joy on Earth like in Heaven.

I saw crime and disgust everywhere I looked. Drugs, prostitutes, blackmail. In Heaven, everything was peaceful, until the disturbance due to Lucifer. I could sense the turmoil in Heaven, even though I'm trapped down here on Earth.

Shaking my head, I tried to clear my thoughts and focus on the task at hand. These past few months, more and more Fallen Angels were appearing here. Since being on Earth, I'd never seen more than a dozen Fallen Angels in one place until just recently. I had to stop them and I have yet to find their operating center. Every time I follow them, they just vanish into thin air. I almost thought I was imagining their presence.

The Fallen had created some type of arrow that could permanently kill angels, completely erasing them as if they never existed. These lethal weapons were called Glory Shots. Somehow the Fallen had inserted actual Angel Glory into the arrowhead. I shivered just thinking of this new development. I had my celestial sword which could kill angels, but they would be sent to Hell, not gone forever. The celestial blades were blessed by the Throne, giving them ultimate power and were only bestowed upon Archangels. My sword is called Kaidel and she is part of me. She was the only thing that reminded me that I was still an Archangel.

I heard shouting and saw a few Fallen Angels pursuing a human. Their aura was a deep black that oozed hatred so they were easy to detect. I angled to the left and began my descent.

As I neared the ground, I reached behind me and pulled out Kaidel. She shone with power and I beamed in her presence.

I landed in a blur of fog with a small thump. My wings immediately folded in, disappearing. The alleyway had a cold wind breezing through as I edged forward. I sent all my focus and strength to my ears, listening. It was eerily quiet, but I knew they were here.

I sensed a force behind me, but before I could react I was flying straight into the dumpster. I smashed into it, wincing in pain. My shoulder harbored a deep cut and my head spun round and round, making my vision blur. In seconds I could already feel power running through my veins, mending my injuries.

I jumped up looking all around me. The fog clouded the air, shadowing the angels.

"Gabrielle …" a voice whispered, filled with malice. It wrapped around my body, suffocating me.

I closed my eyes with a sigh. "Phillip, what a nice surprise," I muttered unhappily. Phillip was high in the ranks and quite deadly. He used to serve with me in Heaven as an Archangel and he was a dear friend, until Lucifer poisoned his mind.

I heard footsteps and I spun around, slashing my sword through the air. My blade sank into a body, cutting through the flesh of one of Lucifer's thugs.

The man had piercing, crimson eyes and a smile on his face which I returned. He tried to come toward me, but the power of Kaidel slowly moved through his body and he burst into ashes. The Fallen Angel was sent back to Hell where he belonged.

I heard someone clapping and Phillip emerged from the shadows. His wings were a dirty gray, his feathers flecked with black. Phillip wore a dark duster coat over his shirtless body. His stomach was toned and his bulging biceps were about to break through the fabric with their size. "Looks like you still got it, Gabrielle," he retorted.

I was about to race forward and finish the vermin, but another angel came out of the darkness, holding a small blade to a human's neck. The human wore shredded clothes, with blood soaking what remained of them.

His eyes were closed, but once they flashed open something inside me changed. His forest green eyes rushed through me, spreading warmth throughout my body. I thought of freshly cut grass and leaves arriving in the spring. The man's eyes were filled with sheer panic, but somehow they still seemed so utterly precious.

And at that moment I knew, I had to save him.

The man distracted me, so Phillip bolted forward, tackling me to the ground. Kaidel flew out of my grasp and I immediately felt the emptiness in my hand, longing for the weight of my sword.

Phillip caressed my cheek as he lay on top of me and my skin crawled. I grabbed his shoulders and spun my body over so I was hulking over him.

He glared at me, trapped under my weight. I quickly held my hand out and Kaidel raced into it. I was just about to cut his throat, when another angel decided to join the fight.

Hands grabbed my leather jacket and yanked me back. I flew backwards, but I flipped my body about and landed safely on top of the closed dumpster.

Phillip just leaned against the wall with the man lying on the ground in front of him. The human clutched his stomach in pain as anger radiated through my body. The other angel was coming toward me slowly, waiting for my next move. I screamed and raced forward as my sword glowed with my rage.

My heart pounded as my battle cry rang through the night. I fell to my knees and slid across the ground. But the angel still kept coming. I held my blade out to the right and when the angel drew near, the metal cut through his waist.

I turned back, my breathing heavy. The angel held his side, glancing up at me right before he burst into cinders.

Phillip grabbed me and tossed me into the alley wall. I hit the wall, falling to the ground. My face smashed into the cement and Phillip dragged me by my feet. My skin ripped off, leaving my face soiled and bloody. I pulled my foot away and then shot it back, hitting him square in the chest. He let go of me with a growl.

I sprung up, but Phillip was already there, nailing me to the ground again. Suddenly, I was a prisoner under his power. "Well, well … the mighty Gabrielle defeated."

Phillip pulled out an arrow and I knew immediately that it was a Glory Shot. It glowed with Glory and my eyes widened in fear. That little arrow could end everything, including my very existence. It would send me into the nothingness of death and I would never reach peace.

Phillip wanted to toy with me first, so he put the tip of the shot against my nose and dragged it down to my jaw. The arrow cut through my flesh, burning my skin and making me writhe in agony. I screamed into the night as pain spread throughout my entire body. My back beat against the ground, hands clenched in pain.

With a cocky grin he got off of me, tucking the Glory Shot within his coat. After one last glance at me, he released his wings and looked toward the sky, about to take off.

"Why leave me alive?" I asked.

"As much as I'd love to be the one to end the magnificent Gabrielle, I am forbidden. Lucifer has a … special end planned for you," Phillip replied, smiling from ear to ear. His pure joy for my death made me cringe, trembling uncontrollably.

I lay on the ground for a while after Phillip left. Tears ran down my face, trickling into my mouth, tasting like salt. Thankfully, the pain went away, along with the scrapes and the cut from the Glory Shot.

I don't know how much longer I can go on alone, I thought.

I spun around, crawling my way over to the human. He lay on the ground shivering, crunched up in a ball.

I edged closer to him and his eyes flew open wide in alarm. He whispered, "Please ..."

"Shh, it's okay," I cooed, hesitantly reaching my hand out to him. I tried to stop, but I couldn't. I rested my hand on his cheek and rubbed his smooth skin, carefully avoiding his injuries. My hand tingled. The feeling was *amazing*. "What is your name, human?"

He looked up at me and spoke, "Blake ... Blake Dawson."

Blake. It was such a wonderful name. I wanted to say it aloud, to whisper it softly, but I didn't think he would be appropriate.

I grimaced and looked away from him. This was wrong. I shouldn't be feeling any emotions for this random stranger. I should just drop him off at a hospital. My only loyalty was to the Throne. These thoughts were unnatural.

I glanced back down at him and something about the look in his eye spoke to me, telling me that I would no longer be alone.

Defying everything I knew, I gathered Blake up into my arms, then stretching my wings outward, I darted off from the ground and into the sky, sailing through the air.

"I'm watching over you, Blake Dawson."

Chapter Two

Blake lay on the couch, covered in blankets like a human cocoon. I studied his face, marveling over his beauty. I gazed at the curve of his lips and they practically shouted, *kiss me!* I touched my own lips, wondering what it would be like to be kissed, to share someone's air.

He shot up in a panic, interrupting my daydreams. "W ... what? It ... I ... kill ..."

I pushed him back down onto the sofa and said, "Calm down, Blake Dawson. You're safe."

Blake was still breathing heavily, but he simmered down at the word safe. Now, he just stared into my eyes. I bit my lip and tore my gaze away from his. "You're s ... so beautiful," he murmured. I smiled widely, shining with happiness. I hoped my Glory wasn't showing — that would only startle him more. Blake cleared his throat and asked, "Where am I? And would you mind explaining what the hell happened? I remember certain things about last night, but it couldn't possibly be true."

I walked to the kitchen with a frown and poured Blake a cup of coffee. Coffee was Earth's most amazing creation.

I walked back and sat in the chair with a sigh. "You'll need this. Now, you may or may not believe me, but I promise this is the truth."

I began to tell him everything: about the war, The Fallen, even about me and what I truly was. I had never told a human about all this. It was the golden rule: never reveal your identity.

When I finished, I was biting my nails, filled with anxiety — another emotion I'd never felt before. Blake stayed silent for a while — too long for my taste— but I let him soak it in. Just as I was about to speak, he burst into fits of laughter. "Are you kidding me? This is freaking ridiculous!"

Blake continued to blabber on as I got up, rolled my sore shoulders a few times, and released my wings. They spread so far that they knocked all my belongings over. I heard things shatter, but I just stood still, waiting for his reaction.

His jaw dropped and he stood and slowly walked toward me. "They're white as snow!" he said. I smiled over at his shocked expression. "Gabrielle ..."

I scrunched my eyebrows together, backing up. "How did you know who I was? I never told you my name," I asked. Grabbing him by the shirt, I lifted him off the ground.

It physically pained me to hurt him, but I had too. "Are you working for them? Tell me now!"

"N ... No! Put me down!" Blake shouted. I dropped him and fell back onto the chair. "I have no idea how I knew that. I ... I just *knew*." My head fell into my hands, but at his last words, it snapped up.

I shot up out of my seat and patted down my skirt. "Well, drink your coffee and rest. I ... I ..." I said, then ran through the kitchen, into my room and slammed the door shut. I sank down against it, putting my hands together in prayer.

My hands trembled as I thought about what I was going to say. God had never answered while I was down on Earth, but He always heard our prayers. What would happen if he knew about my strange feelings for Blake?

**

I stayed down on the floor for hours. Once I saw the moon streaming its light through my bedroom window, I got up and braced myself to face him again.

Slowly opening the door, I tiptoed out into the living room where he sat, drawing a picture. I coughed, trying to make my presence known and he jumped. Blake quickly shoved the piece of paper behind him with a startled expression on his face.

I crossed my hands in front of me, swallowed my unease, and edged closer to him. I eventually made it to the couch, inches away from him. It felt as if hummingbirds were flying around in my stomach, trying to break free. I couldn't comprehend *why* he made me so damned nervous.

Blake's mouth opened a few times, but only on the third try did he actually say something. His voice was golden, "Uh ... hi there," Blake stammered awkwardly, and I let out a soft chuckle.

"Hello, Blake Dawson," I murmured.

He ran his hand through his hair and I bit my lip, fantasizing about doing that myself. "You can just call me Blake," he replied.

I nodded at him, then there were more uncomfortable moments of silence.

"Um ... so ... thank you for patching me up," he said, pointing to his injuries.

"It was no problem," I said with a smile. He returned the smile and his teeth shimmered. I looked away, then spoke, "What were you drawing?"

Blake's smile froze and he stuttered, "N ... nothing!"

"Show me, please," I said.

He shook his head.

"I wasn't asking." I extended my hand and he hesitantly handed over the sheet of paper.

I gasped when I saw the drawing. It was *me*. The soft locks of hair were draped across my face perfectly and I had a seductive smile plastered across my face.

"Do you like it?" Blake asked.

I cleared my throat, trying to find an answer. As soon as I opened my mouth the room began to shake. I was almost grateful for the disturbance so I wouldn't have to respond to his question.

I shouted, "Get down! Hurry! Get under the table!" I grabbed his shoulder, then we crawled over to the kitchen table and hid under it.

Blake and I watched as my apartment slowly fell apart. My flower pots fell to the ground and dirt covered the white tile. A five-foot long bookcase toppled over, smashing into the glass coffee table. I knew I should have been nervous and mad, but Blake had his arms wrapped around me, protecting me from the earthquake. His frantic eyes met mine and Blake calmed immediately. The world was shattering around us, but we were trapped in our own little bubble of bliss. He reached over and stroked my cheek, and slowly traced my lips.

Just as his head began to lean down to my mouth, the earthquake stopped and I jumped back away from him, hitting my head. I knew it was wrong. It took every little bit of my willpower not to dart over to him and pull his lips to mine.

I scurried out from under the table before anything could happen. "What the hell was that?" Blake asked, scurrying out from under the table.

"It was Lucifer," I said. Walking over to the window, I moved the curtain aside so I could see outside. I stared at the stars and continued. "His army is growing stronger. These quakes are his forces fuming, preparing for battle."

"You're going to stop him, right? I mean ... we'll all die if you don't save us, won't we? Angels, humans, everything ..." Blake's voice trailed off.

I squeezed my eyes shut. Everything rested on my shoulders. The fate of everyone was mine to bear. I whispered under my breath, "Michael, I need you."

"What?" Blake asked.

I closed the curtains and turned to face him. "Nothing. Go on and take a shower. You're filthy. There are fresh towels and a set of clothes waiting in the bathroom," I replied. I actually liked the shaggy, sweaty look he wore, which in reality should have grossed me out.

Blake studied me. "Are you sure you're ..."

"I'm fine," I interrupted sternly, my lips pursed together.

"There's something about you, Gabrielle. I can't place it, but you just feel ... right," he said with a smile, shaking his head.

Blake disappeared into the bathroom and I sank down onto the couch with my face in my hands. I heard the shower start and I moaned, for all I could think about was his buff body under the hot water.

I spotted the drawing of me, covered in dust. Picking it up, I brushed it off, then looked at the bathroom door.

"Blake Dawson, you could be the death of me … or my savior."

Chapter Three

Blake had been stayed on my couch for the next three weeks now. He didn't seem to want to leave and I never mentioned anything about him going. I loved getting to know him. All his routines and quirks were marvelous to me. In the morning, he had terrible bed head, but it was sexy. Blake always did thirty pushups after breakfast, saying it helped him stay fit. I just laughed.

I brought him to the dojo I rented to train and let off steam. Once he saw my five hour work-out, his view of exercise changed drastically. He tried it one day and it didn't go to well. After one hour of my intense boxing, cardio, treadmill, weights, crazy-ass workout, he collapsed on the mats, heaving, completely drenched in his own sweat. He said, "Damn, girl, you're one fierce angel."

I *love* how he embraced my angelic side. Blake never shied away from me. In fact, I think he adored me more for it. Never had I imagined a human would take to my being an angel so easily. He always asked to see my wings and to hear stories. The way his eyes lit up every time he saw my wings unfurl sent flurries of butterflies throughout my stomach.

We never really said it out loud, but it was obvious that we loved each other. It was electric. Every time we walked by each other, sparks flew. He always found ways to touch me; a hand on my lower back guiding me along, running his hands through my feathers, rubbing my arms while I cooked for him, hugging me when I was sad, caressing my cheeks.

I wasn't entirely sure how I felt about us. Was I ready to leave my Archangel life behind for a human life? The first night that I took him flying was the night that I knew the answer.

We were coasting over New York City around eleven at night. The whole city was alight with the buildings shining bright, creating the famous New York City skyline. I held him close as my arms wrapped around his waist and our legs intertwined. Blake stayed silent the entire time, but I knew he was in awe. He glanced up at me sometimes, our cheeks touching. I began my descent and spun us around. Blake shouted, "Woo-hoo!" I laughed, my giggles echoing in the night. We flew out of the city and over the Hudson River. The moon shone, lighting the water on fire as the stars guided our way along.

Blake reached his hands out and skimmed them along the cool water. "Gabrielle?"

"Are you alright? Too cold? We can go back ..."

"I'm perfectly fine ... *wonderful* actually." He spread his arms and let out another, "Woo-hoo!"

Blake flipped his body around and I almost dropped him into the water. "Blake!"

He put a finger to my lips and I froze. "Gabrielle, you gorgeous angel, I think I've fallen in love with you."

I looked up to the sky, to the stars twinkling in the night. His words made my heart beat faster and slower at the same time. My breathing become shallow and I gasped for air, but somehow it was a good feeling. I quickly glanced back down at him. His green eyes demanded my gaze and I was sucked in, mind, body, and soul.

I opened my mouth to speak, shaking, "I'm afraid." I didn't want to say that, but it was the truth. I was scared silly. Usually I was afraid of nothing, but this was completely new territory. I wasn't meant to love anyone but the Throne. To an angel, this was immoral, but it seemed as natural as the wind.

Blake showed me his hundred-watt grin. His hand was freezing as he trailed his finger along my face, but somehow his touch warmed me up. "I am, too. Life's a rollercoaster,

Gabrielle. You have to either scream or enjoy the ride. Which is it?"

I looked toward the skyline. It truly was the city that never sleeps. It is the city that was alive and full of vibrant, crazy people who were in love. Why shouldn't *I* be?

I crushed my face to his, and our lips met with intense passion. I let out a tiny whimper and melted into him, pulling his face closer to mine. I kissed him with a newfound craving inside of me. Our bodies pushed against each other, memorizing this. Blake's hands roamed roughly down my back and landed on my hips, squeezing tightly.

Air suddenly pushed down on us and we crashed into the water, landing with a big splash, shocked. Swimming to the surface, I searched for him. "Blake?"

"Boo!" Water splashed me from behind. I spun around and there he was, our noses touching and our hands finding each other under the water.

"I love you, too," I finally replied, but it came out all jumbled, *Iloveyoutoo.*

Blake chuckled, rubbing my hair away from my forehead. He murmured, "Good," before kissing me again. I let myself go, getting lost in my first kiss, *our* first kiss.

I was an Archangel and Blake was a human. It seemed impossible, but our love would conquer all. Love doesn't need to be perfect; it just needs to be true.

Chapter Four

"Gabrielle ... It's time ... Wake now, sweet one ... Gabrielle ..."

I jumped up, startled from sleep. Quickly, I hopped out of bed with Kaidel already in my hand. Seconds ago, I was sleeping, but now I was alert and ready to fight. Someone was here, and it wasn't Blake. He was visiting his grandmother. Someone was here for me, and I was glad Blake was gone.

I sent all my strength to my eyes and ears. I didn't want to risk turning on a light, which would just be a beacon saying, "Come kill me!"

I slowly edged forward, right foot in front. Concentrating on my footwork sometimes helped distract me from my fear. It was silly having the word fear in my vocabulary. Ever since I lost Michael, I was filled with nerves before fighting.

"Gabrielle ... "

A loud, flowing melody rang throughout the apartment. I did a 360 degree turn searching for something, anything. In my mind, I pictured a lethal angel playing the harp just seconds before he was going to murder me. I wanted to laugh at the thought, but then I realized what the sound really was.

An Archangel was sending me a message.

Immediately, I stood up, patting down my hair and straightening my pajamas. I saw the pattern on them and scowled. Having singing pink poodles on your pajamas didn't really scream lean-mean-Fallen Angel-killing machine.

A foggy mist formed in front of me and I took two steps forward. Suddenly, the scene changed to white oblivion. There was endless white without anyone, anything in sight.

"Gabrielle ... "

I turned slowly around, finally recognizing who the voice belonged to.

It was Michael.

The huge expanse of my brother's beautiful, white wings filled the room. His armor was glistening so brightly that it almost blinded me. His brown, curly hair was cut short, different from the time I last saw him when it was long. Michael's topaz eyes watched me as I took in every bit of him. It was *sixty* years since I saw my brother.

"Michael ..." Before I could say anymore, he was right in front of me, his toned arms surrounded my fragile body. I started crying, and then it turned into full on weeping. He released me and gave me an odd look.

I wiped my tears away and took a deep breath before I saying, "When you've been on Earth for a while, you begin to act like them."

Michael didn't even acknowledge that. "Gabrielle, I'm in Pennsylvania. I've found out where they main operating base is ... where Lucifer is."

My jaw dropped at the news. He'd found him! He'd found Morning Star.

"You ... found ... him," I muttered, staring at the ground, my lips pursing together.

"Yes! We must leave immediately. I'll explain more once we get there. Oh, sister this is it! We can finally go home and say goodbye to this dreaded place forever," Michael said, his voice filled with hatred for my new home. I just stared at the white nothingness. "Gabrielle, this is what we came here for. Speak!"

My eyes met his and recognition flashed across his face, and was quickly replaced with disgust. He wrenched his arm out of mine and stormed away, as I crumpled to the floor, crying again. "Michael!"

"Ugh, how could you, Gabrielle? How could you love a mere human? I was told of this so called attraction and how we would be tempted, but never once did I think this would distract us! Damn, Gabrielle!"

"I ... I'm so ... so sorry! I c ... couldn't help it! H ... he ... I love him! I can't l ... leave," I stuttered, unable to speak properly.

Michael raced over to me and dragged me up off the floor. We were face to face as he said, "Gabrielle, you must be in Lancaster by the thirteenth of September or let the whole human race, all of the angels, and the Throne die! Become nothing! You hold the key to existence. Don't you dare waste it on a human! We did not come here to experience puppy love like real, live humans!" With that, Michael vanished and I was catapulted back to my apartment

I was silent for a while as I stared at the walls, but eventually tears slid slowly down my cheeks. I had five days left. And if I went to fight with Michael, I knew I would never see Blake again. Ever.

Chapter Five

I hadn't let Blake see me for days. I told him I had to do some angel business and he bought it, promising not to bother me. He was so trustworthy and I felt like a monster, ruining his life. I'd tried to keep him out of my head and, of course, I failed epically. He clouded my thoughts constantly. There wasn't a moment that he wasn't in front of my eyes distracting me.

I went on my rounds, searching the area for The Fallen and everyone I saw had Blake's sweet, genuine face. One guy had his dark, scruffy hair. Another had his brilliant, green eyes. I tried watering my plants, but the scene of him first seeing my wings unfurled appeared before my eyes. I sat down to read, but all I saw was my bookcase falling and the two of us huddled together under the table.

It was the twelfth of September and I couldn't avoid him any longer. I ran to my balcony and pulled the doors open, almost ripping them off the hinges. I pushed my right foot against the chair, which shot me upward, helping me land my left foot on the edge of the railing. I brought my feet together and dove into the air, my body spiraling downward, my eyes closed with my arms crossed against my chest. My hair was flapping around me with the ground nearing.

I stretched my arms out, my eyes opening. I let my wings unfurl and it felt so amazing to stretch them out. I beat them up and down, propelling myself higher into the air, then started to fly toward Long Island where Blake was with his parents.

After mere minutes, I landed in a tree right in front of Blake's parents' giant mansion on Cherry Crest Court. The whole house was made of brick with dark blue shutters and a big, wrap-a-round porch with thick white columns. A small grin spread across my face. How easy it must have been to grow up as a human. Nowadays, I wished that I could have had the same normalness that Blake had.

I don't know how long I was perched in the tree staring at his house, but when raindrops began to fall, I was startled out of my funk. As I looked up at the sky, I began to cry along with it, tears mixing in with the drops of water.

I'd been wandering this planet for too many years all alone with the weight of the world on my shoulders. Each day was a day that I feared Lucifer would strike and I would fail everyone. I needed something to help me and that came in the form of a human.

I had never met a more interesting person than my Blake. Humans used to be little blips on my radar, nothing important and certainly not worth my time. The night I met Blake, he was battered and bruised and I thought I could save him, but he wound up saving me.

We spent the whole summer under the trees laughing, loving, and just living. Blake showed me everything, like how beautiful the world really was. The world was filled with color, and not just the black and white void I used to see.

I love Blake Dawson, but my love for him wasn't normal, wasn't allowed. I was here for a mission and I had to honor that, but every part of me told me not to.

Suddenly, a door slammed and my eyes snapped up. Blake walked out of the house and started his little, black Audi.

The car pulled out of the expanse of his driveway, and I jumped out of the tree, beating my wings hard. I sailed over his car for a while until he reached the forest, then it was safe for me to stop and go to the ground.

I sped forward and lightly landed on the hood of his car, making him jolt to a stop. His eyes were wide, his knuckles white, holding a death grip on the steering wheel. Once Blake saw my smiling face, his head dropped down in relief.

Blake threw his car into park, set the brake and hopped out. "You scared the shit out of me! Geez, Gabrielle! I thought I hit something or I ... I ... ah ... I don't even know ... you just scared me! I was actually coming to see you. I know you wanted some alone time, but I've been worried about you," Blake said.

I leaped off the hood, hitting the pavement hard. Blake moved forward to kiss me, but I just gazed downward at the ground, then spit it out, "Michael, he ... uh ... uh contacted me. It's time to finish our quest."

Blake nodded his head too many times, his face distraught, knowing exactly what this would mean. Once I was finished, I would never be able to come back to Earth ... to him ... unless the Throne sent me back, which would never be allowed.

"Good thing he's alive," Blake murmured, his hands in his pockets.

I moved forward, taking his face into my hands, forcing him to look at me. "I don't have to go." I knew the words were a lie, but I had to say them. I figured if I said it enough, it could be true.

Blake scoffed, rolling his eyes. "Of course you do! You can't let this war happen. You said so yourself. Lucifer is almost ready to strike. It's only a matter of time."

Tears slipped down my cheeks and I furiously wiped them away. "I can't lose ..."

"I know," Blake muttered, reaching into his car for a little box. "Here, I got this for you for ... for when you had to leave. I knew eventually you would have to go, so I thought you could have this to remember me by."

I wanted to shout that I would *never* forget him, but instead I just opened the little velvet box and inside glistened a silver heart. I took out the long chain swinging around. The little heart was a locket. I opened it and whimpered at the picture of us both inside. We looked so happy, so full of bliss.

"Blake, I ..." I tried to speak, but his lips smashed to mine with intense hunger. I longed for him more than ever, knowing that this would be our last kiss. My hands ran up his arms, his neck, his face, and into his hair, trying to memorize his whole being. Blake's hands were squeezing my waist, to the point of pain, but I wanted him to squeeze even harder and never to let me go.

"Gabrielle!"

Blake and I parted like we were electrically shocked. Both of us turned, with tears in our eyes, to face the man who spoke.

I gasped, and more tears rolled down my cheeks when I saw Michael in all his splendor standing before us with an angry expression on his face.

I tried to explain, "I was coming, Michael ..."

"No! You were going to stay with him! I know it!" Michael faced Blake, "Do you love her?"

Blake looked startled to see him, but he remained confident, "Forever."

Michael glanced to the side and I almost thought he changed his viewpoint on love with that one word, but then his head jerked back up. "Let's go, Gabrielle."

I nodded, but didn't move. Blake had to pry my hands off of him. "Go."

"I love you, Blake Dawson," I said, my voice shaky as I spoke.

He smiled, recalling how I always called him by his full name when we first met. "I know. I always will, too, Gabrielle. Always."

And with one last kiss, Blake turned and sulked as he walked to his car. I lifted my head high and walked over to Michael.

Michael looked down at my sad face and a flicker of emotion filled his expression, but he immediately went back to his stoic attitude. "It's for the best."

Michael burst off the ground as I let my wings extend out. I glanced back once more at Blake, who never took his eyes off me, as I flew up into the blue sky.

I was depressed and sad yet again. *Was I ever really happy before just with the Throne?* I thought. *No,* I said in my mind. Everyone needs to love and to be loved, or else there's no point in anything. At that moment, I knew that I'd find my back to him, knowing that I would *never* be without love again.

Chapter Six

Michael and I were on our stomachs on top of some abandoned warehouse with the moon shining down on us. Right across from us in another building with no roof, were dozens of The Fallen and their leader, Lucifer.

Michael had somehow found these warehouses in the middle of the forest. They were old factories from back in the day … the perfect spot to hide hundreds of The Fallen. I didn't know how he found it. Michael barely spoke to me since he saw me kiss Blake.

When I first saw Lucifer, I couldn't believe my eyes. He had aged forty years, now a shrunken man with wrinkles and constantly hunched over. His hair was a dark, greasy black and his hairline was receding. His nose was long, pointed downward, and his lips had a sinister curve that screamed evil. The nails that grew from his fingers were like claws ready to rip you apart. Lucifer wore a light gray suit with black ash covering it. I shuddered at the thought of all the angels he had killed, creating the ash on his jacket. Lucifer was once the most beautiful of all angels. Now, he was the most ugly, withered angel of all.

Michael whispered, "Gabrielle, this is it. He's right *there.*"

I took a deep breath before I answered, "It doesn't feel right, Michael."

He scowled, "You just want your human. This is it!" Michael let his Glory loose and raised his sword, Durendel, into the air, screaming battle cries.

I closed my eyes as I jumped off the building, spiraling downward. I flapped my wings, sending me flying straight to The Fallen with Michael on my right. Suddenly, The Fallen noticed our presence … and so did Lucifer.

All of The Fallen rose up into the air, but Lucifer stayed on the ground with a few select Fallen Angels, including Phillip. I knew the ones he kept with him were Fallen Archangels. As his army flew up, Lucifer crossed his arms, wearing a giant grin.

I tore my gaze away, looking at The Fallen waiting for us.

Though I walk through the valley of the shadow of death, I will fear no evil: for Thou art with me, I prayed.

It seemed like decades, but finally Michael and I merged into the big group of The Fallen. I held Kaidel to my left and it sliced through at least ten of them at once. Ash clouded my vision so I twisted to the side and flew straight to the ground.

I glanced behind me and saw five of The Fallen chasing me. My eyes widened as I saw each of them with bows, loaded with the deadly Glory Shots, ready to fire.

I flapped my wings as hard as I could upward, giving them the perfect position to nail me from below. They lined up side by side, bows raised up to me. One of them shouted and a flurry of shots raced through the air toward me.

Suddenly, I wrapped my wings around my body, trapping me in a cocoon. With no wings supporting me, I fell through the air. Once I reached the line of shooters, I let my wings extend out and I glided horizontally, dragging Kaidel through their waists. I saw dust below me and above me from where the shots hit one of The Fallen instead of me.

They all burst into ash, but I had no time to celebrate victory because many more of The Fallen were still attacking. Michael was fending off ten at a time, his black blade easily defeating The Fallen. His lips were in a square shape, baring his bright teeth.

I raced to the ground as many of The Fallen pursued. Landing with a loud bang, I stayed on the ground with my knees bent and my head down. My hair cascaded around my face, as my heavy breathing shook my body.

As I sensed the others file around me, a small smile broke across my face. I jerked up, shouting as the first of them came at me. One of their blades went for my shoulder and I easily dodged it, sending my sword into his heart.

Turning around, two of The Fallen hustled toward me. I jumped into the air, my left leg gaining height. I knocked down one of them with a roundhouse kick, sending him down and then I hit the other, as well.

A young angel with striking eyes came forward, but before he could touch me, a sword shot through his chest, making him vanish. Once the ashes faded, Michael was standing there with Durendel pointed forward. He grinned at me, "Thought you might need some help."

"Oh, yes … please do help," I retorted, full of sarcasm as I dragged my sword across the Fallen Angels' chests, finishing them off.

As soon as I stood straight up, a mass of Glory Shots bolted through the air. I bent back and the shots flew right over my stomach. I almost fell to the ground, but I used my strength to send my body swirling like a tornado to the left. I hit some of them and they went down, then I let my wings beat and I brought Kaidel down through their necks.

A Glory Shot whizzed past my cheek, inches away from my skin. Another struck my arm. I dropped Kaidel and my hand squeezing my bicep. The shot had only skimmed my skin, leaving a cut, but it still hurt like hell.

I was blinded by agony and didn't see the angel come forward. I heard the Glory Shot speed through the air, but couldn't make a move to stop it. I anticipated its arrival, but dark metal moved in front of me, stopping it. I saw Michael's face looming over me.

"Gabrielle!" he screamed.

"Keep fighting!" I yelled, exploding off the ground and into the cool night air. I still held my arm which luckily didn't bleed like a human wound. I heard them on my tail close behind, but I flew upwards.

I closed my eyes and took a long, deep breath, before glaring at my pursuers. I let go of my arm and reached out, and Kaidel suddenly appeared in my hand.

The angels each bore smug smiles and held large, rusted blades. With a firm battle cry, I dove down as metal hit metal. I struck Kaidel as hard as I could against each of them. It took time, but my strikes left them without weapons, leaving me to move in easily for the kill.

The last one took a while to finish. I saw he was the Archangel, Fredrick. He continually used his feet to kick me. Fredrick landed his foot in my jaw and sent me sailing backward. I did a back flip and sprinted back at him, when he hit me with another kick, leaving me seeing stars.

Fredrick was about to finish me off, but I played injured. He raised his sword over his head and used both hands to bring it down on me. At the last moment, I brought up Kaidel, keeping her horizontal. His blade hit mine and in his moment of shock, I brought my blade on top of his. Pushing down in the shape of a sideways U and thrusting forward, I caused his own sword to pierce his abdomen.

Fredrick let out a pained gasp. His eyes twitched as he slowly looked down and saw his death. Fredrick turned to black ash and soon was forgotten.

Michael and I fought on for hours, killing more of The Fallen than I could even remember. Each one disappeared in a cloud of ash, and was blown away by the wind.

I finished off my last angel and landed on the warehouse floor. Michael hit the ground next to me and in perfect synchronization, we stood up with swords bared in front of us, ready to end Lucifer.

I glared at Lucifer, sitting on his make-shift throne, surrounded by three Archangels who I immediately recognized as Alice, Jeremiah, and Phillip.

Lucifer let out a giant laugh, as he clapped his hands and stamped his feet. "Ha-ha! Michael and Gabrielle! What a wonderful surprise! Oh, how I've missed the two of you! We had such good times up with you know who!"

Michael bared his teeth and said, "Our brothers and sisters died for a fraud. You should be ashamed."

Lucifer retorted. "I feel fine! Actually, I feel *perfect!*"

I scowled, "You laugh and joke when your army is all dead. You watched as we killed them and now you *laugh?* Whatever happened to our beautiful Morning Star?" I shook my head, shocked when tears fell down my face. I furiously wiped them away. How dare my body actually shed a tear for this monster?

Lucifer pursed his lips, clasping his hands together. "Well, I got bored, raised hell, became banished, and … well … you know how it goes. Especially you, Gabrielle! What happened to you? Now that you've found love and happiness? I thought you *only* loved the Throne?" Lucifer shook his head in mock disappointment, but he still wore his crooked grin.

My face froze. *He* knew. Lucifer knew about Blake.

"I do," was all I could mutter, so I tried to change the subject, "Why aren't you more afraid, mighty Lucifer. Your army is gone, and here we stand seconds from killing you. Tell me, do you fear death?"

Lucifer merely chuckled and said, "Do you honestly think that was all of my forces? You won the battle, my dear, but we're going to win the war."

Lucifer raised his hands about his head and clapped his hands. Immediately, the room began to shake and walls fell apart. Michael and I fell down, clawing at our ears, for there was an eerie screeching sound that was tearing us apart. My eyes watered, but I could still see Lucifer and his three most prized Fallen Angels, flying out of the building, running away. "Ta-ta dearies!" Lucifer said.

Michael screamed, "They're getting away!" He tried to get up, but he fell back down, curling up into a fetal position.

After what seemed like days of utter agony, the noise stopped. For a few minutes after, I still clutched my head, as the sound still rang in my ears. Michael came to me, letting me know it was over. I sat up, my eyes stinging from the dust. It must have been one of Lucifer's earthquakes, plus that awful noise.

Lucifer was now able to conjure dark magic. It meant only one thing: Lucifer was at his strongest.

I jumped up, remembering what he said about Blake. I extended my sore wings and tried to take flight, but Michael grabbed my ankle.

"He knows, Gabrielle. There's no protecting Blake ... no helping him. You can't save him," Michael said.

I kicked him off my foot.

"Just you watch me," I said, then I tore off the ground and flew into the clear, morning air. I flew as fast as I could to reach my love with only one thing going through my mind — the same thing I thought the first time I laid eyes on Blake: *I have to save him.*

Chapter Seven

My wings flapped furiously up and down, gaining speed faster than I had ever flown before. I tried to control my ragged breathing, but all I could think of was Blake. Had they found him? Was he dead? Surely I would have known, wouldn't I?

I neared my apartment building and saw Phillip waiting in the front of the door, holding a bow and a Glory Shot in his hand. I swerved and spiraled straight toward him.

Phillip smiled and his eyes following my body as it descended. He spoke, "Hello dear, I ..." Phillip didn't get to finish his sentence because I struck him in the heart with Kaidel. Phillip's eyes fluttered unable to comprehend how I killed him so quickly. I didn't know myself how I got to him so fast, but I was grateful I did. "You ... I ..."

I grinned evilly, actually happy to kill him. "Goodbye, Phillip," I said, yanking Kaidel out of his body, then hurried to pick up what he had dropped. Phillip ripped his shirt open before he burst into ashes. I was flying away before his remains even settled on the ground.

Reaching the north side of the building, I curled my legs up, smashing straight into my kitchen window. I felt bits of glass pierce my skin, but nothing could distract me or hinder me from getting to Blake.

I slowly edged around the wall, as Kaidel glowed a brilliant white. Once I saw what was behind the corner, I nearly dropped my sword.

Lucifer was here ... with a blade at Blake's throat.

Blake's eyes shot up to me, filled with sheer panic. He opened his mouth, but nothing came out. Tears ran down his face, glistening as they hit the metal dagger.

Lucifer chuckled. "Gabrielle, Gabrielle, Gabrielle! You should have known better than anyone *not* to fall for the illusion of love. But I must admit, he *is* a handsome one," Lucifer said, trailing his hand down the side of his face. Blake's winced and closed his eyes.

"Don't you touch him," I snarled, moving closer.

Lucifer shook a finger at me, smiling widely as he inched the blade even closer to Blake's neck. "Uh, uh," he said, taunting me. I stopped in place. My feet begged me to rush forward, and my hands tingled in anticipation of the kill.

"Just let him go, Lucifer. This is between you and me," I spoke as calmly as I could, even though my heart was beating through my chest. I glanced from Blake to Lucifer and back again. Blake's eyes showed fear, but said how much he loved me.

Lucifer rubbed his chin, then said smugly, "I don't think so."

And just like that, the small blade slid against Blake's throat, creating a thin line, killing the man I love.

I wanted to cradle him within my arms and protect him from all the evil that I had brought upon him, but I just stood frozen, as the life drained out of Blake's body. My jaw dropped and my heart cracked in half. *No!*

Lucifer dropped his lifeless body to the floor as blood streamed out, creating a pool of red around him. "No," I whispered.

Lucifer clasped his hands together and spoke with mock sadness, "What a pity. He has such a pretty face … well … *had.*" Lucifer used his foot to touch Blake's face, turning it to the side. His green eyes stared at me, lifeless and cold.

I shouted at him, "Don't touch him! Don't …" I was shaking uncontrollably, as rage burned through my veins.

Lucifer threw the bloody dagger at my feet. "Keep it as a souvenir, doll."

I screamed a blood curdling shriek of fury, and quickly reached behind me for what I retrieved from Phillip — a Glory Shot.

Suddenly, Lucifer's face showed alarm, but he quickly composed it, putting his arms in front of him, preparing to deflect it.

I arched my arm behind me and threw the arrow like a spear right at Lucifer. He easily dodged the arrow with a mere chuckle. "Gabrielle, you ..."

Lucifer gasped as spasms of pain spread across his face. Lucifer's eyes widened and now it was my turn to smile. In the millisecond that he repelled the arrow, I surged forward and shoved a second Glory Shot right into his stomach.

"What a pity," I recited what he had said earlier. "Go to Hell."

I wrenched the arrow out of him and he stumbled back, clutching his stomach. His head arched back in pain and his yellow teeth crunched together. I worried that it might not kill him, as it wasn't thrust into his heart, but I didn't think a monster like him even had a heart.

Suddenly, a blinding light appeared behind him and Lucifer turned to it. I panicked, thinking that he was being given mercy, but once his head fell, rolling onto my floor, I knew what it was.

Michael was beaming as his smile stretched from ear to ear with Durendel pointed outward.

I walked over to him and he wrapped his arm around my shoulder. We both watched as Lucifer became nothing, erupting into dust. I was in amazement that it was over. It was really, truly over.

As soon as the ashes vanished and the air was clear again, I saw Blake's still body. Horror immediately crashed over me like a tidal wave. "Blake! Blake! Oh, no ... Blake ..."

I grabbed his body and pulled it onto my lap. I tried to ignore the horrible pale skin and the wide gash across his throat. Instead, I rubbed his hair out of his face and stared into his gorgeous, green eyes one last time.

I sensed Michael kneel down next to me. He put a hand on my shoulder and said sincerely, "I'm so sorry, sister. I truly am."

Before I could say anything, Blake disappeared and we were jerked away from my apartment by a strong force, shooting upward. My eyes closed, and the world turned to black.

Chapter Eight

I muttered, rubbing my eyes. Michael was lying beside me and I stood up, dragging him with me. "What is this?

"Heaven, my child," a voice said.

My eyes snapped open to see God. It was really Him.

I stared up at the Throne in shock as Michael immediately fell to his knees. I stood frozen and Michael tried to yank me down. I slowly sank to the ground and bent my head down. "My Lord."

"Rise, my friends," His voice boomed, loudly. Michael and I rose to our feet. "You have done a wonderful job, my children. Lucifer has been sent to Hell where he rightfully belongs. The Fallen are trying to come back into the folds of Heaven. There is *peace* in Heaven once again! All thanks to my two strongest soldiers. Michael and Gabrielle, we thank you. *I* thank you."

Michael grinned widely, but I only let a small smile break across my face. I couldn't celebrate victory with Blake's death still fresh in my mind.

Michael mumbled, "It was an honor to serve you, my Lord."

God smiled down at him and spoke, "Leave us please, Michael. I must speak with Gabrielle alone. Again, I thank you."

Michael bowed down to God, cast me a large smile, and strutted away. I looked around, but there was no one else here. I was surprised not to see angels everywhere. It was just me with the Throne.

"Child . . ." He whispered, making me turn to face Him, then continued, "I understand you experienced love down on Earth."

I stuttered, "Y ... yes, but I never lost my loyalty to you!" The words were a lie. I would have never returned to Heaven if I could have been with Blake down on earth forever.

"Gabrielle, I know you. I know your tendencies, your actions, your thoughts. Blake meant the world to you and I *understand*. I feel love. I know its power. That is why I have granted you a gift, my child," God said.

He swept his hand to the right and I almost died right then and there, for Blake was smiling at me, with wide, white wings sprouting from his back. His body beamed, filled with life. I couldn't do anything. I couldn't speak or even thank the Throne. All I did was run to him ... run to my love.

I slammed into him. My arms snaked around his entire body, trying to consume him into my soul so I wouldn't lose him again. I sobbed, "Blake ... I ... I'm so ... so sorry!"

"Love, don't fret. It's alright," Blake soothed, rubbing his hands all over me. I shivered in his touch, never thinking that I would ever feel his warmth again.

I pulled back and Blake wiped my tears away. "But, I ... I didn't protect you! I let y ... you die!"

Blake crushed his lips against mine, his hands entwining in my long hair. His body was smashed against mine, so close I could feel our hearts beating in sync. It felt so wonderful to be in his arms again, knowing that I didn't have to leave him.

"It's meant for me to be here with you, love," he replied, caressed my cheek, setting my skin felt on fire. "I love you," Blake told me, gazing into my eyes.

"I love you too, Blake," I whispered, leaning my forehead against his.

"You *saved* me, Gabrielle, and that's all I ever wanted."

THE ANGEL I BELONG TO
By: Sky Diamond

Quickly, I packed my messenger bag with today's homework, a pen, whiteout, my phone, iPod Shuffle and a book I was reading. My parents were in the kitchen down the hall, trying to — unsuccessfully — quietly argue, for about the millionth time today, but I heard every word that was being said. This was what I had put up with for the past seventeen years, and over that time, I've heard more than enough to know I didn't want to hear any more of it. The arguing was a daily occurrence in this house. I swore I could remember hearing my parents arguing from the day they brought me home from the hospital.

With my bag over my shoulder, I walked down the hall and leaned against the door frame with my arms crossed over my chest as I watched them both arguing. I was waiting for Mum to notice my presence so I could tell her I was going out. My eyes rolled when she didn't. So I headed down the hall, out the door and down the stairs of the veranda. I could still hear them outside the small, white-and-blue-painted house.

It was a wonder the police hadn't been called by now, like they had been so many times before. The neighbors were probably more than used to this, and knew better than to bother.

Looking down to the dull and dying summer grass, it crunched under my feet as I walked over the lawn. I shook my head, walking on the footpath leading down the street to the little cafe just a couple of blocks away from the house.

In the front of the red-orange brick building, hanging over the entrance and patio were medium sized white flags dancing in the gentle summer breeze. In the center of the flags was the cafe's red logo of a teacup and saucer. White chairs and tables in rows of two were outside under white umbrellas with the same logo on them.

Walking through the already open black, steel gates, I headed down onto the brown-painted, wooden patio and down to the corner where I always sat near a little goldfish pond placed in the corner, against the wood-on-wood railing. Long grasses reached out of the goldfish pond. Small water lilies grew on the surface of the pond. One of the lilies was about to flower a soft baby pink-and-white pedaled flower. Goldfish with the colors of deep orange, black and white swam gracefully through the water under and around the lily pads, nipping at leaves, where flies rested. Water from the fountain ran down the carefully placed rocks, creating a trickling stream. It was calming, relaxing. Something I desperately needed more of.

Being in that house wound me up like the strings of a yoyo. I was quite happy to have this little quaint café just a few walking minutes away from home. This was the usual place I came to clear my mind and focus on my homework. I knew all the staff here, too. They were friendly, though knew nothing of my life.

I smiled, watching the fish as I sat back on the dark, chocolate picnic table, placing my messenger bag beside me on the seat and pulled out my homework. I started with English — it always seemed to help me ease back into the mind set of focusing on what I learned at school.

I hated school, but even *I*, had to admit it had its perks. I didn't mind learning English or attending drama class. I just hated being the center of attention whenever I did well with my work. I liked being alone and invisible to everyone. There was less trouble that way.

If I did okay in school, the teachers wouldn't notice, nor would my parents or any of the students. But if I did bad, I'd be downed upon — my parents would be called and my teachers would take notice of me more with trying to improve my grades — and pretty much the same thing would happen if I did well in school. It was a fine line between the two, but somehow I managed it.

Halfway through my homework somewhere in the middle of math, I heard the familiar voice of my best friend, Keira, calling out my name.

"Lara! Hey, what are you doing here?" she asked, quickly walking up to where I was sitting.

Few people knew I came to this café. My parents didn't and neither did Keira — until now. I liked it that way. I could focus without distractions. No one thought that a teenage girl of my age would be hanging around an old café, even if it was nice. They all thought I'd be shopping or out with boys. Even the people who owned the cafe had said that.

I smiled slightly at her as she sat across the table from me. I instantly noticed the gossip magazine she had in hand. She slid it across the table between us.

"Just doing my homework," I replied, writing in the last answer. Then I slipped everything back into my bag.

Keira sighed and said, "I don't know how you get by. You need to chill. Be a teenager for once, Lara. Forget homework and have some fun once in a while. I never see you shopping, and we don't even hangout afterschool. I haven't even seen your house in the five years we've been friends."

I rolled my eyes and huffed. I wasn't a typical teenager and didn't want to be, besides, I knew my father would flip if I went shopping for clothes more than once a month and even then, he resented it.

"And not to mention," Keira continued, "you really need to find yourself someone so you can go out and have fun ... and we can't forget the cute clothes he would buy you if you don't have the money to buy them yourself." She winked and pulled the gossip magazine open.

I scoffed. "Yeah, that's just what I need," I muttered sarcastically, pushing a loose strand of hair to the side. Keira wasn't even paying attention now. Her nose was stuck in the gossip magazine, like it usually was.

"It wouldn't be that hard to find you someone. There're plenty of good guys around here. What about Tyler or Jack?" Keira continued absentmindedly.

"Oh please, Keira. They're both nineteen and sleaze balls. They'd both take out the first girl who asked them. I'm not interested in guys anyway." *Not to mention that they were crazy with drinking and partying*, I thought. I didn't need someone like my father and I had already had enough of him.

No one, especially not Keira, knew what my father was like and that was how I planned to keep it. If anyone knew, I would be the center of attention and then the pity parties would start — *poor Lara, I feel so sorry for her.* Ugh! I hated just hearing it my own head!

Keira shook her head, giving up with a sigh. She ran her hand through her long, straight blonde hair as she kept her other hand on the magazine. She was pretty, fair skinned, tall, and model-like, but her blue eyes were what usually attracted the guys. I had seen them in action far too many times. All she had to do was flutter them innocently and it was like watching a cartoon where the guys would fall back and you could literally see their hearts flying out of their eyes. It kind of made me sick to even think about it. Not that I would say it to her face or behind her back, but it made Keira look desperate.

"Well, if you're not going to get a boyfriend, at least choose some kind of celeb to have a crush on and be a little more like a typical seventeen-year-old girl, Lara. You need some normality in your life, girl."

I rolled my eyes at that, too. Like snobby celebs were any different to any guy I knew. Seriously, though, I thought

I could swear off men for the rest of my life and turn into a nun for all I cared about them. I sighed, rolling my eyes once more at Keira, basically giving her the death stare. Why did she care whether I was a typical teenager or not? It wasn't affecting *her* life!

I groaned, palming my forehead. I closed my eyes and placed my finger on the page of the magazine, just wanting to get it over and done with. It didn't matter to me who my index finger picked, as I wouldn't continue on with the whole crush thing any further after Keira left. It seemed pretty immature to me anyway. The celeb crush thing was more for thirteen year olds.

"Fine, him," I muttered bitterly.

"Justin? Oh no, Lara," she said, shaking her head with a disapproving look.

"What's wrong with him?"

"Girls either love him or hate him. Plus, in my option, he's a stuck-up brat and has everything given to him."

Did it really matter what the other girls thought of who I crushed on? Plus, weren't all celebs stuck-up brats anyway? I really couldn't understand her reasoning.

I watched as she flicked through a few more pages and placed the magazine back between us. There was a whole page of guys, but none of them seemed to stand out in my opinion. Once again, I let my finger do the talking and closed my eyes and pointed to one. Keira picked up the mag again, raised her eyebrows and nodded.

"Perfect," she said. *Finally*, I thought, looking up to the roof of the cafe, thanking God. "Daniel Taylors is *very* down to earth and not to mention the sweetest guy on earth!" she gushed.

"Uh huh," I murmured, highly doubting a word she had said, crossing my arms over my chest. The way I figured it, if they were all a pain in the ass, they wouldn't get any work, so all of them would have to act like the sweetest guy or girl on the planet. They were actors, after all … it was their job.

"Hazel brown eyes," Keira read, "five-foot-eleven and a half, short black hair and currently single. Never had a girlfriend nor has any parents. They died in a car crash — aw, that's so sad. Daniel was placed in a foster home at the age of six and was spilt up from his little sister, Cassie. He currently lives … oh my God, Lara!" she gushed loudly with wide, excited cat eyes.

"What?"

"He lives here in Sydney! You might run into him!" she gasped.

"Yeah right, Keira. You do realize there's like a million or more people in Sydney and just as many — if not more — places to go, right? Plus, I'm sure he's in Los Angeles most of the time, and filming more than at home," I tried to reason, but then I wondered why. "I gotta get home. Mum's going to be freaking out otherwise."

I grabbed my bag and rose to my feet, slinging it over my shoulder. It was almost night now, though it was summer. With the night, it seemed to have turned even more humid than throughout the day. It was such weird weather. A very light and refreshing breeze blew through my shoulder-length brown hair before disappearing again. I loved the summertime and wished it could stay around longer, but I didn't like the humid nights so much. They were nice to wake up to at five in the morning, though.

"Alright, night Lara," Keira said sweetly with a kind smile and a hug. I smiled back at her and slowly headed home.

Keira was a good friend, even though she could be a bit pushy. I guessed it was just because she cared and wanted me to be okay — I often forgot that. I wasn't used to being cared about by anyone other than my mother, and even then she ignored my thoughts and wishes — or me altogether — when it came to arguing with my father.

Now that the sun had set, there was still a light blue hue of daylight, allowing me to see. The finer details of the homes I passed were now impossible to see.

There was a large house on a corner that always stood out whenever I passed it. I stopped on the footpath, admiring it once more. It was a two-story house, with honey-colored wood and a deck on the second floor, facing the horizon. The railing of the deck was lined with tubing cables, making the whole house look modern and tropical. On the corner of the deck, was a Yucca plant growing in a black, square pot with Mondo grass planted around the base of it. Palm trees reached up to the deck from beside the garage, where black pebbles had been placed around its bearings. More Yucca plants grew along the black-steel-fencing, splitting off the red and black bricked driveway to the neighbors. On the other side of the driveway was another garden with more Yucca trees running down the driveway before making an upside down L down to the entrance of the house, which I could not see. The bases of both gardens were made of a dark, stained honey colored bamboo — the very same color as the house.

The garage was sandstone, painted a dark-blue grey with a dark honey colored opening. On either side of the door were two small palm trees planted in two tall, glossy black pots. The whole place was lit up — all the gardens, the driveway, the garage and the deck. The place always amazed me. Each time I passed it, I wondered what it'd be like to live in a house like that, though I knew we could never afford it.

Things like this house were the things I wanted in life right now — not to be out shopping or hanging out with my friends or boyfriends. I was more the simple type of girl, happy with most of the things I already had, happy to stay home whenever my parents *weren't* arguing, but at times wanting to live a little more of the glamor life, like the –

without a doubt – expensive house that looked nice instead of a house that looked like it was still being put up for over fifty years with bare dirt gardens, and dead grassy spots in the lawn.

It was depressing to think about, and to know that maybe we could have a house like that — if my father wasn't so tight with his money and didn't drink so much. The worst part was that my mother insisted on staying with him, so I would have a father figure in my life. I didn't see the point when he was only a bad influence upon me. It showed me that this is what you had put up with in a marriage, when in reality it was only an option. It was just making me see the worst of what men could be like. He was the reason why I didn't have, nor wanted, a boyfriend.

Not having a father in my life wouldn't upset me. But having to live with him was upsetting, and it wasn't like my mother and I couldn't get a job and live on our own.

She was more than capable of working at a store or at a crystal shop in town. She knew everything to do with angels, crystals and tarot cards. But of course, my father had her in his mitts, making her think she would never be able to get a job with his belittling comments. He was demeaning in every way, putting her down every chance he could.

If I hadn't grown up with him in my life, and if my mother had come to her senses and left my father years ago, I wouldn't be the way I was today. Maybe I would have friends and a boyfriend, and maybe even a stepfather that would treat me like a daughter, instead of ignoring me completely by the likes of my supposed to be father, Darren. Sometimes, I wished I was adopted, or even better, that something kinky had happened between my parents and Darren really wasn't my father.

Shaking my head, I sighed, pulling my iPod out of my bag and placed the earplugs into my ears. I turned it right up to block out my depressing thoughts about my life. I shoved my hands into the pockets of my white denim shorts as I headed back toward the direction of my house, staring down at the footpath as I went. There was no rush in my step to get back to the House of Hell.

A strong gust of wind came up and blew my white blouse against my skin and my hair past my shoulders and into the air as I kept walking. A few flyaway hairs went into my eyes and over my face. I looked up to pull them out of my sight when a massive wolf-like dog ran toward me. I put my hands up defensively in front of me, hoping the dog would get the hint and leave me alone. I wasn't much of an animal lover when it came to dogs, especially ones this big. I could thank being bitten by a dog when I was younger for the fear of them.

With a loud bark, the dog jumped up and forced me down to the footpath. Something hit the side of my head as I put my arms over my face protectively. In my foggy state, I could hear a gentle guy's voice. My music faded into the background as my earplugs fell out.

"Jack, leave her alone!" a guy shouted in an even tone.

I felt a warm lick on my elbow and the dog ran off.

Thank God, I thought, leaning forward, trying to gain back my balance and not make a fool of myself in front of this guy, but the dizziness was too much to withstand. I groaned, closed my eyes and placed my palm against my forehead and winced. Looking down to my palm, through the haze I could see it was grazed and bloody. *Great! Just what I needed!* I thought to myself.

"Hey, you okay?" he asked gently.

I tried to look up at him, but my eyes turned foggy and my head was spinning. I shook my head very slowly to answer him, but wasn't able to think clearly enough to speak. An electric shock went through my arm where his hand lightly gripped my wrist. My head snapped up and my eyes looked into his, as if a compulsion had been placed upon my body. It was an urge I could not disobey nor think twice about. It was instant, automatic.

For a split second, I stared into his hazel brown russet eyes and my vision turn clearer than crystal, the fog and dizziness in my head had disappeared along with the pain. It felt like nothing in the world existed outside of us, almost as though the world had stopped moving within that moment.

His eyes reminded me of melted chocolate. I hadn't ever seen anything like them before in my life. I had met so many people in my lifetime, but there was something about his eyes … compelling. I could almost lose myself within them if I kept staring, but I didn't want to look away, either. I felt blissful, safe and relaxed.

"Aw, your head," he murmured softly. His voice echoed from miles away.

He pulled my hair to the side, bringing me from my blissful, dazed state. The fog and dizziness had returned, too, though it was ten times worse. I could hardly hear a thing he was saying and everything seemed to be turning dark.

"What's your name? I have to get you some help."

"L … Lara," I murmured. I had to think through the fog to remember my name. My head was heavy and pounding and everything was getting worse by the second. If I didn't know better, I could have sworn I could feel the earth moving under me a hundred times faster. Then suddenly, everything went black as the fog consumed me completely, against my will.

Later, I awoke to bright, white lights shining down upon me, as my eyes opened slowly. They were foggy, but not like before. At least my head wasn't spinning anymore. I looked around to see a bright white and pale-blue room around. The bed that I was sitting on had crisp, white sheets and a matching pale-blue curtain was pulled around the bed. No doubt, it was a hospital room. The sterile smell was the giveaway.

As my senses began to strengthen and come back, I quickly became aware of a warm, smooth and unfamiliar hand around my own as another shock of electricity went through my hand. I moaned, closing my eyes again. I quickly snatched my hand back and placed it against my forehead, then I heard his voice.

"Hey, you're okay," he stated matter of fact. Hearing his voice, my eyes opened and fixed on his deep, hazel eyes. They were like molten, melting chocolate with runny hazelnut mixed through; so sweet and kind, gentle and rich with life, giving warmth and comfort.

"W ... who are you ... and ... where am I?" I asked, a little panicked.

"You're in the hospital. My dog knocked you over and you hit your head hard on the pavement. My name's Dan Angel. I'm an EMT here. I bought you in," the man said.

"Oh," I murmured, looking down to my hands clasped in my lap.

Dan's words repeated in my head. After a few moments, I realized there was a world where other people apart from Dan and myself actually existed. I gasped at the realization, remembering my mother, and looked franticly at the bedside table for my mobile phone. It had to be around somewhere. I knew I had it when I left the cafe.

"Where's my phone? My mother will be freaking out," I said quickly, patting the pockets of my jeans. I couldn't even remember where I had put the thing.

My cheeks grew hotter by the second. He must have been amused. It was pathetic, really. First, a girl gets knocked over by a dog at the age of *seventeen*, not *seven*, then hits her head and now she can't even find her phone. Yep, pathetic!

"Here," Dan spoke gently, catching my attention. My gaze went straight to his eyes again. What was it about them that was so ... so alluring and captivating? When I looked into his eyes, I felt peaceful, relaxed and happy. I felt like there was a magnet between us. No one in the world ever made me feel this way before.

Slowly, I came out of my dazed state, as Dan slowly pulled my phone out of my messenger bag and handed it to me with a warm smile that reached his eyes. They seemed to sparkle. My cheeks burned even more than before as I looked down at my phone. I glanced at him and looked away again, trying to focus on calling my mother's mobile number. Gently, Dan rested my messenger bag on the bed and handed me my water bottle. Pressing the call button, I held the phone up to my ear and took a sip of the water.

I wished I hadn't come out of the world where only Dan and I existed. It felt so much easier, peaceful and safe. Realizing what I was thinking and feeling, I mentally rolled my eyes at myself. I wasn't being myself! I never wanted a boyfriend. I didn't even believe in love. There was no point of it. You only loved each other for a while. Once you grew up, the serious life set in and it was nothing more than arguing about ridiculous stuff like money and not spending enough time with each other, even though you couldn't stand to be around each other.

My body was starting to take control over my brain and doing exactly the opposite of what I believed. I was saying one thing and doing another. It had to stop. I could already see I was getting too close to Dan and I was only going to get hurt.

My mum picked up on the second ring. "Lara? Lara? Are you okay? I'm down at the cafeteria. I'll be right up now."

My eyes narrowed at Dan as my head turned in his direction. He gave a faint, though sweet, smile. I shook my head. "Yeah, Mum. I'm fine. Don't worry, okay?" I closed my phone and looked to him.

For the first time, I actually saw what he looked like, instead of gawking at him like a love-struck puppy, staring into his eyes all the time. His hair was black, cut short and looked as though he had been swimming and left it to air dry. Though it was slightly messy, the style suited him. He wore a washed out grey t-shirt and jeans, which made him look very lean and fit. I guess that all came with being an EMT. After all, they had to be fit and up to the job when they were called. He looked tall, even when sitting down. *About six-foot,* I thought. His lower lip was plump, almost pouty for a guy and a very light pink, which looked perfect against his russet, tanned skin. His face was lean, too, like the rest of him, without a mark or blemish. I thought he could easily be a model with his physic — tall, dark and handsome. He looked mature, even for a teenager, or at least I thought he was.

"You didn't tell me that you already called her." I whispered, staring down at the sheets of the bed.

Dan just shrugged his shoulders. "I thought it'd be better if she heard your voice," he murmured. "She was very worried about you."

I sighed, nodding. Well, I guess he had me there. At least he was thoughtful. I hoped my father didn't know, or I'd get a lecture about being after dark on a summer night, even if it was still light out when I passed out. I bit my lip at the thought. Then I wondered, *if he knew, would he even care?* I didn't think so. He was too self centered to think about anyone other than himself. He showed that daily with my mother. I bit my lip harder, hating the thought of it.

"Are you okay?" Dan whispered in a soft, warm voice, his eyes filled with concern.

I closed my eyes and nodded, trying to be strong and hold back the tears. I didn't want him to see me cry. No one saw me cry anymore; not even my own family.

His hand lightly took my hand into his own. I instantly felt better, but the stinging of tears was still there. My head snapped up hearing a light knock on the door. I smiled slightly when I saw my mum with a container of food in hand, along with a fruit smoothie cup in hand. She put the food down, walked over to the bedside, and hugged me tightly. My arms wrapped around her just as tightly.

"Are you okay, Lara? You had me so worried," Mum asked.

I nodded, then replied, "I feel fine, Mum, really." I smiled slightly, blinking a few times so she couldn't see my tears. Dan smiled too, watching us both. Mum sat down on the end of my bed, and took my hand for a second. She smiled once and then looked at Dan.

"Thank you for bringing my little girl in," she said lovingly, as tears welled up within her blue eyes. Then she looked between Dan and me as if she thought something was going on. She then got up and pulled another chair over.

"It's the least I could do," Dan murmured with a smile aimed in my direction. My cheeks warmed as I glanced toward Mum. She was looking at Dan again, with a puzzled look. I swore his smile could light up a room or anyone's day, no matter how dark or hard it had been. It was already lighting my life. I mentally shook my head at the thought.

"Here, drink up, Lara. You need your strength," Mum said, handing me the smoothie drink. Sighing, I took a drink, tasting mango and apple. It was nice and refreshing.

Hearing another knocking at the door, a woman dressed in a white coat entered the small room. Her hair was long, straight and auburn. Her eyes were a gemstone green and deep with emotion. Her smile was small, but very sweet as her eyes went from my mother to where I sat. She looked pale between her bright hair and the white coat. In my option, she would look beautiful with lighter hair. She wasn't tall or short, built up or skinny. She looked to be in her early thirties or even in her late twenties. There was an uplifting presence about her, but as she sat down between my mother and Dan, sadness filled her eyes as she glanced down at the chart she held in both of her hands. I noticed Dan smile at her, which made one of my eyebrows lift in confusion.

"Lara, I am Doctor Taylors. How are you feeling now?" her voice was gentle and soft.

"Fine, thanks," I smiled slightly.

"Well good. You can go home now. You may have a headache later on, but you don't seem to have any signs of concussion, which surprises me, considering the hit you took."

"Guess I'm lucky," I replied, glancing toward Dan as I smiled at her, a smug smirk lit his lips before disappearing completely.

Dr. Taylors nodded and replied, "Maybe so, but you were very lucky." Then she looked to Dan. "Daniel, please keep Jack on a safe lead from now on, will you please?" she asked in an even and deep tone of voice. It was more of a tone I thought a parent would use with a child rather than a coworker.

"Of course, Dr. Taylors," he said, then turned his attention to me, "I'm sorry, Lara." His eyes were intense and warm.

"Well, I'll leave you to get ready to go home, Lara. It was nice meeting you and I hope I don't have to see you anytime soon under such bad circumstances."

"Thank you, Dr. Taylors, and you, too."

She smiled once again and left with the chart in her hand. Looking to Dan, his gaze followed her down the hall, then he glanced back to where I sat, leaning against the rising head of the mattress.

I leaned over and grabbed my messenger bag from against the foot of the bed. Then from nowhere, a black feather fell out of the bag and onto the sheets. I looked at it confused, and picked it up. I hadn't been around birds to have a feather in my bag.

My fingers ran along the perfect quill, as a dark green and purple shimmered through it. There wasn't a tear nor break in it to be seen. My mother watched, smiling. But I knew what she was thinking and what she was about to say.

"There must be an angel watching over you, Lara," she murmured softly, taking the feather from my fingers to look it over. "An angel who may have fallen off the right path."

I nodded hearing Mum. Dan glanced up to her for a moment as she spoke. His expression was shy, confused and surprised, as though she had spoken a secret no one knew, apart from him. Then he quickly turned his head in the opposite direction. My mother smiled, having caught the look in his eyes. Then she handed the feather back to me. I placed it back into my messenger bag and got out of bed.

I couldn't help but wonder if Dan thought my mother was crazy. Most people thought that about my mother, including my own father, but I didn't think that at all. For all the things she had seen and told me about, there was no doubt in my mind that she was probably seeing angels.

Pulling on my shoes, Dan took my bag and helped me out of the hospital to my mother's car. Sitting in the front seat, I smiled sadly at him. I waved, not sure whether I would ever see him again or not. I may not have been looking for a boyfriend, but a friend would do, especially someone like him. I felt as though I could really trust and depend on Dan. It was a feeling I had never felt so soon after meeting someone for the first time.

That night, I dreamed of Dan being my angel and having black wings, taking me away from all that was upsetting in my life. He was my guardian angel. When I woke in the morning, I shook my head and smirked at the black feather on my bedside table sitting on my messenger bag, just where I had placed it the night before.

Dan wasn't an angel. *But he's close to it*, the little voice in the back of my mind whispered. I rolled my eyes and shook my head as I got up and prepared for school.

Thankfully, my father hadn't said a thing last night about why I had been so late getting home. I could have sworn he would have, I guessed he was just caring less.

It had been a long, stormy day. It was already steamy out with thunder and lightning not long after I had got up. I heard thunder in the distance as I walked out of the school grounds and along the footpath, passing kids getting onto busses to go home.

Looking up to the sky, it was dark toward the north and I spotted a strike of lightning snake through the skies to the ground. It was way off, though. I could easily have my homework completed and be home before it hit.

Sadly, the cafe was closed today so I thought the park would do. It would be quiet and if I was lucky, only little kids would be there. No kids my age hung out at the park, unless it had a skateboard ramp.

Sitting down on a dark green picnic table, I set out my homework and quickly got to work. Thankfully, I didn't have much to do today. Before I knew it, I was finish. I smiled at myself, glad it was over and packed it all back into my bag, but it was too early to go home yet. It was only four o'clock. I began wondering what I would do. Going home wasn't an option.

I heard a dog barking in the distance and quickly became wary. The wind picked up in a gust, sending my hair flying into my eyes as I turned around. Pulling my hair off my face, I looked up just in time to see the very same wolf-like dog as last night. But this time, he jumped into my lap and stayed there.

"Whoa," I gasped, feeling its weight upon my legs. The dog turned his head around to look at me and panted innocently.

"Jack! Get down!" Looking up, I smiled as Dan ran up from the other end of the park. He wore a white tank top with dark, washed out jeans and runners. He smiled back, grabbed Jack from my lap and clipped him onto a lead.

"Sorry about him, Lara," he said, sitting down. "How are you feeling today?"

"It's okay," I said, jumping back as Jack was attempted to jump back up. "He's exuberant, isn't he? Yeah, I'm fine, thanks."

Dan laughed and patted the dog's head. "Yeah, he is. He always gets into trouble. What are you doing out here, anyway? It's pretty hot and stormy out today." He leaned back against the table and looked up at the sky and then his gaze then met mine.

The wind picked up, rustling the gum trees above our heads. I shrugged my shoulders, not really wanting to answer that question. "Just find it relaxing and quiet out here, that's all."

"Uh, huh … so … what's the real reason?" he asked with a smirk, watching my face.

I turned red and giggled. How could he do that to me? I never laughed, genuinely laughed, let alone giggled.

"Do you not like it at home?" he questioned, holding my gaze. I swallowed hard, feeling as though he knew more than I had mentioned.

Without thinking or even wanting to answer, I shook my head and closed my eyes. My own body was answering without my permission. I didn't like anyone knowing my life at home. It wasn't that bad, really, but after years and years of putting up with it, and not seeing a silver lining or change anywhere in sight, it got to the point of being unbearable. I didn't know why Mum put up with it.

A crack of thunder echoed around the park. Jack jumped up from sitting happily between Dan's legs to under the table in an instant.

Dan sighed and he leaned down on the picnic table's seat to pet Jack.

"C'mon. It's okay," he said softly, tugging him by the lead until he was out in the open. "Guess I'd better get going," he murmured, as disappointment colored his voice.

I huffed at the thought of going home as lightning flashed in the distance, followed by more thunder echoing throughout the park. I could have sworn I felt the ground move under my feet from the thunder's intensity. Many times, I had heard thunder rattle the windows at home.

Everything was eerily quiet a second later. The air was warm and the breeze had stopped. There was a faint scent of rain. I didn't hear cars, kids playing, or even the birds singing.

Hearing the sound of something like a small stone fall onto the rooftop of a two story home across from the park, I looked over and then felt the heavy drops of rain upon my head. They were cold, like ice.

Grabbing my messenger bag, I held it over my head in protection, as Dan pulled the hood of his shirt over his head. He grabbed my hand in a gentle grip just like yesterday, and I felt the same electric shock go through my hand and up my arm as I did before. I shuddered hard at his warmth as it pulsed through my muscles, in sharp contrast to the cold rain hitting my skin. I was blinded by the force of the weather coming down as we ran from the park. Gusts of wind began to blow.

I didn't know how Dan could see. When I glanced up at him, I saw he had a pair of black, wrap-around designer sunglasses on. My face grew hot again, seeing them. They suited him well. Suddenly, the rainbow lenses reflected another flash of lightning.

I looked back down to the cement footpath, watching my feet as we walked quickly to shelter. I asked Dan where we were going, but because of the intensity of the rain, I couldn't hear my own voice. I didn't bother trying a second time.

My back and skin ached from the force of the rain. Finally, it started to lighten up until it had almost disappeared altogether.

"I'm glad that's gone for now," Dan murmured, taking his glasses off and slipping them down into the V of his shirt. He stopped and let my hand go.

I ran my wrist over my eyes and watched as he grabbed a remote of some kind from his jean's pocket. No longer blinded by the rain, I saw we were standing in front of that two-story house I had always admired with the Yucca plant on the deck.

"Wait, this is *your* house?" I asked.

He smiled, then answered, "Sure is." Pressing the red button on the little black remote, the black steel gates opened. Memorized, I looked around at all the things I had seen before, though now, up close and personal.

I stopped at the bottom of the stairs leading up to the deck. Dan looked down to where I stood on the first step, with a confused and questioning expression in his eyes.

"I shouldn't be here," I muttered.

"Why?" he asked, worried.

"Because, I don't know you and my parents don't know you either."

He smirked and quietly scoffed, shaking his head. "Your mother knows me better than you think, Lara," he spoke softly, almost a whisper. I tilted my head to the side listening, as if it was some kind of an inside joke. He shook his head again and opened the door, allowing himself and Jack inside.

I was just about to say no and turn back and go home, when the rain started up again. It was just as heavy as before, only this time it was accompanied by hail.

Suddenly, a piece of hail hit my arm like a knife, cutting my skin open. I winced sharply and ran up the stairs and into the house where Dan was standing at the door with Jack. The dog barked quietly and wagging his tail, welcoming me into his home.

Dan closed the door just as the hail came down harder. Pieces of ice hit the roof like bombs being dropped. I thought maybe it would bring the roof down.

I dropped my bag at the door, shivering wet. Then I rubbed my arm and winced.

"Are you okay?" Dan asked, grazing my wrist with the tips of his fingers. My skin was ice cold. I glanced down to my arm, shaking my head. There was a small, bloody gash below my elbow.

"I'll fix it," Dan said, then quickly walked down the hall and into another room. I gazed around while he was gone, trying to get my mind off the sharp pain.

The hall was wide with a red runner reaching down to the staircase at the end of the room. Four doors lined the hallway, all closed except for the one Dan had disappeared into. There was also a fifth door, opposite to the deck's door, also closed. The walls were a very warm, rich brown. The frames of the doors were painted a cream-white, as was the ceiling and railing of the stairs.

A few seconds later, Dan came back with a small white bag with a red cross on it. He sat down on the floor where I rested my arm on my leg, and began cleaning the gash. He then pulled out some ointment and smeared it over the wound before wrapping a bandage around it twice.

"Thanks," I whispered, smiling shyly.

"No problem," he smiled back and then sighed. "Well, my sister is out apparently."

"Oh ... well ... I should be getting home anyway," I murmured.

Dan looked into my eyes oddly. "It's still hailing out. Why are you so nervous? I understand you don't trust people easily but …" he dragged his teeth over his lower lip, then turned away.

"But?" I watched his face, wondering what he was about to say.

"But nothing," he said, sighing quietly. "I'll drive you home, if you like."

"That'd be great, thanks," I said, eyeing the look of disappointment in Dan's usually bright and cheerful eyes as he rose to his feet. He offered me his hand with a small, pained smile. I took it and stood as he led the way downstairs.

The hail outside had disappeared completely the thunder was also gone. I could no longer hear the rain. Dan opened the door at the bottom of the stairs and turned on the light in the garage.

"Watch your step," he warned.

Glancing around quickly, I entered the garage. It was neat and tidy, with not a speck of dust in sight. The garage was huge, big enough to hold three vehicles.

I looked to my right and felt my jaw drop, seeing a white Lexus LFA. Dan unlocked the car and opened the door. I knew these cars were expensive and I didn't think someone like Dan, at his age, would own one.

"This … is … your car?" I stuttered.

Opening the driver's door, he smirked. "Sure is."

"And you're taking it out in the rain?"

He shrugged. "It's a car, Lara. It's meant to be used. I can wash it, anyway."

"Right," I whispered, walking slowly over to it. I knew if I owned a car like that, I wouldn't be driving it out in the rain … ever.

Pulling the car door open, I hopped in, smelling the strong scent of leather and smiled. I loved that smell. I couldn't help myself from running my hands over the white leather seat. It felt so soft and smooth. It felt rich … like I was in a small limo.

Dan pressed a little black button above the windscreen. Hearing a sound, I looked behind us and saw the garage door opening. Dan backed out at a perfect angle, then turned around to face the road. Pressing the button again, the garage door closed.

As he drove out of the driveway, the gates of the house closed behind us. I blinked, watching them. That house had everything. *Almost like the houses you see in movies or in Hollywood,* I though:.

Sitting up and watching the road, Dan turned on the air-con and pushed another button to bring down his window. The coolness of the leather on my skin felt nice as the mix of cool and humid air entered the car.

"How'd you afford this?" I blurted out accidently, running my hands over the leather dashboard. I glanced to him, shyly, realizing what I had said. His lips formed a tight line.

"I inherited some money from my parents, when I turned eighteen," he answered painfully.

"I'm sorry, I shouldn't have asked."

He shook his head and gave me a comforting, small but pained smile. I could see by the dull and sad look in his eyes how he felt about them — he missed them, dearly.

"Forget :t. It happened a long time ago. Thirteen years ago, to be exact."

I stared down to my hands in my lap and glanced up at him again. "What happened?" I breathed, hoping I wasn't going to make him feel worse.

"I was six and my sister and I were fighting. It was raining heavily — to the point that you couldn't see anything — and we were on a highway. None of the traffic ahead was stopping so we couldn't either. We had distracted Dad and he veered onto the wrong side of the road as a truck came along … it was my fault."

I bit my lip, listening to his pained voice. Somehow, I knew that Dan could remember it like yesterday. Hearing his last words, I shook my head. "No, it wasn't," I spat. I didn't know how I knew, but I *knew* for sure that it wasn't *his* fault.

Dan stared at me for a moment and smiled. Looking back to the road, his smile grew a little more. "You know how your mother said you had a guardian angel watching over you … at the hospital? Well, that's what they said to me. In the accident that killed my parents, I died and they brought me back. I believe what your mother said. You do have someone watching over you, Lara," he said softly, giving me another smile.

I watched Dan, memorized by what he had said. Then, for some reason, the black feather I had found in my bag flashed before my eyes. It was falling from my fingertips and onto a white surface, then it turned white, too. I shook my head at the image, unsure of what it meant.

"So, you just live in that house with your sister?"

"No, our adoptive mother lives with us, too."

I gazed over to Dan, surprised. "You're adopted?"

He nodded, turning a corner that was just five minutes away from my house. "We were sent to foster homes after the accident. We didn't have any family outside of our parents. I was separated from my sister until I was twelve when we were both adopted and reunited. No one seemed to want two kids."

"So, you only have your adoptive mother?" I asked, truly curious.

"No, we had a father, but he kicked us out along with our mother a few years later."

"I'm sorry. It must have been hard."

"It was, but it's in the past now, so it doesn't really matter," he said, smiling slightly.

I looked out of the window, watching my neighborhood slowly pass by. The car slowed down as the rain began to fall once more. It pattered heavily against the car. I couldn't hear much other than the windshield wipers and rain.

I couldn't help but think of just how down to earth Dan was for the life he had lived so far. It really got my brain thinking. At least my father hadn't thrown my mother and myself out of the house ... yet. He easily could have, too. In the end, I realized how alike Dan and I are. Obviously, his adoptive father didn't care at all. I was curious about what he was like, though. Was he anything like Darren? Or worse?

"This is my house," I whispered. He pulled up on the street as I got out. "Thanks for driving me home."

"No problem, Lara. Do you want me to come in?" Dan asked, putting the car into park.

I nodded without thinking, but then I heard my parents arguing inside, over the sound of the rain.

"No, its fine," I said quickly, forcing a smile on my face. I waved and turned my back, then ran inside before he could protest. I ran straight to my room and closed the door with a bang. From my window, I saw Dan's car turning around and going back from where it came. I sighed as I threw my muddy shoes off and kicked them under the bed. From there, I went to take a shower in an attempt to drown out the sound of my parent's arguing.

In the bathroom, I took off the bandages from the side of my head. I gasped, seeing it had healed already. Taking off the one on my arm, my eyes widened. It was healed, too. I hadn't ever healed that fast before in my life.

That night, it was still storming out, but I sat happily on the side of the bed, watching the lightning flashing in the sky, when I heard Mum knocking on my bedroom door.

"Come in," I whispered, staring down to the black feather in my hands and placed it on my bedside table. I slipped into bed and pulled up the sheets.

"I'm sorry about your father earlier, honey," Mum murmured, sitting down on the side of the mattress. Spotting my black feather, she picked it up and carefully ran the tips of her fingers over it. "I saw Dan drop you off earlier. That was nice of him."

I nodded, agreeing. "Yeah it was."

"You seem different around Dan," she whispered quietly, without looking up.

"What do you mean?"

"You seem happier, more relaxed around him," she replied.

I sighed, looking at the sheets on the bed. I couldn't deny it. She was right. "I am, I guess, but I don't want to feel that way around him ... I don't want to change for some *guy* and wind up hurt."

Mum smiled. "Love does that to people, honey. It changes us. It captures us for the better or worse and can set us free ... whether we like it or not. I know how you feel about your father, but Dan isn't him, baby. He's different than anyone I've ever met. Just remember that, okay?" she cupped my cheek while speaking softly. She smiled and leaned down, placing a kiss upon my forehead.

I nodded and smiled, realizing how true her words were. Since the first time I met Dan, I felt ... free. "I will, Mum. Night.

"Night, baby," she whispered, walking out of my room. Instantly, I fell asleep with a smile upon my face, thinking of Dan.

In the morning, I woke to the sound of a car pulling up outside. Yawning, I slid out of bed and went over to my window. I pulled the curtain back to see Dan's car parked outside by the footpath. Upon seeing him, I smiled, realizing that it was still raining. *Oh well*, I thought, at least there was something good about it raining before school — having Dan drive me there. My mother's words from last night echoed in my head.

Quickly, I pulled on a white summer dress from my bedside table. Flinging open the mirrored doors of my wardrobe, I found my tan cowboy boots and put them on. Closing the doors of the wardrobe, I looked in the mirror to see how it all went together. My deep, dark chocolate brown eyes stood out the most. My straight, shoulder length hair hung to my shoulders. The white summer dress hugged my figure neatly and went perfectly with my sun tanned skin. I smiled slightly, then quickly put some lip gloss on my pouty lips. Keira said they looked like the lips of a movie-star, but I disagreed. I was ordinary compared to movie-stars.

I grabbed my school bag and threw it over my shoulders before taking one last look in the mirror. I could see my bed in the reflection of my mirror, and then the rest of my room. It was only a small cream room, but the biggest thing in my room was the wardrobe, it was big enough for all my needs. My iPod player sat beside to my bed along with my lamp. My one stuffed animal sat at the head of the bed, amongst the mess of sheets and blankets. Sooner or later, I would actually think of making the thing. I closed the door and ran down the hall, passing the kitchen where, once again, my parents were unsuccessfully "quietly" arguing, and outside into the sprinkling rain.

I smiled, seeing Dan in his car. He looked up and got out of the driver's seat an opened the door for me.

"Morning, Lara." he smiled brightly.

"Morning, Dan. Thank you," I said, sliding easily into his car. He got back into the driver's seat and started up the engine. I couldn't help but smile again. "So why are you picking me up so early?"

He smiled. "Well, I thought we could have breakfast on the beach, before school. But seems it's raining, so I guess it'll have to be on the beach in my car, if that's okay with you?" he asked, glancing in my direction.

I nodded shyly, staring down at my hands in my lap and then glanced up at him once I knew it was safe. A second later, I could feel my cheeks warm. I could already smell the delicious scent of bacon and eggs.

After driving for a few minutes, Dan pulled up in a parking lot. I gasped, seeing the view from where we were parked on a small cliff. The entire view of a sea storm flashing wildly on the horizon and the whole beach was right before us. Trees lined the footpath. The sand thinned out and reached up to the trees as the wind blew through their branches. Waves violently clashed against rocks and cliffs, and there was no one on the beach or in the water.

"It's amazing," I gushed, smiling as I looked around.

Dan smiled. "I thought you'd like it here. It's peaceful, even on a day like today."

I nodded in agreement and opened my bag of food. He was right. There was just something about this place that seemed perfect, even on such a stormy, windy and wet day.

As we ate, the rain let up and rays of sunlight broke through the clouds. Getting out of the car and walking down to the beach with Dan at my side, I could hear some light rumbles of thunder. The wind was a hot and humid northerly. Glancing up to Dan, I leaned back into him as his arms wrapped around my waist.

"I guess I better get you to school and myself to college," Dan murmured with a disappointed sigh.

"I suppose so," I replied, not wanting to go to school now — which I never felt before. My arms wrapped around Dan's neck, feeling the warmth of the sun on my face and the fresh sea-wind through my hair. Slowly, his hand lightly grazed my own before he gently took it and led the way back to the car.

"Thank you for that, Dan," I smiled shyly as connected my seatbelt up.

"You're more than welcome, Lara," he smiled. Glancing up at him from behind my hair, I smiled, too.

As Dan turned around and headed back toward the city, I noticed the dark and heavy clouds looming overhead. Before long, it was raining again. I sighed, looking out the back window of the Lexus to see the rays of sunshine back at the beach, but even those were beginning to be consumed by the storm.

A few moments later, we were parked outside my school. I stared at him, shocked.

"How'd you know this was where my school was?" I asked.

He shrugged casually. "I've seen you leaving a few times now. My university is just up the road."

"Oh. Right."

He got out of the car and pulled the hood of his white shirt off his head. The rain lightly soaked his shirt to the point it was hugging his body, but something under the material caught my attention. It was black and outlined his whole back from his shoulders down.

"What's that, on your back?" I asked.

Dan turned around and looked over his shoulder. "Oh, that's my tattoo. I got it after my parents died. Thought it was appropriate," he answered softly.

With his back turned to me, he quickly pulled his shirt up to the top of his shoulders. I gasped, seeing the tattooed angel wings on his back. It was hiding many barely noticeable, light, pink scars over his skin.

"It's beautiful," I whispered with a small smile.

"Thanks," he said, pulling his shirt back down as he turned around. I gasped again seeing a long scar running from his ribs down over his hip before his shirt concealed it completely. Getting out of the car, he walked us up to the undercover picnic tables of the school. Keira was sitting at one.

Noticing my presence, she glanced up and smiled as I sat down across from her. She blinked twice when she saw Dan sit down, as well.

"Morning, Lara," she chocked slightly.

"Keira this is Dan. He's my friend," I announced.

"Nice to meet you, Keira," Dan said, smiling kindly, then shook her hand. She nodded and gave a small, shy smile. I had *never* seen Keira shy before around anyone, especially a guy.

Her cheeks burned as she looked back down at her netbook. She quickly typed in something and then turned the thing around to where I sat. I sighed seeing Daniel Taylors name.

"Look, Lara, the paparazzi caught Daniel out at a club last night."

I glanced at the photo and nodded, seeing he was spotted at one of the popular Sydney clubs. Dan leaned in and laughed quietly. My face turned red with embarrassment and then turned the netbook back around to Keira.

"What's so funny?" I asked Dan.

"Nothing, I just thought teenage girls weren't worried about celebs anymore." He got up then and asked if he could pick me back up again later. I thanked him and smiled.

"No problem. Later." He waved as he walked off and winked at Keira who was peaking up from the netbook before he caught her. She ducked her head back down, pretending to still be staring at the screen. My eyes rolled at how she was acting. The school bell then rang, forcing Keira to close the netbook and we headed into school.

It was another long day. Half of the time I was staring at the clock above the teacher's desk, just waiting for three o'clock to come, so I could see Dan again. The second the bell rang, I headed down to the lockers.

I looked up, hearing someone running down the hall, and a few seconds later, Keira was at my locker with a magazine open in her hand. "Here," she smiled innocently. "I found this last night and thought you'd like it."

I took the magazine and blinked a few times, thinking I was seeing things. There were posters covering two pages, both marked Daniel Taylors, only, it was my Dan. In one poster, he was posing with his shirt off in a denim vest and I could see the very same scar running down his ribs to the V of his hip, where washed out almost-white jeans hid the rest of the scar. In the other poster, he had his back to the camera, looking over his shoulder with a sexy pout. His eyes were bright and vigorous with life and passion. But the look he gave the camera wasn't what stood out to me the most ... it was the angel tattoo on his back. I now knew why he had been laughing earlier. He was laughing at me, thinking I was crushing on some celeb, who I already knew and was too stupid to know it.

I smiled at Keira with pain in my eyes, nodding as I took the magazine. "Thanks, Keira," I said, forcing back the tears, not wanting to make a scene. "I'll see you later then."

"Sure. You're welcome, Lara."

I quickly walked out of the school before anyone else was able to. Looking around, I didn't see Dan, so I headed straight for the park. It was empty as I glanced around, but then I looked up and saw Dan. He was smiling that room-brightening smile that I loved.

But his smile disappeared the instant he saw my expression.

"Why didn't you tell me, why didn't you tell me you're really Daniel Taylors?" I cried, shouting, flinging the magazine at him.

"Lara, calm down," he said, glancing down to the paper and then back up to my face. "I'm sorry, I was going to tell you but ..."

"But? But what? You lied to us! I thought I could trust you … rely on you … and I was just starting to believe it and now I know I shouldn't have even thought about it!"

"Lara, you have no idea what it's like trying to find *true* friends that want to know me for me and not for my fame. I wanted you to know me before I told you so you would understand where I was coming from. I'm sorry if I've hurt you. I didn't mean to, Lara."

Tears ran down my cheeks like small floods. I couldn't remember the last time I had cried this hard, let alone in front of someone. It felt like a volcano exploding within me.

"You lied about who you are and what you do for a living! You think people just get over that?" I ranted, unable to stop, letting all my anger pour out.

Dan tilted his head to the side as his eyes narrowed. "I am an EMT Lara. It's a job on the side … I want to help people like they helped me. Acting and modeling isn't something that makes me feel good, Lara, but being able to help people does. Acting and modeling was just something I wanted to do and was I lucky enough to be able to do it. I want to make a difference to the world, and I think I can do that … with fame, I can help people and spread awareness about things that has no voice," he said with a sigh and shook his head. He looked around the park. It was still deserted apart from the two of us.

"Look, I'm really sorry I hurt you." He took three steps closer to where I stood and wiped the tears away. "I didn't mean to, Lara. Truly. My full name is Daniel Angel Taylors. I use Dan Angel when I'm an EMT so people just don't freak out and stop me from doing my job. No one seems to recognize who I am when I'm in uniform."

Looking into his eyes, I could see the truth. I sighed, nodding, then leaned into his muscular arms and I glanced up to his face. "So that doctor … Doctor Taylors … she's your mother?"

"Adoptive, yes. That's another reason why I don't use my real last name while I'm working. People would put it together and she would never be able to work, either. It's hard being you when everyone wants a piece of you."

"I understand ..."

I hadn't even noticed it was raining again. We were both soaked to the bone. I smiled slightly seeing Dan's hair spiked up from the rain. Water ran down over his perfect cheek bones and down to his chin where it dripped to the ground.

"Come on, I'll take you home before you catch a cold," Dan said.

"Kay."

His arm wrapped around my waist as we walked back to the school parking lot, where I spotted his car, literally shining in the darkening light as more storms were on the horizon.

"So, you do work as a model, actor, EMT and you go to university, too?" I asked, resting my head on his shoulder.

"Yup. After my adoptive father kicked us out, we moved and Mum was able to find work as a doctor, but she didn't get much work at first. That was when I started modeling and making enough money to support her and my sister."

"Oh, wow. That's a lot to take on ..."

We got into the car and closed the door just as the rain pelted down upon the car roof. A sudden crack of thunder echoed through the parking lot. I shuddered at its sound and my wet clothes clinging to my skin.

Dan got in and turned on the heater and I smiled at his thoughtfulness. Pulling out of the parking lot, I watched the skies lighting up with forked lightning. But somehow, even with the thunder it felt calming. The air was humid and warm, but cool at the same time.

"Why didn't you ever tell me about your father?" Dan asked suddenly, catching me completely off guard.

My eyes grew wide with shock as I stared at him in the driver's seat. "How do you know about that?"

"Word gets around," he answered casually.

Staring down at my hands in my lap, I played with my fingers while chewing my bottom lip, not knowing what to say.

"I never tell anyone ... not even Keira knows. I don't want pity parties or to be the center of attention, like I would be if people knew. Enough of our neighbors know already," I mumbled.

"I can understand, Lara ... more than you realize. I can see he's hurt you, emotionally and mentally. I know that you don't trust people easily, and I don't blame you. But not everyone is like him. You can trust *some* people," Dan said with kind eyes.

I smiled slightly. He sounded like my mother now. I glanced up at Daniel and met his smiling gaze already upon my face. "Like you?" I questioned in a low voice.

He smirked crookedly, nodding once. "Like I told you, you have someone watching out for you." He winked, smiling.

Pulling up at the house, Dan quickly got out before I could ask him what he meant. I tried to wrap my head around what he said when I heard a noise coming from my house. Looking out the window, most of our stuff was on the lawn or packed up in boxes. My eyes narrowed as I got out, seeing Mum quickly coming out of the house with a large box in her hands.

"Mum, what's going on?" I asked, heading up to the veranda, glancing over the boxes.

"I've had enough of your father. He's kicked us out and I'm happily leaving him," she spoke in a slur of words. My gaze snapped up from a box to her face. I felt my insides do a happy cartwheel as my eyes opened wide. Finally!

Dan came to stand by my side. "Are you okay, Marina?"

Mum looked up at him with tears in her eyes — I wasn't sure whether they were happy or sad — and nodded. "Better than ever, Daniel. I should have done this years ago," she said.

I never thought mum would admit that. Well, at least she was being true to herself — something I that I thought my father had taken away from her.

"Get what's left in your room, Lara. There's only a few boxes," she said calmly.

"I'll help you," Dan said urgently, walking up the stairs behind me and followed me into my room. It was empty. There was no bed, no bedside table, dressing table or clothing lying on the floor. The room actually looked big now. I picked up the lighter of the two boxes and Dan took the other. Going back outside, we set them down on the lawn.

"Where are you going to stay?" Dan asked, running his hand through his wet hair.

"We'll find a motel or something for the night, Daniel," Mum murmured.

"No don't. Come to my place and stay until you find somewhere to live. I don't mind and neither will my mother or sister," he gestured kindly.

Mum looked suspiciously between the two of us, then smiled a faintly and nodded.

"Alright, if it's okay with your mother, then we stay just for a few days if you have room."

He glanced at me and then back to my mother, offering her his hand. "Daniel Angel Taylors, by the way."

I watched and held back laughing out loud as I watched my mother's jaw drop in shock. Slowly, she shook his hand while practically gawking with the widest eyes I've ever seen.

After my mother stopped playing twenty questions with Dan, he helped us pack our car and his with boxes before leading the way to his house. Taking most of my things from

Dan's car, he took the rest upstairs and inside where he placed them in an empty room down the hall of doors. There wasn't a thing in the room ... only a window at the far end, opposite to the door that looked out over the neighborhood. The walls were all a gloss cream and the carpet was the same color.

Neatly, we piled the boxes up against the wall and then he helped my mother bring in the furniture. My bed went in the opposite corner from the window and my dresser went near the door. Even with the furniture in my new room, it was much bigger than the old.

I smiled, sitting down on the side of my bed as I looked around, finally feeling comfortable in my own bedroom. The bed felt softer than before. And for once, I smiled without having a reason to.

Waking up to another cloudy day outside, I heard Dan at my door. I yawned, sitting up and rubbed the sleep out of my eyes as I peered up at him. I couldn't believe he was already dressed at five-ten in the morning, but it was already light out. He smiled softly and sweetly, half leaning in the doorway. I smiled back and stretched.

"Morning, would you like to have breakfast on the beach again?" he breathed.

"Yeah, that'd be nice. I'll be right out," I replied, feeling right at home.

"Kay," he said, disappearing from sight.

Getting up, I went to my dresser and pulled out a pair of denim shorts and a brown tee with gold glitter splashed over the front in thick, shimmering ribbons. Pulling on some black sandals and running the brush through my hair a few times, I headed out the door. Dan was standing on the top step of the stairs. Seeing me approach, his face lit up.

"Pretty nice, Lara," he smirked crookedly.

My face flushed. "Thanks." I wasn't used to getting complements from anyone.

Dan offered me his hand from where I stood. Shyly, I took it and we headed out the door. Once outside, Daniel pulled his wrap-around glasses out of his jean's pocket and put them on. He looked completely different. I guessed they were so the paparazzi wouldn't recognize him or bother us.

He kept hold of my hand as he led the way down to a small, private beach not far from his house. There was no one to be seen. Some waves lightly lapped to the shoreline where others crashed into small rocks. A dim, but brightening light was being cast across the beach as the sun slowly rose. I smiled, content, taking in the warm sea air.

Releasing my hand, I watched as Dan pulled a picnic blanket out of a small cane basket I hadn't even noticed he was holding. He spread the red-checked blanket out over the sand and sat down, placing plates of eggs, sausage and bacon with buns and some pancakes with berries and cream over them. I licked my lips at the pancakes. I hadn't had them since my grandmother died seven years go. She cooked the best pancakes in the world!

Asking me what I wanted, Dan dished up some pancakes for me with some of the cream and berries. I smiled happily, tasting them for the first time in years ... just how I remembered my grandmother's.

Later on, lying back in Dan's arms that were warmly wrapped around my waist, I leaned back into him watching the sun rising through the clouds over the horizon. The sky was a strong, deep orange and mauve purple with hints of royal blue further up where the stars were slowly disappearing.

"I wanted to ask you," Dan murmured quietly, sounding quite shy. "I've got a premiere tomorrow night and I was hoping you could come with me. You don't have to, if you don't want to."

I turned around to face him. His gaze set upon my face and I could sense that he was trying to read my thoughts. "I'd love to, but ... I don't have anything to wear," I said, embarrassed. Dan's features seemed to brighten. He leaned over and pulled a small, flat box out of the picnic basket.

Taking it, I looked down at the silver box with the black ribbon tied into a neat bow and then to him. His smile widened and his eyes sparkled. "Well, I'm glad you *didn't* have anything to wear. Open it," he said, suddenly excited.

I gasped, covering my mouth in shock as I took the lid off the box and looked down to see the perfectly folded dress laid out over tissue paper. I rose to my feet, pulled the dress out and gushed. It was a perfect silk white dress with a gold glitter shimmering through it.

"I love it! Thank you, Dan!" I said loudly, placing it safely back over the tissue paper and leaned down to hug him tightly, with tears of happiness in my eyes.

He smiled broadly and wrapped his arms tightly around my back. I couldn't stop smiling and my cheeks were actually beginning to hurt.

"I'm glad you like it," he whispered.

I pulled away just enough to rest my forehead on his. His eyes were brighter then I had ever seen them. I felt like I could see his soul and willingly lose myself within them. They were, hypnotizing — perfect.

As his hand reached up and cupped my cheek. The warmth of his palm sent an electric current through my muscles and nerves — the exact same feeling I had experienced the first time I met him just a few days before, though it felt more like years. I had complete and utter trust in Daniel.

Slowly, his smooth, warm lips brush against mine. I giggled quietly at the sensation and held him tighter within my arms. He smiled against my lips as his fingers twinned with mine. He held the kiss for a moment and then he kissed me again, slowly, tenderly and sweetly. My heart beat in an upbeat pace that rang within my ears.

He pulled back after a moment and gazed into my eyes. "What are you thinking about?" he whispered huskily, tilting his head to the side.

I smiled slightly, though sadly. "About how much I love you ... and at the same time, wondering what is the point of love ... when it never lasts."

Dan shook his head. "We wouldn't be like your parents, Lara."

"How can you say that? When you don't actually know?"

"Because, you're different from your mother and I'm different from your father. I would never hurt you, and I will never leave you alone. I love you too much to."

"I love you, too, Dan," I said, smiling, with tears of happiness in my eyes. Leaning down, I rested my head on his chest. His arms stayed tight around my own. He kissed my temple once as we finished watching the sunrise.

Going home after school, Mum was in an ecstatic mood — practically dancing around Daniel's house humming a song I hadn't heard. She then explained she got a job at the local Crystal and Angel Therapy store and with it, our own permanent home to live in. She would start first thing Monday morning.

I truly couldn't believe it. Everything in my life seemed to finally be changing to how I wanted it to be, and I could only thank Dan for it. He seemed to have been the start of it all. Maybe he was even my *new* lucky charm.

That night, I had butterflies in my stomach, not quite sure of what to expect of the premier tomorrow. I was excited and nervous at the same time. I kept reminding myself of how Dan seemed to be so calm and thought, *Well, if he's not nervous, I shouldn't be either.* It helped somewhat. I knew everyone would have their eyes on Daniel. They probably wouldn't even notice me. I couldn't believe that I was actually going somewhere, where I knew there was a chance I would be the center of attention.

At five o'clock the next afternoon, butterflies were swarming my stomach as I quickly got ready for Dan's premiere. I was so nervous, wondering what was going to happen.

Taking in a deep breath, I sat on the end of my bed and put my head in my hands as I stared down at the cream floor under my feet, just trying to relax and calm my nerves. I didn't know how Dan could stay so calm. If I was him, I'd be a nervous wreck a thousand times over by now.

Hearing a knock at the door, I looked up and flushed when I saw Dan. I grabbed the sheet of my bed and wrapped it around myself.

"Sorry, Lara. I didn't mean to pry," he whispered, coming in and sitting on the bed. "Are you okay?"

I nodded. "Yeah, it's just ..."

"Nervous? I know. I'm not as confident as I act," he said with a wink, then kissed my cheek as I felt something light and cold wrap around my neck.

"It was my mother's," he spoke though a smile.

Glancing down, I saw something gold around my neck. I gasped and stood, seeing in my dresser's mirror a gold necklace in the shape of angel's wings wrapping around my neck. The end tips of the feathers ended in the middle of my chest. Where the wings would have joined to its owners back, wrapped around the back of my neck. In the dull light of my room, the gold glistened like glitter in the sun.

Dan stood and wrapped his arms around my shoulders, holding my haze through the reflection of the mirror. "Do you like it?" he whispered huskily.

I nodded, as tears of happiness sprang to my eyes once more. "I love it, thank you. It's so sweet."

"Only for my angel," he whispered. I turned around, looking down at the necklace and then up to him, and kissed him softly.

I went over to my bedside table and grabbed the little silver box. Taking my dress out, I slid into it and held the front as Dan zipped up the back. I smiled widely seeing myself in the mirror. Everything fit and went together, perfectly. The dress hugged my torso and came out at my hips. Like the necklace, the dress' fabric shimmered gold with movement. My gold and white eye shadow picked up the colors in my necklace and dress. I slipped into my white sandals with a pale gold buckle and three dainty studs placed in a triangle at either end of the strap around my foot.

"You look perfect," he breathed into my ear, wiping the tears of happiness out of my eyes.

I smiled, feeling slightly embarrassed, then thanked him again. I'd never dressed up like this before.

Dan smiled, too, and left so I could finish up. I painted my nails white with gold tips. When Dan came back, he was dressed in a light-grey suit with a navy-blue shirt underneath it, and a matching light-grey tie. I shyly looked away, trying not to smile or bust out giggling. He looked … too good.

"Ready?" Dan asked and I nodded. We headed downstairs and out to the garage. Glancing at the white Lexus LFA, Dan passed it and pulled off a tarp to reveal another Lexus LFA beneath it. This one was pure midnight black. For the first time, I felt my jaw drop and got in. The interior was pure black and leather, too. But the leather scent was stronger compared to the white car.

"So, no limo?" I joked as Dan started the engine.

He laughed. "No, I don't care for them."

Holding my clutch handbag tightly, I glanced down at it and bit my lip hard as the car came to a stop a few minutes later. Already, there were camera flashes going off. I was glad the windows were tinted black.

"Ready?" Dan asked, touching my hand, as I took in a deep breath.

"Yeah," I croaked, as my cheeks flushed again. He smiled and kissed the redness away as security got our doors.

Getting out, I blinked at the flashing cameras, then felt the gentle touch of Dan's hand. I smiled at him as his hand went from mine to my waist. My eyes adjusted to the flashing lights as I looked around and spotted Mum in the front row, taking photos. I waved to her shyly.

We were both standing on the red carpet in front of Dan's car as security drove it away. Paparazzi and fans were taking a thousand photos a second. The atmosphere was ecstatic with the excitement of screaming fans. I was already starting to feel my ears ringing, and at the same time, out of place. I was just a normal girl no one knew, standing on a red carpet with someone millions of people knew. I smiled at the thought, knowing some people would kill to be where I currently stood.

Dan murmured into my ear that the media wanted photos and interviews first and then he would have to sign some autographs. For the little I heard him over the noise, I nodded and stood by his side. The media asked for casual photos on the carpet, but behind the security fence, I could hear paparazzi shouting questions about who I was. Daniel smirked hearing them.

"Want to make it official?" he said into my ear.

I nodded, placing the back of my hand up to my mouth, trying to cover my giggle. My cheeks glowed along with the smile I attempted to keep hidden, but failed greatly.

Slowly with his warm hand resting on my cheek, I could feel the smile on Dan's lips as he softly and slowly kissed me and I kissed him back. Though it was only brief, the cheers from the crowds tripled. I giggled and leaned into Dan's side as he wrapped his arm around my shoulders. I knew I could easily get used to this new life with him, and I could see how

Dan could put up with this life — just his presence made his fans happy.

While heading to bed, brushing my hair out, when something fell to the floor and caught my attention. Placing the brush on my dresser, I turned around, leaned over, and found a white feather. A perfect, thick and shiny quill, just like the first black one I had found. I smiled, looking it over as I turned it over between my index finger and thumb.

With a knock at my bedroom door, I looked up and smiled when I saw Dan leaning in. He caught my glance and looked down at the feather. His smile then grew as he took it from my finger tips into his own. For a moment he looked at it, turning it over between his fingers and then kissed my cheek, murmuring softly, "You must have an angel watching over you." He winked. I giggled as he said goodnight and closed the door.

Lying in bed that night, I thought of the day that had been. It was nothing short of amazing.

Seeing how generous and sweet Dan was while having photos taken with his fans and then signing autographs made me realize just how lucky I was to have him. I laughed silently, knowing Keira would be flipping over backwards tomorrow when she saw the photos of us together.

I smiled widely at what Dan had just said and all he had given my mother and I so far. I did have an angel watching over me, and that angel was Daniel Angel Taylors. The angel I belong to.

Acknowledgements

A special thank you to all the authors who are featured in this anthology! You truly are angels!

Monica Blanton
Susan Burdorf
Ashlea Burns
Callie Cool
Sky Diamond
Sara Drake
Stephanie Greenhalgh
Beth Hoyer
Theresa Oliver
Jennifer Paquette
Dana Piazzi
Nikki Shah
Melissa Somoza
Kim Stevens

Many of these authors have books coming soon from Write More Publications!

www.ingramcontent.com/pod-product-compliance
Lightning Source LLC
Chambersburg PA
CBHW031316170626
46807CB00002B/443